FRENZY

By Eva Carmichael

Best Wishes

Eva Carmichael

First Edition

Kindle: ISBN 978-1-9998113-3-4

Cover Design by Chris Hart

Also Available as Paperback

Nitere Publishing: ISBN 978-1-9998113-2-7

1EDCHAMZ2310

Acknowledgements

Grateful thanks to Chris and Tracey, without whose tireless help and guidance this book would not have been published. You've both done a fantastic job. Thank you.

Also, I must thank my beta readers. This year I have had advice from Jane, Maureen and Claire. Thank you, ladies. You have been brilliant.

As always, Billy and Judy have gone out of their way to enable me to promote my work on Redcar Market. Also, Jackie and Helen at The Gypsy Rover have been brilliant selling my books in the pub. Sincere thanks to all of you.

A big thank you also to my husband, Derek who's still providing the tea, coffee and occasional wine, and thank you to my family for their continued encouragement.

Last, but by no means least, I would like to thank the people of Redcar and the surrounding area who have bought my books over the past three years. The wonderful comments of support I have received make all the hard work worthwhile.

Thank you everyone!

PROLOGUE

***I'm not mad. Don't ever think me mad.
What I did was necessary. It had purpose.
Surely you can see that.***

***Anger explodes inside me, flowing
like a gigantic tsunami throughout
my body. I am rendered powerless to
resist. I do not have a choice.***

The urge to kill becomes irrepressible.

1

Detective Chief Superintendent Andrew Bainbridge arrived early at the Redcar station on Monday morning. He went straight to his office. A few minutes later, Sergeant Brown entered carrying a mug of coffee.

"Thought you might fancy a coffee, sir," he smiled, placing the mug down on the desk. Bainbridge nodded his thanks as he reached out for the mug.

"How was the holiday?" the sergeant enquired. "I've always fancied the Greek Islands myself, but the wife won't hear of going anywhere else but Benidorm."

Bainbridge smiled. "The two months I spent in Corfu were great. I can recommend it." He sipped at the coffee as he pulled his in-tray closer. "Anything interesting been happening whilst I've been away?"

Sergeant Brown shrugged. "No, not really. That bunch of lads causing all the trouble with their quad bikes got sorted. The court ordered the bikes to be destroyed and the three lads involved have been given community service."

"Good. Let's hope it sends out a message." Bainbridge began sifting through the papers. "Has Inspector Mason settled in? It was unfortunate we only had a couple of days handover before my holiday."

There was a slight hesitation. "Inspector Mason is doing fine, sir," he commented without emotion.

Bainbridge raised an eyebrow. "But?"

"Well sir, since you ask. The lads are always a bit wary of officers who've been fast-tracked. There's no doubt the inspector knows all the theory from the books, but when it comes to being street-wise and actually catching villains… well, no amount of learning can prepare you for that."

"So, you're saying you don't think he's up to the job?"

"No, I'm not saying that. He might turn out to be the best copper in Redcar for all I know. I just think his lack of experience on the streets may prove a disadvantage."

"We'll just have to wait and see then, won't we sergeant? By the way, I'm assuming that the anonymous call I got before I took my leave was a hoax?"

"It looks like it, sir. There have been no bodies found in Redcar, murdered or otherwise."

"That's a relief. I suppose there are always going to be a certain amount of nutters out there desperately seeking attention after a case like that."

"Yes, sir. It's all part of the game I suppose. Do you want me to send the inspector up when he comes in?"

Bainbridge frowned as he opened an internal envelope marked 'Confidential.' "Give me an hour to go through this lot first," he said.

"Very well, sir." The sergeant headed towards the door. "By the way, it's good to have you back."

Bainbridge smiled. "It's good to be back, sergeant."

Jack Mason rushed into the kitchen of his neat semi. His wife, Annika, was at the breakfast bar buttering toast.

"Have you seen my blue tie? I've been through all my ties, and I can't find the blue one."

Annika shrugged. "Wear the green one then," she suggested, "or the red one."

"No, it has to be the blue tie. The old man's back from his hols today and I want to give a good impression."

Annika put down the butter knife and walked to the door. "I'll find it," she sighed. "I've made you some breakfast. Make sure you eat before you go to work."

Jack shook his head irritably. "I haven't time for breakfast. I don't want to be late, not today of all days."

"Relax," Annika smiled. "I'll find your tie." She left the room. Jack took a sip of the coffee she had poured and a bite of the toast.

"Here it is," she said triumphantly, holding up the elusive blue tie. "It was at the back of the drawer." She handed it to her husband, and he quickly put it on.

"Thanks, love," he slid into his suit jacket. "I don't know what I'd do without you." He kissed her lightly on the lips as he headed towards the hall. "I'll see you tonight," he opened the front door. "I should be home for six."

Smiling, Jack hurried out of the house and within minutes was behind the wheel of his Audi, heading in the direction of Redcar Police Station.

***

Bainbridge reached over his desk, arm outstretched, and shook Mason's hand. "How are you settling in, Inspector? Redcar must be a big change from Leeds?"

Mason smiled. "I'm enjoying the challenge," he said, "and my wife is loving being by the sea."

"Good. I'll have to arrange a meal one evening and get to meet her."

"She'd like that. By the way, sir, I didn't have the chance to tell you at the handover how much I admired your work with that business with the missing girls. You did a brilliant job."

"Thanks, but it was a team effort. Everyone played their part. Fortunately, incidents like that are rare. I don't think it likely we'll be seeing anything like that in the town again."

"Let's hope not. The publicity couldn't have helped the tourist trade much."

Grinning, Bainbridge leant forward, steeping his fingers. "Actually, it increased tourism. The town had never been so busy for weeks after the trial. We had television people coming from all over the country to see where the murders had taken place. I even heard there was an organised bus tour visiting the sites."

Mason shook his head slowly. "There are some sick bastards about," he said.

"I can't argue with that! Anyway, to business." He picked up a report and handed it to Mason. "This was waiting for me when I got in this morning. It was marked confidential and sent directly from Headquarters."

Mason studied the document. "Its details of a prison release," he read. "Shaun Dyson." He tilted his head and looked enquiringly at Bainbridge. "Is there a problem?"

"Shaun Dyson is the most vicious little bastard I've ever come across," Bainbridge almost spat, the muscles on his neck tensing. "He got sent down six months ago for robbing a bookie at the racecourse. Hit him over the head and half killed him."

"How much did he get away with?"

Bainbridge hunched his shoulders. "Freddie Roberts, the bookie, said there was about five thousand taken, but I have it on good authority that it was nearer fifty. Not a single penny was ever recovered."

"Do you want me to arrange surveillance?"

"You can try, but Dyson's too clever to lead you directly to the money. What I want you to do is pay him a home visit. Read him the riot act, point out the terms of his parole. Make sure he's aware he's being watched."

"Certainly, sir. I'll do it right away."

"Oh, and I think I should warn you about Leanne."

"Leanne?"

"That's his wife. She's fiercely loyal to her husband and extremely aggressive. Make sure you take someone with you."

"I'll take Walker. She seems a capable officer."

Bainbridge nodded his approval. "Dyson is a complex character. He..."

The desk telephone rang, and Bainbridge picked it up at once. "Bainbridge. Oh yes, Chief Constable, right away, sir." He replaced the receiver onto its cradle. "Summoned on high," he said, a broad grin spreading across his handsome face. "Let me know how things go with Dyson."

2

Walton Street in Redcar, was a shabby terrace tucked in behind the abandoned steel works. Less than half of the twenty houses were occupied, the rest had been boarded up, ready for demolition. Number thirteen, the registered address of Shaun Dyson, was in the middle of the row. It had a dingy, red-painted door with the house number painted in the same colour on the brickwork. Two overflowing refuse bins were beneath the grimy bay window.

"This is it," Mason announced as he parked the police car close to the house. "Not much of a place, is it?"

PC Lisa Walker placed her uniform hat on her head as she got out of the vehicle. "Don't let this place fool you, sir. I'm sure they've got money squirrelled away somewhere."

Grinning, Mason got out of the car, walked towards the door, and knocked with intent. It was flung open a few seconds later by a scruffily dressed boy of about ten years old. He stared defiantly at the two officers then turned his head. "Mam, it's the filth," he shouted. "Two of 'em."

Before either officer could respond, a woman of about thirty, with long, unruly black hair and large brown eyes, grabbed the boy and pushed him into the house before turning menacingly to face the officers.

"What the fuck do you want this time?" she snarled, inhaling deeply on the half-smoked cigarette between her fingers. "Come to accuse my Shaun of something else he hasn't done, have you?"

Mason stepped forward. "Mrs Dyson, is your husband at home? I need to speak with him."

"No, he's not, so piss off or I'll call my solicitor. This is harassment, that's what it is." She flicked ash from her cigarette, and grinned as it landed on Mason's shoe. "My Shaun's done his time, even though he was innocent, and you're still hounding him."

"Nobody's hounding him, Mrs Dyson. Shaun is on parole, and I need to speak with him."

The woman took another drag from her cigarette before tossing it into the street. She huffed, placing her fists on her ample hips. "Well, you can't. He's not here."

"When will he be back?"

She shrugged. "How the hell do I know? I'm not his fucking jailer. Shaun's out and he'll come back when he's ready to come back, not before."

Mason reached into his pocket and removed his card. "Tell him to give me a call," he said. "Will you do that?"

She grabbed the card. "I can ask him. Whether he does is down to him." Before Mason could respond, she slammed the door shut.

"I told you she was feisty," Walker said as they walked back to the vehicle. "Not a woman to be meddled with is Leanne."

Mason got into the car and took out his handkerchief, cleaning the ash from his shoe. "It sounds like her and Shaun are well suited."

Grinning, Walker turned on the car engine. "You can decide that for yourself when you meet him, sir."

3

Chief Superintendent Bainbridge arrived back at the station from his meeting with the Chief Constable as Inspector Mason returned from Walton Street.

"Well, how did it go?" Bainbridge asked cheerily as he walked through Reception. "What did you think to Shaun Dyson?"

"Dyson wasn't in, sir," Mason said. "I spoke briefly with his wife. She's going to pass on the message."

"Well, good luck with that, but I wouldn't hold my breath. If he's not reported to the station by the end of the day, I suggest you bring him in by force."

"Yes, sir."

"By the way, I've been informed by the Chief Constable that we'll be getting four new beat constables next week straight from Training School, so you can choose an experienced uniform to help out in CID for a few weeks."

"Oh, that's great. I could certainly do with an extra pair of hands."

Bainbridge began to ascend the stairs. "I've heard Superintendent Barraclough is retiring at the end of the month," he said. "He used to work here in Redcar before his move to Middlesbrough."

"I did meet him briefly when I first arrived," Mason said. "He seemed a decent bloke."

"He is. Anyway, he's having a farewell do for senior officers at The Grey Horse in Marske next Friday evening. Perhaps you and your wife would care to come along?"

"That's kind of you, sir. I'd love to. I'll give Annika a call now and double check."

Inspector Mason returned to his office and telephoned his wife. There was no reply. He checked his watch. It was eleven-thirty. PC Walker entered his office carrying a mug of tea.

"Thought you might fancy a cuppa, sir," she said smiling.

"Thanks," he replaced his mobile into his pocket.

Left alone, Mason picked up the internal phone and dialled the front desk. "Sergeant Brown? Could I have a quick word when you have a minute?"

Sergeant Brown left PC Walker to staff the front desk and made his way to Mason's office. He knocked lightly on the door and stepped into the room. "You wanted to see me, sir?" he asked.

"Yes, sergeant, please take a seat."

Sergeant Brown plonked his chubby frame in the leather chair across from the inspector and looked at him expectantly. "Yes, sir. What can I do for you?"

"I've been informed by DCS Bainbridge that the station will be getting four new recruits next week."

The sergeant huffed. "It's about time. We're running on fumes at the moment."

"Yes, it's tough for all of us. Because of the new recruits, the boss has agreed for one experienced uniform to be assigned to CID."

"Who did you have in mind, sir?"

"I thought PC Beaumont might be suitable. He seems a bright lad. He's been on several courses and I know he's applied to join CID at least twice."

"Beaumont? Are you sure you want Beaumont?"

"I take it you don't approve, Sergeant?"

"Wayne Beaumont is a capable officer, there's no doubt about that," he admitted. "He did a really good job with that Duffy business a few months back, but… well there have been certain issues with him."

"What sort of issues?"

"Beaumont's a handsome, popular bloke. Girls like him."

"There's nothing wrong with being good-looking and popular."

"No sir, there isn't, as long as it doesn't affect your work."

"What exactly are you implying, Sergeant?"

"There have been rumours about his liaisons with women. Married women. Just last month the optician on the High Street came to the station threatening to make an official complaint about Beaumont hanging around his missus."

"I didn't hear anything about this."

"No, sir. I had a chat with the gentleman and promised him it wouldn't happen again. I severely reprimanded Beaumont threatening to have him transferred. He gave me his assurance he would stay well clear of the lady in question, and insisted it was the woman who had done all the chasing."

"Have there been other incidents with married women?"

The sergeant shook his head. "No, sir, nothing specific, but like I said, there have been rumours."

Mason leant back in his chair, steepling his fingers. "Unfortunately, CID are desperate for more officers and Beaumont would seem the most qualified."

The sergeant stood up. "As you think fit, sir."

"Ask him to pop into my office when he's back in the station, will you?"

"Yes, sir. He's due in for his meal break at twelve."

After phoning his wife twice more and getting no reply, Mason began working through his in-box. It was twelve fifteen when Police Constable Wayne Beaumont tapped on his door and tentatively entered his office.

"You wanted to see me, sir?" he asked, his six-foot-two frame filling the doorway.

"Yes, come in Beaumont. Take a seat."

Beaumont sat on the chair across from the inspector, his hands clasped tightly on his lap.

"Relax man, it's good news. How would you like to join CID for a couple of months on a trial basis?"

Beaumont ran his hand through his thick black hair; the look of relief on his handsome face was clear. "That… that would be great, sir," he faltered. "When can I start?"

"Next Monday. I understand you've already done several courses on CID procedures?"

"Yes, sir. The last course was in January."

"I see from your file you're a bachelor?"

"Yes, sir. I have a girlfriend and we share a flat, but… well, I'm only twenty-nine and I don't know if I'm ready to settle down yet."

"That's your business of course. I just need to make sure that my officers are in a stable home environment."

"Oh, Jodie and me are sound. We've been together nearly two years now."

"And you think she'd be happy with the strange hours working in CID would entail? I only ask because some officer's partners can't cope with the disruption to their lives."

Beaumont grinned. "Oh, there'd be no conflict on that front, sir."

"Glad to hear it." Mason leant forward, elbows on his desk, his fingers laced. "There is one matter of concern which has been brought to my attention," he dropped his voice to reinforce confidentiality.

Beaumont tilted his head. "Oh, what matter is that sir?"

"I understand you have a liking for the ladies... other people's ladies."

Beaumont inhaled and threw back his head. "If you mean Maureen, the optician's wife, it was her that did the chasing. The woman's a nymphomaniac. It got to the point where she was actually stalking me."

"That may well be, but let me make this clear, Beaumont. If you are to work for me in CID I don't want to hear of any further incidents of this nature. Are we clear on that?"

"Yes… yes of course, sir."

"Very well. Report to Sergeant Brown and we can get the ball rolling."

Beaumont stood up and held out his hand to Mason. “Thank you for this opportunity, sir,” he said. “I won’t let you down.”

Mason shook his hand. “I’m sure you won’t, DC Beaumont,” he smiled. “I’ll see you on Monday morning.”

4

It was six-fifteen in the evening when Jack Mason got home. The aroma of his favourite curry greeted him as he pushed open the front door. “Mm… something smells good,” he commented playfully as he joined his wife in the kitchen.

“Had a good day, darling?” Annika asked as she scooped the rice onto the two plates. “How did it go with Super Cop?”

Jack kissed his wife on the cheek and took off his coat. “If you’re referring to Detective Chief Superintendent Bainbridge, it went well. He’s a decent bloke.”

“The way everyone in the town talk about him you’d think he could walk on water.”

“He’s a good copper. People recognise that.” Jack walked through to the lounge. “I’m having a drink. Should I pour you a vodka?”

“Gin and tonic, please,” she answered. “I’ve gone off vodka.”

“Since when? You always have vodka.”

Annika banged the spoon down noisily on the worktop. “I don’t think the bloody sky will fall in if I have gin for a change. Do you?”

Jack poured the drinks and returned to the kitchen. “Is everything all right, love? You seem a little tense.”

Annika turned to face her husband. “I’m sorry, Jack. I… I don’t know, I didn’t sleep well last night. I’m a little tired.” She took the gin to her lips and swallowed it in two gulps.

"Is something bothering you, Annika? You would tell me if there was, wouldn't you?"

Annika snorted as she began to put the curry onto the plates. "I've told you, I'm fine. Just a little tired that's all, so please stop fussing."

She took the plates through to the dining table and poured a glass of wine for herself and one for Jack.

"What have you been up to today?" Jack asked. "Anything exciting?"

Annika pushed the food around her plate. "Exciting in Redcar? You must be joking."

"I thought you were happy here?"

"I am. I love walking on the beach."

"Is that where you were this morning, walking on the beach?"

Annika huffed. "What do you mean?"

"I rang you a couple of times and got no answer. I wondered where you were."

"Are you checking up on me?"

"Of course I'm not."

Annika pursed her lips. "If you must know, I joined a book club at The Galleon. I'm going tonight as a matter of fact."

"A book club? I didn't know you were a reader."

"Well, I am. I enjoy a good book."

"Good for you," Jack said.

"Then I called in the hairdressers."

"Oh? Your hair looks fine to me."

"I wasn't making an appointment. They're advertising for a stylist, and I applied."

"Why do you want to go back to hairdressing of all things? There's no reason for you to go back to work at all, but hairdressing? You said you hated it when we were in Leeds."

"Well, I've changed my mind, just like I have about vodka."

There was an uneasy silence. It was Jack who spoke first. "There's a bit of do going on in a couple of weeks at The Grey Horse. Superintendent Barraclough is retiring, and all the senior officers and their wives are invited. I thought we might go along."

Annika pouted. "If you want, but I'll need a new dress."

Jack reached over and took Annika's hand in his. "You can have as many dresses as you want, love. You know that."

Annika smiled and squeezed Jack's hand. "I'll go over to Middlesbrough later in the week," she said. "There's a new boutique opened in The Cleveland Centre. I've been meaning to go and have a look."

"You enjoy yourself," he said smiling. "By the way, which salon have you applied to?"

"The one on the seafront. It's called 'Maria's Hair & Beauty.' They're putting me through my paces tomorrow."

"Putting you through your paces?"

"It's part of the interview. I'll probably be asked to do a shampoo and set, maybe a cut. Things like that."

Jack was about to pour a second glass of wine when his mobile rang. "Mason," he answered. His body stiffened and the muscles in his face tensed. "I'll be right there."

Jack picked up his coat, replacing the phone in the pocket. “I have to go,” he said. “There’s been a serious incident in town.” He rushed towards the door. “I’ll probably be late in, love,” he said. “Don’t wait up.”

“What sort of incident?” Annika said, but Jack was already through the door heading towards his car.

5

An ambulance and two marked police cars were outside Benji's Wine Cellar, a small off-licence at the end of Queen Street. As Mason drew up, the ambulance crew appeared from the shop carrying a man on a stretcher.

"That's Benji Myers," PC Porter remarked, as he joined the inspector. "It looks like he's in a bad way, sir."

"Who found him?" Mason asked.

"The woman over there, sir. Her name's Sheila Thompson." Mason looked over at the woman slouching in a doorway smoking a cigarette. Early forties, he guessed, with dark, lank hair and an unhealthy pallor.

"Have you taken a statement from her?"

Porter shook his head. "No, sir, not yet. Sheila's... Sheila's drunk. She's not making much sense."

Mason turned to PC Jones. "You go to the hospital with Mr Myers. "Let me know the minute he regains consciousness."

"Yes, sir," the constable climbed into the ambulance.

Mason strode over to the woman. "Ms Thompson?" he asked officiously.

"Bloody hell, I only get called Ms Thompson when I'm in front of the Beak, love. You can call me Sheila."

"Did you see what happened here tonight, Sheila?"

Sheila hunched her shoulders. "I didn't see Benji get clobbered," she slurred, "but I saw someone come dashing out of the shop. He nearly knocked me over."

"Did you recognise him?"

"Is there a reward if I did?"

"If you know who did this, you have to tell me."

Sheila shook her head. "It all happened so fast. The bastard came pushing past me and ran off down there." She pointed in the direction of the town. "He was a big bloke, and he wore a leather jacket. That's all I know."

She began to sway forward and grabbed Mason for support. "I need some fags and a bottle of White Lightening," she demanded. "Who the fuck's going to serve me now Benji's gone?"

"I'm sorry, Sheila, but the shop is closed for now," Mason explained as he tried steering her away from the doorway. "I think Morrisons are still open though."

Sheila sniffed loudly. "I can't afford their prices. Can't you get me twenty fags and a bottle off the shelf? I've got money," she said, pulling out an assortment of coins from her coat pocket.

"Sorry, Sheila," Mason refused, firmly taking hold of her arm. "This officer will take you home and tomorrow, someone will call round and take a statement. Is that all right?"

Sheila snorted and pulled away from Mason. "It'll bloody well have to be, won't it?"

Mason turned to PC Porter. "Make sure Ms Thompson gets home safely. "I'll stay here and wait for Forensics."

"Very well, sir," the constable said, taking hold of Sheila's arm. "Where do you live, love?" he asked. "I'll walk you home."

Sheila began to chuckle. “It’s a long time since a young man walked me home,” she laughed and reached for his backside. “I hope you’re not planning any funny business.”

Porter shot an anxious look in Mason’s direction before heading off with Sheila down Queen Street.

Alone in her flat, Sheila walked to the window and furtively pulled back the curtain, her eyes darting up and down the deserted street. She reached into her pocket and took out a mobile phone and selected a number.

“It’s me,” she said, “I saw what you did. If you want me to keep my gob shut about tonight, it’s gonna cost you.”

6

DCS Bainbridge was already in Inspector Mason's office when he arrived at the station the following morning.

"Good morning, Inspector," he said cordially. "I hear there was some excitement down on Queen Street last night."

"Yes, sir. The proprietor of an off-licence, Benji Myers, got taken to hospital. Someone hit him over the head."

"Any witnesses?"

"A woman saw someone rushing out of the shop. Unfortunately, she could only give a vague description, but I've arranged for PC Porter to take her statement this morning."

"Good, keep me informed." Bainbridge made his way to the door, and then turned back. "By the way, have you spoken to Shaun Dyson yet? I wouldn't be surprised if last night's caper was down to him. Bashing someone over the head fits his M.O. perfectly."

"Dyson hasn't been to the station yet, sir."

Bainbridge huffed. "Interviewing Dyson should be your first priority. Make sure you speak to him today as a person of interest."

"Yes, sir," Mason agreed. "I was planning to do that this morning."

"Inspector, I don't want you to think I'm interfering with your investigation, but I intend to keep a close eye on this case. I'm sure you'll benefit from my guidance."

"Yes, sir," Mason said. "I'm sure I will."

It was an hour later when Mason's phone rang. It was PC Jones calling from the hospital. "Sir, Mr Myers has just died. He never regained consciousness."

Mason inhaled deeply. "All right, constable. I'll be along shortly." Mason rushed up to Bainbridge's office. He knocked lightly on the door and entered as DCS Bainbridge was replacing the phone handset on its cradle.

"I've just heard," he said. "Did Myers have family?"

"His wife is at the hospital now. I'll go over there and speak with her."

"Take Walker with you. She's good at that sort of thing."

"Yes, sir."

"Have Forensics come up with anything yet?"

"Nothing useful, I'm afraid." Mason turned to leave the room. "I've sent PC Porter round to take a statement from the witness, Sheila Thompson. I'm not hopeful she can tell us much though. She had been drinking heavily last night. I understand she has a real problem with drink and drugs."

"Sheila Thompson, eh? I've had dealings with her in the past. A bit of a wrong 'un was Sheila in her younger days. Keep me informed."

***

Accompanied by PC Lisa Walker, Inspector Mason found Mrs Myers in the Family Room at the hospital. He quietly approached the arm of her chair. "I'm Inspector Jack Mason," he introduced himself softly. "I'm so sorry for your loss, Mrs Myers. It's a terrible thing that's happened."

Irene Myers was a small, thin woman in her late fifties. Her grey hair was tied back in a bun and her watery-blue eyes were red and swollen. She turned to face the police officer. "Who would do this to him?" she asked. "Benji was the kindest man you'd ever meet." Tears began to trickle down her cheeks as she slowly swayed backwards and forwards. "Have you arrested the bastard who did this?"

"Not yet," he said, "but we will."

PC Walker crouched down in front of Irene. "Can I get you anything?" she offered, "tea or coffee perhaps?"

"No thanks, love. If I have any more tea, I'll start floating."

Inspector Mason walked over to the window. "Did your husband have any enemies, Mrs Myers? Had anyone made any threats towards him that you know of?"

Irene shook her head. "No, I've told you, Benji was a good man. Everyone liked him."

"How long has he been running the off-licence?"

"About a year. When the steelworks closed, he was employed as a night watchman. for a while, but then he fancied a change, so he bought the shop."

"And there's never been any trouble until last night?"

Irene shook her head. "No, not really. Kids would try it on with fake ID sometimes, but Benji was strict about that."

Mason walked towards the door, and then turned to face the police officer. "Take Mrs Myers home when she's ready to leave," he requested, "then report back to the station."

"Yes, sir,"

***

DI Mason left the hospital and headed back to Redcar. He got to his office as the phone on his desk rang. "Mason," he said, positioning himself behind his desk.

"Sir, it's Leo Cutts in Forensics."

"Yes, Leo? Any news?"

"None any good, I'm afraid," Leo said. "I've checked the CCTV in the shop, but it's poor quality. There's a blurred image of someone entering the shop. It looks like he was having an altercation with Myers. They both go off camera, and then the bloke can be seen rushing out of the shop about three minutes later."

"It's definitely a bloke?"

"I'd say so, sir. He's wearing the compulsory hoodie of course, but I'd swear it's a bloke."

"No prints?"

"Hundreds of them I'm afraid, but none to identify which belong to the thief. There's no sign of any weapon either."

"Well, keep searching. Whoever smashed Benji's head in used something heavy. According to the pathologist it's probably a hammer."

"Okay, inspector. If there's a hammer in this shop, I'll find it. There is one thing which seems a bit strange though."

"What's that?"

"There's nearly two hundred pounds in the till, so whatever the bloke wanted, it wasn't the takings."

"And the stock's intact?"

"Nothing seems to have been disturbed. We can check with Mrs Myers later about that."

"All right. You finish off there. I'll speak later."

"Very well, Inspector."

7

PC Porter entered Inspector Mason's office half an hour later.

"Sir" he said as he nervously stepped into the room. "I've been to Sheila Thompson's flat this morning to get her statement, but she's not answering the door."

"Then knock louder," Mason snapped. "She's probably in a drunken stupor."

"I banged on her door, sir, front and back. I even knocked on the windows, but there was no reply."

"What about her phone? Did you try ringing that?"

"Yes, sir, several times."

"Perhaps she's gone out shopping."

Porter shook his head. "I was there at eight o'clock this morning, sir. I don't think Sheila would be out at that time. It's more likely she went out last night and bunked down somewhere."

"Well go back in a couple of hours. We have to get her statement."

"Yes, sir," Porter said as he turned to leave, almost colliding with Sergeant Brown who was entering the office. "Sorry, sarge," he apologised, stepping to one side. Sergeant Brown glared at the young constable, but said nothing as Porter scurried out of the office.

"Shaun Dyson is in Reception," the sergeant informed the Inspector.

Mason raised an eyebrow in surprise. "Good, it saves us bringing him in. Take him to the interview room, sergeant. I'll be along in a minute."

"Very well, sir," the sergeant said.

***

Shaun Dyson was in his early thirties, tall and muscular with fair hair and pale-blue eyes. He was leaning back into the chair, legs outstretched before him, hands behind his head, when Inspector Mason entered the room and sat in the chair opposite. Sergeant Brown was standing by the door, his arms folded across his ample chest.

Mason nodded an acknowledgement as he took his seat across the desk.

"Good of you to take the time to call in, Mr Dyson," he said.

Dyson sniffed. "I didn't have much choice, did I? The missus said you wanted to see me."

"Yes, that's right, I did." Mason carefully placed a buff-coloured folder on the table between him and Dyson, taking out several sheets of paper. "I see you've recently been released from Durham prison."

Dyson yawned his indifference. "Yeah, that's right, but I was framed. I got sent down for something I hadn't done."

Mason gave a dismissive wave. "That's not what the jury thought. They believed the two eyewitnesses who saw you batter Freddie Roberts over the head in the car park and make off with his tote bag."

Dyson banged his fist on the table, anger flashing in his eyes. "They were lying. It wasn't me. I was at home with the wife."

"No, you weren't. Leanne will say whatever you tell her to, we both know that."

Dyson glared at Mason, his mouth tightening, the veins on his neck pulsating.

Mason turned back to the documents. "You have quite a temper, Mr Dyson."

Dyson hunched his shoulders, but said nothing.

"I see the money was never recovered. Where did you hide it, Shaun? You know you'll never be able to get your hands on it. The minute you try, you'll be re-arrested."

"I don't know what you're talking about. I've told you; it wasn't me."

"You were arrested soon after the assault so you can't have got to it. Why don't you come clean and give it back?"

"If I had that money, don't you think I'd be long gone instead of hanging around here?"

"Oh, Redcar not good enough for you now?"

Dyson pursed his lips. "I never said that."

"You will be watched, Shaun. You do know that? If and when you attempt to retrieve the cash…"

"Good luck with that," Dyson sneered. "Can I go now we've had our little chat? I have things to do."

"Not yet. There is another matter I wish to discuss with you?"

"What's that? Somebody pinched the town hall clock?"

“Where were you last night between six and eight o’clock?”

“Why? What are you trying to fit me up with now?”

“No-one’s trying to fit you up with anything. Please answer the question. Where were you?”

“At home with the wife,” Dyson said. “We had tea and then watched the telly.”

“Who else, besides yourself and Leanne were in the house?”

“Nobody, just us.”

“What about your son? Wasn’t he at home having his tea?”

“He was out with his mates. He didn’t get home till about ten o’clock.”

“That’s late for a young lad to be out, isn’t it?”

“What the fuck’s it got to do with you what time my kid gets in?”

“Are you saying there’s nobody, other than Leanne, who can confirm your alibi?”

“That’s right. We don’t have many parties these days. Why, what am I supposed to have done this time?”

“Have you heard of Benji’s Wine Cellar?”

“Course I have. It’s on Queen Street.”

“Benji was attacked last night in his shop. I was informed this morning that he died from his injuries.”

Dyson jumped to his feet. “Are you accusing me of killing Benji? That’s crazy. I was nowhere near Queen Street last night.”

"No, of course not. You were at home having tea and watching the television with Leanne. Isn't that right?"

"If you're accusing me, I want my solicitor. I'm not saying another word until he gets here."

"Calm down, Dyson. No-one's accusing you. Not yet anyway. There's a witness we have to speak to first."

"You bastards are all the same. It wasn't me; I tell you and you can't prove it was."

"I will need to speak to you again, Mr Dyson," he said, "both you and Leanne."

"Yeah, whatever," Dyson grumbled as he got to his feet and marched towards the door followed by Sergeant Brown. "This is bordering on harassment," he shouted, "and you know how the press love a good story of police harassment."

8

Inspector Mason closed the file and prepared to leave the interview room when DCS Bainbridge entered.

“I see Dyson’s been in,” he observed. “How did you get on?”

“The usual denial,” Mason tapped the file on the desk. “He’s using Leanne as his alibi for last night.”

“What do you think to him? Feisty little bugger, isn’t he?”

“I’ve sent for his file from HQ, but it hasn’t arrived yet. What can you tell me about him, sir? You’ve known him a long time.”

Bainbridge sighed and sank into one of the chairs. “I first met Shaun Dyson soon after I came to Redcar,” he began. “Shaun would be about ten years old then. His dad, Joseph, had a record as long as your arm. You name it and Joseph Dyson had a conviction for it.”

“So, what happened?”

“Joseph Dyson’s favourite sport was knocking seven bells out of his wife, Julie. She was in A&E every other week, but the stupid cow never made a complaint against him.”

Mason tutted. “The loyalty of these women never ceases to astound me.”

“Oh, believe me, it had nothing to do with loyalty, it was fear. The law didn’t work in the woman’s favour back then. Julie knew if she made an official complaint against her husband, he would be released, bailed, and then come after her.”

“So, she kept quiet?”

"That's right. She never said a word against him. One night Dyson got pissed and went home to Julie. He kicked and punched the poor cow so hard he ended up killing her. In his drunken state, he decided to hide his crime by setting fire to the house."

"He burnt the house down?"

"That was his plan. Unfortunately, the stupid bastard forgot about the two kids upstairs; Shaun and a six-week-old baby."

"Bloody hell."

"The house was well alight. Joseph got out leaving Julie and the kids inside. Shaun was a brave lad. He got to the bedroom window and lowered the baby down to the crowd of neighbours who had gathered in the street below. Then he jumped down himself."

"He was lucky to get out alive."

"Yes, he was. Unfortunately for him, he landed badly and crushed his right leg. He was in splints for about two years."

"The poor kid."

"When he came out of hospital he went into care of the local authority."

"What about the baby?"

"The baby was soon adopted, but Shaun was never even fostered. That's when the violent behaviour started. He was in a young offender's institution from the age of fourteen."

"With a father like his, the poor sod never had a chance."

"Joseph got sent to prison for life. He only lasted two years before somebody knifed him. A good end to bad rubbish really, I suppose."

"Yes sir, exactly."

"Shaun's violent behaviour caused so much concern that he was been seen by psychiatrists and psychologists. In fact, the whole bloody circus. They all say the same thing. He showed all the classic signs of a psychopath."

"That's a big label to put on a child, isn't it sir? I mean it seems to me the lad had been through hell with his father. He wouldn't know how to behave any differently until he had been shown."

Bainbridge shrugged. "You might be right, Inspector, but Shaun Dyson is an extremely dangerous individual. I don't think we appreciate yet just how dangerous."

There was a knock on the interview door and Sergeant Brown stepped into the room. He addressed Bainbridge. "Sir, a lady called Sophie telephoned. She asked if you could call her back at your convenience."

A broad smile spread across Bainbridge's face. "Thank you, sergeant."

"She said you have her number."

"Yes, that's right." Mason noticed a slight flush in Bainbridge's cheeks as he strode towards the door. "Let me know when you catch up with Sheila Thompson, Inspector. I don't think she'll be much help, but you never know."

"Yes, sir," Mason said as he picked up the file from the desk and followed Bainbridge from the room.

Back in his office, Andy Bainbridge closed the door and walked over to his desk. Taking out his phone he dialled a number.

9

It was seven-thirty in the evening. Annika was setting the dining table when her husband arrived home.

"Darling, you look exhausted," she said as she walked towards him, arms outstretched. They embraced and Jack kissed his wife lightly on the cheek.

"It's good to be home. It's been a shit day. I'm knackered."

Annika linked arms with Jack and steered him towards the couch. "Dinner's going to be a while yet. I'll get us a drink and then you can tell me all about it."

Jack sank into the deep-blue velvet couch and closed his eyes. "What have you been up to today, love? Anything exciting?"

Annika plopped down next to him, a glass of red wine in each hand. She handed one to Jack. "Well, as a matter of fact, I've had a great day. I called in at the salon and Maria put me through my paces, so to speak. I did a full head of foils, then a cut and blow and..."

"I take it you got the job then?" Jack said, sitting forward and bringing the wine glass to his lips.

"Of course I did. Why wouldn't I? I probably have more experience than that lot put together." She got to her feet and marched through into the kitchen, Jack in pursuit.

"Sorry darling, I didn't mean… so, when do you start?"

"Next week. The salon doesn't open on Monday, so I start on Tuesday morning."

"That's great," Jack said smiling. "I hope it works out all right this time."

"What's that supposed to mean? Of course it will work out. I happen to be an extremely good hairdresser."

"Of course you are, darling. It's just that... well you soon get bored with routine, that's all I meant. I wondered if perhaps hairdressing isn't challenging enough for you."

The timer on the oven began to bleep. Annika opened the oven door and removed the dish from inside. "Sit down and relax, Jack. It looks like the casserole is about ready."

The meal was eaten in silence. Jack through exhaustion and Annika was still sulking.

"Would you like custard or ice cream with the apple pie?" Annika asked, once they had eaten the beef casserole.

"I don't mind. What do you want?"

"Ice cream, I think," Annika said as she collected the two empty plates from the table. She returned a few minutes later with two bowls, each one holding a generous slice of apple pie and a scoop of vanilla ice cream. She placed one in front of Jack. "You haven't told me about your day. What happened to make it so bad?"

Jack ate a spoonful of the pie and took a sip of the wine before he spoke. "Well for a start, the bloke who got attacked at the off-licence last night died this morning. The poor sod never regained consciousness."

Annika shrugged. "I suppose that's a hazard of working in an off-licence at night. You get all sorts of weirdos in and out."

"I suppose so, but the odd thing is..." Jack stopped abruptly.

"What?" Annika pressed. "What was odd?"

Jack took another sip of wine. "I'm sorry, love," he sighed. "I really shouldn't be discussing my work with you."

Annika slammed her dessert spoon down hard into her bowl. "Oh, for fuck's sake, Jack, I'm your wife. If you can't talk to me, who can you talk to?"

Jack got up from the table and walked over to the couch, taking his wine glass with him. "He was an old man," he said, perching on the edge of the couch. "Some bastard hit him over the head with, what we think was a hammer. But the odd thing is, they didn't take the cash from the till."

"Maybe they got disturbed," Annika volunteered, "or maybe they got scared. They probably didn't mean to hit him so hard."

"If it's the bloke responsible that we think it is, he meant it all right, and I don't think he's the type to get scared."

"You have a suspect?"

"Some 'scrote' with a history of bashing people over the head. We're waiting to interview a witness to confirm it was him."

"There was a witness?"

Jack inhaled. "Some woman who was outside the shop at the time. She was too pissed to be interviewed properly last night, and today she seems to have disappeared. I've got the night shift out looking for her."

"Maybe she doesn't want to get involved. You can't make somebody give evidence if they don't want to, can you?"

Jack's hands curled into fists. "We're talking about murder, not some minor transgression. Of course she must get involved. It's her civic duty."

"Well, I think..."

"For goodness sake, Annika, stick to hairdressing love and leave police work to me, eh?" Jack got up and headed towards the hall. "I'm knackered. I'm going for a shower, and then I think I'll have an early night," he said.

Annika shrugged. "Suit yourself. There's a film on at ten I want to watch."

"All right, but don't be up too late."

"Good night, Jack."

"Good night, Annika."

10

It was five o'clock the following morning when Jack was awakened by the shrill ringing of his police-issue phone. "Inspector Mason," he yawned, reaching out and turning on the bedside lamp.

"Good morning, sir," said Sergeant Brown. "Sorry about the early call, but a woman's body's been found by the boating lake."

"What?"

"PC Porter says he's sure it's Sheila Thompson."

Mason jumped out of bed. "I'll be right there, sergeant. Have CSI been informed?"

"Yes, sir. They've just arrived. I've cordoned off the boating lake and…"

"Good man. Hold the fort; I'll be there in about ten minutes."

"Yes, sir. Oh, by the way, DSC Bainbridge is already in attendance."

"What's he doing there?"

"He was in the station when the call came in. Would you like to speak to him?"

Mason grunted. "No. I'll do that when I get there."

He hurried to the en-suite and closing the door, turned on the light. When he came out a few minutes later, Annika was still sleeping.

Mason could see the police activity as he pulled up on the slipway at the side of Redcar Boating Lake. Sergeant Brown, wearing a white forensic suit, was waiting for him. He handed a similar suit to him. "It looks like the poor cow's been hit over the head. I think she's been out here all night."

Mason put on the suit and walked over to where a white tent had been erected on the path at the side of the lake. Inside the tent, Leo Cutts, the Forensics Officer, was bending over the body.

"What can you tell me?" he asked, joining Leo and looking down on the crumpled body that was once Sheila Thompson.

"We'll get her back to the lab and do a proper examination, but I don't think there's much doubt about what killed her." He turned Sheila's head slightly, revealing a bloody wound above her right temple. "Somebody wasn't messing around. They hit her with such force it's cracked her skull and…"

"Enough," Mason interrupted, crinkling his nose. He stood up and made to leave the tent. "Do you have a rough idea of when this happened? Last night? This morning?"

Leo shook his head. "To be accurate I'll have to get her back to the lab; but if I were to make an educated guess… well I'd say she's been here at least six hours, probably seven."

Mason left the tent and took off his mask, breathing in deeply the crisp morning air. He turned to see DCS Bainbridge approaching. "Good morning, sir," he said.

"Well, Mason, are you thinking what I'm thinking?"

"I… I don't know what you mean, sir."

"This woman is the sole witness to Benji Myers's attack, isn't she? Do you think they're connected?"

Mason shrugged. "It's a bit too early to speculate, sir. Sheila Thompson never actually said..."

"I've been talking to Colin Wright, the bloke who discovered the body. He was taking his Labrador for a walk when he came across her. He thought it was a bundle of rags at first. Apparently, his dog had a pee on the shopping bag she had with her."

"Where is Mr Wright now? I'll need to speak to him."

"I've already done that. I took his statement and sent him on his way. He's at work at seven so there was no point in him being late. I'll let you have his details so you can speak to him yourself later."

"Very well, sir," Mason said. "Is this Sheila's shopping bag?" He indicated a crinkled plastic B&M bag lying on the grass.

Bainbridge nodded. "There's a half full bottle of White Lightening in there and a packet of cigarettes."

"I don't suppose there's a receipt in the bag?"

"Not that I could see."

"Forensics can take it to the lab and undergo an examination."

"Forensics? I wouldn't trust that bloody Cutts bloke to examine a boil on my arse."

"Leo? He seems efficient enough to me."

Bainbridge huffed and turned to walk away. "Make sure you double-check everything he gives you. Don't take anything at face value. Check, and then check again. The man's a liability."

Mason watched as DCS Bainbridge strode over the grass to his car parked on the far-side of the road. Sergeant Brown came over and stood by Mason's side. "I see the old man's still not forgiven young Cutts for what happened, then?"

"Am I missing something, sergeant? What is it between them?"

Sergeant Brown cleared his throat before he spoke. "Well, sir, DCS Bainbridge holds Leo Cutts responsible for what happened to Jilly... eh, Inspector Cooper. There was an investigation at the time, and Cutts was cleared of gross negligence, although he was instructed to tighten up on his procedures."

"And has he tightened up?"

"From what I've seen of the young man in recent months, there isn't a more diligent and thorough young man in Forensics."

"I take it you've started the house-to-house, sergeant?"

"Yes sir. I've got men knocking on doors along Newcomen Terrace. It's a big job because most of the houses have been converted into flats."

"What about the path between the lake and the beach? That's usually busy with dog walkers and cyclists."

"I have two constables on the promenade speaking to everyone passing."

"Was there anything happening in the "Tuned In" last night? Someone might have seen something."

The sergeant shook his head. "The Tuned In has been closed for the last few days sir. There's some electrical maintenance being carried out. The kids disco was cancelled and the night classes were moved to a local school. It's not due to re-open until sometime next week."

Mason gave a cursory look around the scene. "Well, everything seems to be under control here. I'm going over to Shaun Dyson's place and see what he's got to say for himself."

"Very well, sir, but can I suggest you take someone with you. I can spare PC Walker."

"Okay, send her over. I'm parked down there." He began to walk briskly back along the path to the slipway where he had parked his car. PC Lisa Walker soon joined him.

"Sergeant Brown said we're going to interview Shaun Dyson again, sir," she said.

"Yes, that's right. He'd better have a better alibi this time other than Leanne. Get in."

***

Shaun Dyson was sitting at the kitchen table reading the local Gazette when Mason and Walker arrived. They were shown into the room by Leanne. "Shaun, the keystones are here again, love," she said, staring menacingly at PC Walker.

"Leanne, that's no way to speak to Redcar's finest," Dyson said mockingly. "Offer them a cup of tea or something. Remember your manners."

"Stop pissing about, Dyson," Mason cut to the chase. "I want you to account for your movements last night."

"Is this about that old slag at the boating lake?" Leanne said. "That was nothing to do with my Shaun."

Walker turned sharply to face Leanne. "Who told you about that?"

"Everybody's talking about it. They say she had her throat cut from ear to ear. Is that true?"

"I've asked you a question, Dyson," Mason said. "Where were you between ten last night and five o'clock this morning?"

Dyson grinned as he reached out and took Leanne's hand. "Cuddled up to my lovely wife, of course," he said, "and before you ask, no there was no-one else there. We're not into threesomes, are we babe?"

Leanne began to chuckle. "That's right. Shaun's the only man for me, and believe me, I'm more than enough woman for him." She moved over to her husband and sat on his lap, placing her arms around his neck.

"I want the clothes you were wearing," Mason said.

"I wasn't wearing any clothes in bed. That's the way Leanne likes it, in the raw." Dyson and Leanne both began to giggle.

"I want the clothes you were wearing yesterday," Mason repeated. "Then I want you down at the station. I'm not satisfied with your answers, Dyson."

"What the fuck for? I've told you. I was here! I don't know anything about some stupid old bitch getting her head bashed in."

"So, you know how she was attacked?"

Dyson huffed. "I know nothing. Nothing, do you hear? This has nothing to do with me and you can't prove that it has."

He turned to Leanne. "Get my jeans out of the wash basket, will you love. The tee-shirt I was wearing yesterday is in there too."

Leanne walked into the utility room and returned a couple of minutes later with the clothes. She thrust them towards PC Walker. "Here, take them," she snarled, "but you're wasting your time. My Shaun was here with me last night. All night."

Dyson got to his feet and reached for his coat. "Let's get this over with. Before I say a word, I want my solicitor. I'm not saying another word 'til I have my solicitor."

11

Inspector Mason was in his office when DCS Bainbridge knocked lightly on the door and entered. "How did it go with Dyson? I heard you were interviewing him this morning."

Mason shrugged. "His solicitor sat in and recommended him that 'no comment' was the best way for him to proceed."

"So, you got nothing?"

Mason shook his head. "He swears he was with Leanne last night. No witnesses have come forward to challenge that so…"

"…so, …you're up the creek," Bainbridge nodded thoughtfully.

"I was thinking, sir, what if Dyson isn't involved? I mean, what motive would he have for killing Sheila Thompson? I would have thought the promise of a couple of bottles of booze and a few fags would be more than enough to buy her silence if she had witnessed him at Benji's."

"Probably, but Benji died, don't forget. We're dealing with murder here, not robbery."

"What I don't understand is what motive would Dyson have had for attacking Benji in the first place if it wasn't for the cash in the till? His file from headquarters was on my desk this morning. According to this, apart from several GBH's, Dyson is little more than a petty thief, an opportunist. That attack on the bookie was the biggest caper he'd ever pulled."

"Freddie Roberts is lucky to be alive after the attack. He's never worked since. I've heard he hasn't left the house since the attack. Dyson did that. He's vicious and ruthless, just like his father was. Violence is in the genes."

"But there's absolutely no evidence to connect him to Benji Myers or Sheila Thompson."

Bainbridge scowled. "He did it, I know he did. We haven't got the evidence yet, that's all. What about the house-to-house enquiries. Anything there?"

"No, sir, nothing. Everybody living in the vicinity appears to have been tucked up in their beds asleep."

"Well keep trying. Somebody must have seen something. Has the pathologist been able to say whether Sheila was killed at the site or was moved?"

"He said Sheila was definitely moved after she had been killed."

"So, we know the killer has some mode of transport. Have you searched her flat?"

"Yes, sir, the flat has been searched thoroughly. Wherever Sheila was killed, it certainly wasn't there. The lab boys are sure about that."

"What about the neighbours? Surely somebody must know something."

"PC Porter has been talking to them but they weren't helpful. Janice Phelps, who lives in the flat opposite, wasn't at home when he called, but Porter will be back again later."

"Maybe it would be best if you go yourself. I know Janice Phelps. She's a decent woman. She's not a snout but she has produced useful information occasionally."

"Very well, sir. I'll call on her on my way home."

Bainbridge got up to leave. "We have to move fast on this. The press is buzzing round already."

"That's understandable, I suppose. Two murders in two days, especially after what happened here last year, it's bound to get press interest."

Bainbridge grinned. "Maybe I should have extended my holiday by another month."

12

Flat 4a, the home of Sheila Thompson, had the distinctive blue and white 'Police Line – Do Not Cross' tape across the door. A uniformed officer was in attendance.

"Good evening, sir," greeted the constable.

"Good evening," Mason said. "Do you have the key to the flat? I want to have a look around."

"Yes, sir," he took out the key from his pocket. Placing it in the lock, he opened the door.

"Thanks," Mason said, stepping inside.

The room was small and dark with beige-coloured flocked wallpaper and grey curtains hanging at the small window. A black leatherette two-seater couch and a tan wing-back chair were in the centre of the room, whilst a glass-fronted display cabinet was on the back wall. A small television set was in the alcove next to the three-bar electric fire. One corner of the room had been made into a kitchen where a sink and drainer had been fitted and a two-ring stove was on a plastic worktop. The sink was full of dirty dishes and empty bottles of cider were strewn about. A miserable little room, Mason thought as he made his way into the bedroom.

A double bed was against the wall facing the window and a hanging rail with half a dozen items of clothing was next to it. Various pieces of clothing were scattered on the threadbare carpet. A small chest of drawers concluded the furniture in the room. Across from the bedroom, Mason could see a small bathroom with a bright-pink plastic shower curtain at one end.

Looking round the flat, Mason noticed evidence of the forensic team's visit with traces of the fingerprint powder left on some surfaces. As there had been no sign of violence having taking place in the flat, the examination had not been too thorough.

Mason left the flat, locked the door and handed the key back to the constable.

***

Flat 4b was directly opposite. Inspector Mason knocked briskly on the cream-painted door, and it was opened almost immediately.

"Yeah?" grunted the occupant, a small, plump woman in her late forties. Her hair was short and a vibrant shade of blue. "You the police?" she asked. "I heard you'd been around."

"I'm Inspector Mason," Jack replied casually. "Ms Phelps?"

"Yeah, I'm Janice Phelps." She opened the door wider and stepped to the side. "You'd better come in," she said.

Mason followed Janice into the surprisingly neat and tidy bedsit. The room was an array of bright colours in total contrast to Sheila Thompson's flat.

"Take a seat," she said, indicating a green and yellow checked chair by the side of the electric fire. "Fancy a cuppa? I've just made one."

Mason shook his head. "No thanks," he declined, perching on the edge of the chair. "I need to ask you a few questions about your neighbour, Sheila Thompson. I understand you two were friends."

Janice shrugged. "I wouldn't say we were friends exactly, but we got on. She's been my neighbour for nearly two years."

"When was the last time you spoke to Sheila?"

Janice furrowed her brow in thought. "Let me think… I saw her last night, about eight o'clock. She came round here on the cadge as usual. She wanted to know if I had any fags and booze she could have. That's when she told me Benji had been attacked in the shop."

"Did she tell you if she had witnessed what had happened?"

"No. She was more upset that she couldn't get her drink and fags."

"What happened?"

"I told her to piss off. She still owed me a packet of fags from last Friday."

"And what did Sheila say when you said no?"

"The usual string of profanities. I'll say one thing about Sheila, she could curse for England." Janice folded her arms and sighed. "The truth is, Inspector, Sheila was a bloody nuisance to all the tenants. She spent every penny she got on booze and then constantly bothered her neighbours begging for money to buy more."

"So, the last time you spoke to Sheila was at eight o'clock last night?"

"Not exactly. I'd been over to Redcar East. It was my friend Elizabeth's birthday and…. well, anyway, I got back about midnight just as Sheila was leaving by the front door."

"Do you know where she was going?"

Janice shook her head. "When I got to the door, I said goodnight and she came out with the usual abuse. She seemed pleased with herself and said I could stuff my booze and cigarettes. She knew where she could get as much as she wanted."

"What did she mean by that?"

"I've no idea. The last time I saw her, she was staggering down Felix Street towards the town centre. I'm afraid I don't know who she was meeting or what happened to her after she left the flat."

Mason leant back into the chair. "Did Sheila have any friends, any special friends who would help her in crisis?"

Janice shook her head. "She was a drunk, Inspector. She didn't have friends. To be honest, most people avoided her."

"As far as you know, did she have any enemies?"

"No. People would go out of their way to avoid her, but they're not enemies."

Mason got to his feet and handed Janice his card. "Thank you. If you think of anything else, please give me a ring."

Janice took the card and waddled towards the door. "I'll do that, Inspector, but I've told you all I know."

"One more thing," Mason said. "Do you know if Sheila knew Shaun Dyson?"

"Shaun? Of course she did. Everybody around here knows Shaun Dyson."

"Were they friends, Sheila and Shaun?"

"I've told you, Sheila didn't have any friends, not real friends."

"Well thanks, Janice. You've been extremely helpful."

13

Annika was about to take the steak pie out of the oven when Jack arrived home.

"Good timing," she said, placing the pie dish on the worktop. "I didn't hear you get up this morning. What time did you leave?"

Jack kissed Annika on the cheek. "Early, a woman's body was found near the boating lake. It was the woman I told you about who was near Benji's Wine Cellar the other night."

Annika gasped, clasping her hands. "What the hell is going on, Jack? Two bodies in two days?"

Jack shrugged. "I don't know, love, but I intend to find out."

"What about the suspect you told me about? Do you think he was involved?"

"Shaun Dyson? Bainbridge thinks so, but I'm not sure."

"What makes him so certain?"

"I think he's basing it on the family history. Apparently, Dyson's father was a vicious little bastard and Bainbridge is of the opinion the apple doesn't fall far from the tree."

"What do you think? Have you interviewed this Dyson? What's he like?"

Jack poured two glasses of wine and handed one to Annika, before he spoke. "Shaun Dyson is perfectly capable of hitting someone over the head. He was convicted of that last year, but that assault had a purpose. He wanted to steal the money the bookie was carrying. The assault on Benji

Myers seems without motive. The till was untouched and his wife says no stock is missing."

"He could have been disturbed before he had a chance to take it," Annika surmised. "After all, people are in and out of the shop all the time I expect."

"The only person who appears to have been in the vicinity at the time was Sheila Thompson."

"Do you think she knew the thief and tried to blackmail him?"

"That's the theory we're working on at the moment. It's hard because Sheila was an alcoholic and didn't have many friends, not reliable ones anyway."

"So, what's your next move?"

Jack grinned. "My next move is to enjoy this delicious looking pie," he smiled at his wife. "I've had enough of police work for today."

***

Leanne Dyson flung the carrier bag down on the Formica kitchen table and turned to her husband. "I've got fish and chips," she yelled. "Where's Arron? I've got him a battered sausage."

Shaun had been lounging on the couch watching the local news. "It's all over the telly… about Benji and Sheila."

"What do you expect? When somebody has their head caved in it's bound to get on the telly." Leanne went into the hall and shouted up the stairs. "Arron, tea's on the table."

“He’s gone out,” Shaun said.

“Out where?”

“How the fuck do I know. He’s always going out.”

Leanne handed Shaun the box containing the fish and chips. “Eat them while they’re still hot,” she told him. “Arron can warm his up later.”

Shaun took the box and opening it, began to eat the contents with his fingers. “What do you think to that copper that came round?”

Leanne sniffed. “He’s a bit of a dick, if you ask me,” she smirked. “I don’t think we’ve anything to worry about where he’s concerned.”

Shaun frowned. “I’m not so sure. They must think a lot about him in Leeds for him to be made up to inspector so young.”

“Well, this isn’t Leeds, is it? It’s Redcar and he knows diddlysquat, so stop worrying.”

“I can’t help it. What with that bastard Benji playing hardball, and then that drunken bitch trying to blackmail me… it’s all getting out of hand.”

Leanne reached over and grabbed Shaun’s arm. “Don’t be such a bloody wimp. Benji deserved what happened to him, the thieving little bastard, and as for her, she’s nothing but a useless drunk. I wouldn’t think the police will spend much time trying to find out who did for her.”

“I hope you’re right, love,” he said. “Once I get this sorted, we’ll be able to live like Kings. Where do you fancy? The Caribbean? Spain? Just name it.”

Leanne leant back in her chair and began to giggle. "This is going to sound crazy, but the place I really want to visit is China."

"China? You don't even like to eat a Chinese takeaway."

"I know, but I've always fancied going to China, ever since I was a kid. I saw this documentary and..."

Grinning, Shaun put his arm around Leanne's shoulders. "Before we can go anywhere, we have to find it."

"Are you sure Benji didn't say anything?"

"No. As soon as I entered the shop the stupid bastard came at me with a hammer from under the counter. I'd no choice. I had to defend myself."

"You shouldn't have hit him so hard though. Dead men can't talk."

"I didn't mean to but… well you know what my temper's like when I get roused. Once I started hitting him, I couldn't stop myself."

"What are we going to do about the other one? He must know where it is."

"I don't think it's safe me going to his house just yet, not with the cops watching my every move."

"Do you want me to go? They're not watching me."

"No, love. Neither of us can risk confronting him, but I know somebody who can."

"No, Shaun. You can't be serious. It's too risky."

"It's worth a try. The sooner we get this sorted, the sooner we can get away."

Leanne stuffed the last of the fried fish into her mouth and reached out for one of the cans of lager on the table. “I hope you’re right,” she said. “Otherwise...”

“Trust me. I know what I’m doing. Now, where’s my phone? I have to make a call.”

14

It was almost midnight. Pamela Reece pulled her woollen dressing gown tightly around her frail body as she opened her front door of her neat little bungalow at 18 Primrose Avenue. Dolly, her black and white cat, rushed past her into the darkness. The wind was strong, and the rain was lashing down as it had done since mid-afternoon. Pamela squinted through the blackness at the bungalow opposite. There was a figure at the door, standing beneath an umbrella.

"I wonder who's visiting Arthur at this time?" she said, hurriedly closing the door. "He hardly ever gets visitors these days."

Her husband, Bernard, was sat in front of the electric fire drinking the last of his cocoa. "It's probably one of the family," he said. "I know Arthur has a brother down in London. I don't think he could get up for the funeral."

Pamela tutted. "Not many came to poor Alice's funeral," she said. "I suppose with her being bed-ridden for all these years she wouldn't have mixed with many people."

"Well, the poor woman is in a better place now. I wouldn't wish MS on my worst enemy." Bernard put the cup down on the table and made his way to the hallway. "Come to bed, Pam. It's late. You can pop over and check on Arthur in the morning."

15

The alarm clock had given its third piercing ring before Jack opened his eyes. His head ached and his mouth felt dry. Peering over at the clock and saw that it was almost seven o'clock. Slowly he swung his legs out of bed. He felt dizzy as he attempted to stand up, grabbing the dressing table for support.

Annika propped herself up on her elbows and gently rubbed her eyes with her knuckles. "What time is it?" she asked drowsily.

"Go back to sleep, love," Jack whispered as he walked unsteadily over to the en suite.

"Are you all right, Jack?" Annika said. "You look a little… unsteady."

Jack rubbed the back of his head. "I feel like I've been hit by a bus. I can't understand it. I didn't have a lot to drink last night, did I?"

"You had quite a bit. You said you'd had a crap day and wanted to forget about it."

"Yes but… Never mind. I'll have a quick shower and a black coffee. That should do the trick."

"I'll put the kettle on," Annika offered, reaching for her dressing gown. "Do you want some breakfast?"

"No thanks, just coffee," Jack said as he stepped into the shower, "and make it strong, will you, love? I think I'm going to need it.

The CID office was quiet when DI Mason arrived. Two DC's were at their desk, heads bent, engrossed in writing up reports. Neither one acknowledged him as he made his way to his office. He was about to take off his coat when DCS Bainbridge, red-faced and slightly breathless, hurried into the room.

"There's been another one," he said. "An old man has been found murdered in his own home."

"What?"

"According to the constable who confirmed the death, it's been a ferocious attack, this time with a knife. The pathologist is already on the scene, and I've arranged for Forensics to meet us there. We can take my car. It's outside."

Mason hurried out of the office with Bainbridge. Neither spoke until they reached Primrose Avenue. Both officers put on white forensic suits from the boot of the car.

"Who found the body, sir?" Mason asked as they made their way up the flag-stoned path to the front door.

"The bloke's neighbour, Mrs Pamela Reece. She lives opposite."

"Have we identified the victim?"

"Arthur Rhodes. He was recently widowed and… ah here's Forensics. We'd better wait out here until they've made their inspection."

The CSI vehicle pulled up and Leo Cutts, together with a second man got out. They put on their forensic suits and headed towards the bungalow.

"Good morning, gentlemen," Leo said, a grim look on his pale, taut face. "This is getting to be a regular occurrence these days, isn't it?"

Bainbridge ignored the comment, turning to Mason instead. "I'm going back to the office. Come and see me as soon as you get through here."

"Yes, sir,"

Mason watched as Cutts and his colleague entered the bungalow. Fifteen minutes later, Cutts came to the door. "You can come in now, Inspector," he said. "Make sure you keep to the footplates. It's a bloody mess in here. I hope you haven't had any breakfast this morning."

Mason huffed as he followed the forensic officer into the building and through to the lounge. He stopped abruptly in the doorway, blinking rapidly at the scene before him. Furniture had been overturned, photographs smashed, ceramics broken. Amongst the debris on the floor lay the crumpled body of Arthur Rhodes. He was lying on his back, the front of his white shirt red with blood. The cream carpet was stained crimson and blood splatters were sprayed over the marble fireplace and up the front wall.

Using the footplates, Mason carefully made his way to where the body lay before crouching down to examine it more closely. Rhodes's white shirt was shredded where a knife had repeatedly penetrated his chest. The backs of his hands bore deep cuts, as he had tried in vain to defend himself. It was the attack to the man's face which Mason found the most disturbing. Slash after slash had been inflicted across his nose and cheeks, but worse of all, the man had been stabbed through both eyes.

"Are you all right, Inspector?" Cutts said. "You're not going to pass out, are you?" A faint grin spread across his face. “You’d be surprised how many policemen swoon at the sight of blood.”

Mason inhaled deeply. “Don’t worry, I’m not going to faint.” He stood up and slowly shook his head. “How can one human being do this to another?” he mused. “I don’t think I’ll ever understand that.”

Cutts shrugged. “I’d like to say you get used to it in this job, but of course you don’t. You never do.”

Dr Carpenter, the Force Pathologist, was sat at the table at the far side of the room writing notes. Mason approached him.

“I’m DI Mason,” he said. “I’m SIO on this case, Dr Carpenter. I don’t suppose you can give me an approximate time of death?”

“Midnight,” Carpenter replied abruptly, “or not much later. I’ll know more when I get him on the slab.” He gathered the paperwork together and placed it in his briefcase. “Right, I’ll be off. Get the body over to the morgue as soon as you can, Cutts. I can get the PM done this afternoon and then I’ll be free from this bloody work for the weekend.”

Carpenter rushed to the door, giving Mason a curtesy nod. “See you this afternoon, Inspector,” he said as he hurried to his Mercedes which was parked across the street.

“He seems in a hurry,” Mason commented as the Mercedes roared into life and drove down the road.

Cutts grinned. “He’s a keen golfer,” he said. “He’ll be going down to Whitby this weekend to play on the links.”

Mason tutted. “All right for some. I’d better speak with Mrs Reece. I believe she’s the one that found the body?”

"Yes, sir. She lives straight across the road at no. 18. She's in a right state, poor woman. PC Walker is with her now."

"Good. I'll leave you to finish up here."

"Yes, sir," Cutts shook his head. "I think it's going to take some time."

16

Inspector Mason knocked lightly on the door of no 18 and, not waiting for a reply, walked straight in. The bungalow was neat and tidy with magnolia-coloured walls and pale-fawn carpets throughout. There was the unmistakable aroma of lavender from the plug-ins in the hall and the lounge.

Pamela Reece sat nervously on the edge of the couch clasping the hand of her husband who was sitting next to her. Her face was pale and taut, and her eyes were red and swollen from sobbing. PC Walker was sitting in an armchair opposite.

"Good morning, Mrs Reece," Mason spoke softly and politely. "I'm Inspector Jack Mason. I'd like to ask you a few questions about what happened this morning."

Pamela made no reply as she stared aimlessly into space.

Bernard Reece put his arm protectively around his wife's trembling shoulders. "Can't this wait?" he appealed. "Pam's already told you people what happened."

"I'm sorry, Mr Reece, but it can't wait, I'm afraid."

Pamela sniffed loudly and patted her husband's arm. "It's all right, love." she said, turning to face Mason. "Ask your questions, Inspector, but I don't think there's anything more I can add."

Mason sat on the armchair and took out his notebook. "It must have been quite a shock, seeing Mr Rhodes like that?"

Pamela dabbed at her eyes with her handkerchief. "Arthur was a nice man," she said. "I don't understand why someone would want to hurt him."

"How long have you known Mr Rhodes?"

"Ever since we moved to this bungalow. How long is that, Bernard? Eight years?"

"Nearly nine," Bernard corrected. "Arthur and I were members of the Redcar Bowls Club."

"And me and Alice, that's Arthur's wife, went to the WI together, that's before she got ill of course. Poor Alice died two months ago. She'd suffered from MS for years."

"They were a devoted couple," Bernard added. "Arthur was heartbroken when she went."

"When was the last time you saw Mr Rhodes?"

"Yesterday afternoon," Bernard said, "just before the rain started. He'd been for his usual pint at The Galleon. He goes there most days."

"Mr Rhodes liked to drink?"

"A couple of pints, no more. He went more for the company. He used to meet up with his mate and they'd have a game of dominoes."

"Neither of you saw Mr Rhodes since then?"

"Yes, I did," Pamela said. "It would be about midnight. I'd put the cat out when I saw someone at Arthur's door. I said to Bernard, who can that be calling on Arthur at this time of night?"

"Did you recognise Mr Rhodes's visitor?"

Pamela shook her head. "No. It was pitch-black and raining heavily. Besides, they were underneath an umbrella."

"An umbrella? Do you know what colour?"

“Black I think, but you couldn’t tell. It was so dark. Arthur had the hall light on, so I could see him clearly, but not the visitor, I’m afraid.”

“Did you have any indication as to their height or build?”

Pamela furrowed her brow. “I would say he was on the short side, about five feet six I would think, and slim.”

Mason put the notebook into his pocket. “Thank you both, you’ve been most helpful. Now if you wouldn’t mind making a statement about what you’ve told me to PC Walker, we’ll leave you in peace.”

Mason walked towards the door, and then turned to face Bernard. “What’s his mate called, Mr Reece? The one he goes drinking with. Do you know?”

“Oh yes, I’ve known him for years. His name is Benji Myers. They worked together on security at the steelworks. Arthur only retired from there last year.”

17

Inspector Mason returned to Mr Rhodes's bungalow and checked that everything necessary was being conducted by his officers. Leo Cutts was still at the scene. On sight of the inspector, Leo bounded towards him.

"Not much to report sir, I'm afraid. There's no sign of the murder weapon, and as for fingerprints…"

"Keep testing," Mason said. "The killer's DNA must be here somewhere."

Cutts raised an eyebrow. "I'll see what I can do," he said, "but I'm not hopeful."

PC Walker came hurrying towards him.

"I've taken Mrs Reece's statement," she reported. "I'll go to the station and arrange for it to be typed up."

"Before you do that, I need a lift. I came here in Bainbridge's car, and he's left the scene."

"My patrol car's over there, sir. Where are we going?" she asked.

"I need another word with Benji Myers's widow. It seems our victim and her late husband were best mates."

Mason climbed into the passenger seat of Walker's patrol car and they drove off in the direction of Mrs Myers's home.

***

Irene Myers was arranging flowers in a vase when Mason and Walker arrived at her house.

"Aren't these lovely?" she said, placing the vase in the window. "They're from the neighbours down the street. People are being so kind."

"Mrs Myers, I..."

"Irene, please," she suggested, sitting on the couch. "Won't you sit down Inspector?"

Mason settled in the armchair indicated, whilst PC Walker remained standing by the door.

"Irene, I understand your husband was a close friend of Arthur Rhodes."

Irene looked puzzled. "Yes, they worked together at the steel works on security. Why do you want to know about Arthur?"

"Arthur Rhodes was murdered last night. We wondered if there could be a connection to your husband's death."

Irene gasped and began to visibly tremble. "Oh, the poor man, that's terrible, but what's that got to do with Benji?"

Mason shrugged. "I'm not sure yet, but I believe there may be some connection."

Irene shook her head. "No, you're wrong. Benji went for a drink with Arthur and an occasional game of dominoes. That's all. They weren't particularly close."

"You say Benji worked as a night-watchman at the steelworks?"

"That's right. He was given the job to see him up to his pension. He'd been injured in a fall at the plant, so he found it difficult to do his proper job."

"And Arthur Rhodes was already working as a night-watchman?"

"Arthur's wife had been poorly for years. Multiple Sclerosis, I think. That's why he took the night-watchman's job… so he could spend time during the day with his wife. Arthur paid a nurse to stay with her while he was at work."

"I see. Tell me, Irene, do you know a man called Shaun Dyson?"

Irene looked puzzled. "I know of him," she nodded. "Shaun worked at the steelworks for a time. Before his accident, Arthur Rhodes was his supervisor. A few years back Arthur had to give Shaun the sack for bad timekeeping."

"So… there was ill feeling between Arthur and Shaun Dyson?"

"No, I wouldn't say that exactly. As far as I know, once Shaun left the plant their paths never crossed. Why do you want to know about Shaun Dyson? Do you think he has something to do with Benji's death?"

"It's a routine line of enquiry," Mason answered. "I take it your husband never mentioned Dyson to you?"

"No, not that I can remember. Benji was a quiet man, Inspector. He kept himself to himself. The only person he really mixed with away from the shop was Arthur Rhodes, and even that was only once, sometimes twice a week to play dominoes at The Galleon."

"Was Benji a heavy drinker?"

Irene looked puzzled. "I'm sorry dear, I don't know what you mean."

"It's just that it's been suggested that Benji was often drunk."

"I don't know who's been telling you that. It's simply not true."

Mason strode to the door. "Well thanks, Irene. I'll leave you in peace now. Do you want PC Walker to stay with you?"

Irene smiled, shaking her head. "No, that won't be necessary. My daughter and son-in-law are coming from Carlisle tomorrow, so I won't be on my own."

"If you change your mind, please call. PC Walker can be here straightaway." Mason offered.

"You're very kind," Irene said. "Just promise me you'll find whoever killed my Benji and poor Arthur."

Mason opened the front door. "I'll do my best. I promise you that."

18

The old man died too quickly. Much too quickly. He told me nothing. Instead, he hurtled toward me brandishing his walking stick. One blow crashed down narrowly missing my shoulders.

He was definitely trying to kill me.
What I did then was in self-defence.
Surely you can see that.
It was him or me.

I must admit though, it did give me a thrill plunging the knife into his flesh, time after time.

I suppose gouging his eyes could be considered grotesque by some, but the adrenaline was pumping through my body by this time.

I couldn't stop myself.
Killing him was bliss.
Sheer bliss.

19

Mason got back to the station to be met by DCS Bainbridge in Reception.

"Ah there you are, Mason," Bainbridge began. "I hear it was pretty ferocious, the attack on Mr Rhodes."

Mason sighed. "Yes, sir. The poor old sod wouldn't have had a chance."

"Got anyone in the frame yet?"

"Not yet," he said. "The neighbour said Mr Rhodes had a visitor late last night, but she couldn't give a good description."

"You can bet this is down to Dyson."

"I've no reason to think so, but I'll bring him in for questioning of course."

"I'd like to sit in on the interview if you don't mind."

"Do you have a reason for that, sir? I assure you I'm more than capable of..."

"Shaun Dyson is a tricky bastard. I should know. I arrested him over the attack on the bookie two years ago."

"There's something I meant to ask you about that, sir. You said Roberts probably had over twenty thousand pounds on him, not five as he claimed. Why was that?"

Bainbridge walked towards Mason's office and indicated for the inspector to follow him. Once inside, Bainbridge leant against the desk. "What I'm about to tell you Mason, is of a most confidential nature. Not a word must be repeated outside of this room. Do you understand?"

"Yes of course, sir," he said. "You can rely on me."

Bainbridge inhaled deeply before continuing. "The Drugs Squad are investigating Freddie Roberts and his family. They suspect them of being heavily involved in the distribution of Class A drugs here in Redcar."

"Why hadn't he been arrested?"

"It's not that easy. The gang is highly organised. It's believed Roberts was one of the ringleaders, but there's not enough evidence for a warrant to search his premises. There were rumours that he distributed the filthy stuff whilst working at racecourse, but he was too clever to ever get caught."

"You say Roberts is still in a bad way since the attack?"

"He claims to be suffering from amnesia. He says he has no memory of what happened."

"I take it you don't believe him?"

Bainbridge shook his head. "Call me a cynic," he said. "It all seems a little too convenient to me. Unfortunately, amnesia can't be proved one way or the other."

"You suspect Freddie is still involved?"

"I do, but I wouldn't be surprised if his two sons, Barry and Lee are about to take over."

"Do you want me to investigate, sir? I could make the excuse for visiting Freddie Roberts."

"With three murders to deal with, I would have thought your time was pretty much taken up, Inspector."

"I'll manage," Mason dismissed the offer. "I'll call on them in the next couple of days."

"Good man. Report only to me, and make sure you don't take any officer with you."

"Is there a reason for that?"

"The Drugs Squad believe someone from this station may be involved. It's a sensitive matter, so we have to be discreet."

"Very well, sir. Leave it with me."

20

"Well, today's the day," Wayne Beaumont said, smiling as he readjusted his tie in the hall mirror. "CID, here I come."

His remark was met with a contemptuous grunt from his partner, Jodie. "Being in plain clothes means you'll be working longer hours, doesn't it? We hardly see each other as it is."

Wayne huffed as he put on his jacket. "For Christ's sake woman, stop moaning. Getting into CID is a big career move for me. More money and more opportunity for advancement."

"But what about us? You're out working almost every night as it is."

"Not every night," Wayne corrected as he opened the door. "Now, paint a smile on and enjoy your day." Before Jodie could reply, he was through the door and heading towards his car.

***

"Welcome to CID," Mason smiled as Beaumont entered the CID office. "I think you know everyone here."

Beaumont nodded an acknowledgement at the three fellow officers who were sat at their desks, a computer in front of each of them. "Yes, sir," he said, "and can I say how grateful I am for the opportunity of working with you all."

"I intend to bring Shaun Dyson in for questioning this morning," Mason informed him. "You can come with me."

"Yes, sir," Beaumont replied eagerly. "What's it in connection with?"

"I think there's a real possibility he could be involved with what happened to Arthur Rhodes."

"The bloke who got stabbed?"

"That's him. It was a frenzied attack on an old man."

"But why would Dyson do that? I know he has a fiery temper, but to attack an old man in such a savage way… well, it doesn't seem his style somehow."

"You might be right," Mason agreed, "but I want him brought in for interview anyway."

***

Beaumont drove Mason to Walton Street, arriving there just before ten o'clock.

"Let me do the talking," Mason said as he knocked on the door. On the second knock, the door was opened by the young boy who Mason had met on his last visit.

"Is your dad in?" he said. Arron drew his sleeve across his nose, staring at the two officers.

"Dad, it's the…" Before he could finish his sentence, Shaun Dyson, wearing only his boxer shorts appeared behind his son.

"What is it this time?" he sneered. "Someone pinch the lead off the church roof?"

"I want you to come to the station to answer some questions."

"What about?"

"Get dressed, Mr Dyson," Mason told him. "You've got two minutes, otherwise you'll be arrested."

Dyson gave a defiant stare, but retreated into the house. "Leanne, get my jeans from the bedroom," he yelled. "It's the bloody cops again. You'd think they'd have something better to do than harass an innocent man."

"We'll sue the bastards," Leanne shouted from inside the house. "They can't keep blaming you for everything that goes wrong in Redcar."

"Leave it love," said Dyson as he appeared back at the door, dressed in blue jeans and a sweater. "I'll be back before you know it." He turned to face Mason, "Well come on then, mate. Let's get this over with."

***

Mason arrived back at the station accompanied by Dyson and DC Beaumont. He was about to enter the interview room when Sergeant Brown hurried towards him.

"Sir, Mrs Myers telephoned. She wants to speak to someone urgently."

"Did she say what about?"

Sergeant Brown looked furtively at Dyson who was standing next to Mason. "Perhaps we could speak in private, sir?" he said.

Mason opened the interview door and steered Dyson inside. "Watch him," he said to Beaumont. "I won't be a minute."

When Beaumont and Mason were behind the closed door of the interview room he turned to Sergeant Brown. "Well? What did Mrs Myers want to talk about?"

"Irene said she has some information about the assault on Benji. She wouldn't discuss it over the telephone, but she sounded agitated."

"Okay, but I have to interview Dyson first about Arthur Rhodes. I want you to sit in on the interview with me and Beaumont can speak with Irene Myers."

"Very well, sir."

Mason entered the interview room with Sergeant Brown. Dyson was sitting at the metal desk, his arms behind his head. The Inspector turned to DC Beaumont. "I need you to visit Mrs Myers," he said. "She wishes to make a further statement. Sergeant Brown will assist me with the interview."

Once they were all seated, Mason turned on the tape and introduced himself, followed by Sergeant Brown. "Also in the room," said Mason, "is a person of interest, Shaun Dyson." Mason turned to Dyson. "Can you tell me where you were two nights ago, Mr Dyson?"

Dyson shrugged. "I can't remember. I don't get out much these days."

"This is a murder enquiry," Mason said. "Answer my question Dyson. Where were you?"

"Is this about what happened to that old bloke? It's got nothing to do with me."

"Then prove it. Where were you two nights ago?"

Dyson huffed as he brought his arms from behind his head, resting them on the desk. "That was the night it pissed it down, wasn't it?"

"Yes, that's right."

"In that case, I was with the wife. We went to The Smugglers for a couple of drinks. We got soaked on the way home."

"What time did you leave the pub?"

Dyson shrugged. "I don't know. It was late. We had a bit of a lock-in. Joey can vouch for me."

"Joey?"

"The landlord. He'll tell you I was there all night."

"Tell me about your relationship with Arthur Rhodes. Did you like him?"

"Did I fuck like him. That bastard got me the sack, did you know that?"

"And you bore a grudge against him?"

"I didn't kill him if that's what you mean. Arthur Rhodes was a mean old bastard, not the saint he pretended to be."

Mason leant forward across the desk, steepling his fingers. "What exactly do you mean by that?"

Dyson straightened his shoulders and stared at Mason in defiance. "I don't grass, not even on a bastard like Rhodes."

"If you're withholding information, Dyson, I will arrest you."

Dyson sniffed loudly. "I'm saying nothing. I didn't kill Arthur, and I don't know who did, so can I go now?"

Sergeant Brown stood up and walked towards the door. “I’ll be checking your alibi. We’ll be in touch.”

Dyson hurried to the door, a broad grin on his face. “I didn’t kill the miserable old bastard,” he said, “…but I’m not sorry he’s dead.”

21

Detective Constable Wayne Beaumont seated himself in the comfortable armchair beside the log-burner in Irene Myers's front room and waited in anticipation for the home-made fruit cake and cup of tea promised by her. She returned to the lounge a few minutes later and lay the tea tray down on the small table.

"Milk and sugar?" she asked as she began pouring the strong brown liquid into the porcelain cup.

"Yes please, love," Beaumont said as he reached out and took a large slab of the cake. "Two sugars and plenty of milk." He ate the cake with relish, wishing Jodie would learn to bake cakes instead of buying them from the supermarket.

"More tea?" Irene proffered, as Beaumont drained the cup.

"Why not?" Beaumont said as Irene began to pour a second cup.

"I understand your daughter and her husband were coming to stay with you," he said.

"They are, but they won't be here until six o'clock. Sonja's husband had some problem at work which needed his attention."

Beaumont drained his cup for the second time before taking out his notebook. "Inspector Mason said you have some further information about the incident at the shop?"

"Not exactly. I don't know anything about what happened there. No, dear. It was something I remembered about Benji and Arthur Rhodes."

Beaumont sat upright, looking expectantly at Irene. "What's that?" he asked.

"A couple of weeks ago, Benji had been out for his usual drink with Arthur. He got home about ten o'clock and he seemed… he seemed upset and agitated."

"Did he say what was the matter?"

"No. He sat in his chair," she nodded towards the chair Beaumont was occupying, "and stared into the fire. He never said a word. After about half-an-hour, he got up and went into the hall. He picked up a large leather bag and took it outside into the shed."

Beaumont scowled. "I'm sorry, Irene, but I don't see what this has to do with Arthur."

"I asked him what was going on and he said it was nothing to worry about. He said he and Arthur had found the bag. Arthur had been holding it for safekeeping for a while, but he wanted Benji to take it."

"Did he say where he had found it?"

"No, not exactly, but I think it was at work."

"Did he say what was inside the bag?"

Irene shook her head. "He locked the shed door and refused to mention it again."

"Where's the bag now?"

"It's still in the shed as far as I know. I don't know where Benji put the key I'm afraid, but Arthur would visit and they would both go into the shed. I wasn't allowed to take them any tea whilst they were in there."

"And you think the bag could have some bearing on what happened?"

"All I know is Benji seemed quite nervous this last two weeks since he put the bag into the shed. It was as if he was scared of something. Always looking over his shoulder. When I mentioned this to him, he said I was being silly and I had an overactive imagination."

"Can you show me the shed, Irene?"

"Of course, dear. This way."

Irene led the way through her neat kitchen and out into the small but immaculate garden. The green-painted shed was in the far corner. Beaumont could see that the only window in the shed had an old newspaper up against it, making it impossible to see inside. A large silver-coloured padlock secured the door.

"You sure you don't know where the key is?" Beaumont asked, examining the lock.

"I've looked everywhere," she said. "The lawnmower's inside and Sonja's husband was going to mow the lawn for me tomorrow."

"I'll have a word with my boss. He'll probably use bolt cutters to open the door if that's alright with you?"

"Of course, dear. We can't leave the shed locked, can we?"

22

Mason headed towards his office after having had a quick snack in the canteen, when he saw Sergeant Brown coming towards him carrying a CCTV disc.

"I've been to The Smugglers," the sergeant said. "The landlord couldn't say for definite if Dyson was in that night, but he was happy for me to take the CCTV footage."

Mason took the disc from the sergeant. "Good. I'll get one of my lads to look through it, in fact, better still, I'll check it myself."

"Has Beaumont got back from Mrs Myers's yet, sir?"

"I don't think so. He's probably stopped off somewhere for a bite to eat."

"Skiving more like," the sergeant muttered as he headed towards the comms room. "I'll get him on the radio and see where he's at."

Mason had begun sifting through the paperwork when his desk phone rang. "Mason," he answered.

"Sir, it's Leo. Leo Cutts from Forensics."

"Yes, Leo. What can I do for you?"

"I'm still at Mr Rhodes' house. I've found something interesting."

"Oh?"

"Drugs, sir. Expensive drugs. The type used to treat MS. You can't get them in the UK. These have been imported from America."

"You say they're expensive?"

“I would guess a couple of thousand at least.”

“You’d better bring them to the station.”

“Yes, sir. I’ll be there within an hour. I’ve finished at the house now. No luck with fingerprints or DNA I’m afraid.”

Mason put down the receiver as DC Beaumont knocked briskly on his office door and entered.

“Ah, there you are, Beaumont,” Mason said. “Sergeant Brown was about to send out a search party.”

“Sorry, sir,” Beaumont said. “Irene… I mean Mrs Myers, is a rather talkative woman.”

“Did she tell you anything useful?”

“I’m not sure.” Beaumont proceeded to tell Mason about the bag inside the shed. “Mrs Myers seems to think there’s something sinister about it.”

“Well, we’d better take a look. Forensics came up empty at the house.”

“I can go if you like,” Beaumont said. “I can get the bolt cutters and take off the lock.”

“No, I think I’d better go. If there is anything of interest inside the bag, it’s best I’m there. You get me the bolt cutters. Sergeant Brown knows where they are, then continue with the house-to-house around Primrose Avenue. Somebody must have seen something.”

When Beaumont left the room, Mason rang Chief Superintendent Bainbridge’s extension. He explained what DC Beaumont had told him. “I thought you might like to join me at Mrs Rhodes house, sir. It sounds like this could prove useful.”

"Give me five minutes," Bainbridge said. "I'll join you in Reception."

Mason picked up the CCTV disc which had been taken from The Smugglers Inn and placed it in his desk drawer, carefully locking it afterwards. "I'll deal with you later," he said as he walked out of the office and down to Reception.

23

"That's the shed, dear," Irene Myers said as Bainbridge and Mason followed her into the back garden. "Like I told that good-looking young man earlier, I have no idea where Benji put the key."

"Don't worry about that, Irene," Mason said reassuringly, "we'll have the door opened in a jiffy." He quickly snipped at the padlock with the bolt cutters, then turned the handle of the shed door. "Would you mind waiting inside the house?" he said. "Leave us to look for the bag."

Irene shrugged. "As you like, dear," she said. "I have to prepare dinner for Sonja and her hubby anyway." She walked briskly back into the house, closing the kitchen door behind her.

Both men put on rubber gloves. "Well, here goes nothing," Mason stepped inside the shed followed by DCS Bainbridge. The shed was gloomy with the stale smell of tobacco. On the floor, between two camping chairs, were several empty bottles of beer. "I thought Irene said Benji didn't drink?"

"Men get up to all sorts their wives don't know about," Bainbridge said as he ripped the newspaper from the window. "There, that's better. We can see what we're looking for now."

One wall of the shed was lined with wooden shelving containing bags of compost, plant food and other gardening paraphernalia. In the far corner stood an old lawn mower and an even older hedge trimmer. There was a metal bench on the opposite wall with more gardening equipment. Underneath the bench, Mason could see a large, brown-leather bag. He reached down and pulled it out, placing it on top of the bench.

"Voila!" he said. "This must be the bag Irene was talking about."

The bag had a thick layer of dust. Along the top, in gold lettering, were the words 'Mr F Roberts – Turf Accountant.' A sturdy lock secured the bag.

"This fits the description of the bag stolen by Dyson. I'll get Forensics to open it."

"Arrange for a thorough search of this shed as well," Bainbridge said. "You never know, there might be something else here we can use."

With Mason carrying the bag, both men left the shed closing the door behind them. Irene Myers was standing in the doorway accompanied by a younger woman and a man.

"This is my daughter, Sonja," she said, "and her husband, Giles."

Sonja looked annoyed. "Would you please tell me what the hell you're doing in Dad's shed?" she said. "You should be out there looking for the bastard that killed him."

"That's what we are doing, Mrs…?"

"Nixon," she said.

"Mrs Nixon, we don't want you or anyone else near the shed until our Forensics team have had a chance to examine it. If you wouldn't mind going into the house?"

Giles Nixon stepped forward. "Can you tell us what exactly you were hoping to find in my father-in-law's shed?"

Bainbridge walked towards Nixon, hand outstretched. "I'm Detective Chief Superintendent Bainbridge," he smiled, shaking Nixon's hand. "Inspector Mason and I are dealing with Mr Myers's murder."

"I don't see how this involves Benji's shed. He was murdered in the shop, for Christ's sake. Shouldn't you be searching that for clues?"

"I see you've found the bag," Irene said. "I'll go and make some tea, shall I?"

"Not for us," replied Bainbridge. "Now, if you wouldn't mind all going back into the house, our forensics people will be here soon."

They all made their way back into the living room.

"Is this going to take long?" Irene asked, "only I'd like Giles to mow the lawn whilst he's here and the mower is in the shed."

"You can have the mower as soon as Forensics have finished their search," said Mason. Taking out his mobile phone, began dialling their number. "They shouldn't be long."

24

Jack Mason rose just before seven the following morning. He was surprised to see Annika already dressed, sitting at the breakfast table.

"You're up early, darling," he said, lightly kissing her on the cheek. "Everything all right?"

Annika scowled. "You've forgotten, haven't you?" she accused.

"Forgotten what?"

Annika banged her coffee mug down on the table, causing the coffee to splash. "Life isn't only about murder you know. Some of us do more ordinary, mundane jobs."

"Oh, darling, I'm so sorry. It's today you start at the salon, isn't it?"

Annika sniffed loudly then took a bite of her toast hastily.

"I'm sure you'll enjoy working there," he said. "You can tell me all about it this evening."

Annika huffed as she took her mug to the sink. "Do you know what time you'll be home tonight? You seem to be getting home later and later."

"There's been three murders in as many days," Jack said. "I thought you understood that my work isn't a nine-to-five."

"For Christ's sake, Jack. Two old men and a drunken hag is hardly worth all this effort, is it? She probably fell down in a stupor and banged her head. From what I heard she was drunk as a skunk."

"Of course it's worth the effort," Jack said as he poured himself a coffee. "I can't believe you hold those views."

"All I'm saying is don't knock yourself out. You must find time for us. That's what's really important, not solving some crime that nobody really cares about anyway."

Jack gulped at his coffee. "I care," he said, rushing towards the hall. "Got to go. I'm meeting the pathologist at eight-thirty."

"Sounds fascinating," she scoffed. "See you tonight."

Putting on his coat, Jack opened the front door onto the drive. "'Bye, darling. Good luck at the salon," he said fleetingly.

***

Dr Ruben Carpenter was standing by the window of his office at the mortuary when Mason arrived. In his late forties, Carpenter was short and plump with dark hair and even darker eyes. He indicated for him to take a seat.

Carpenter thrust his hands deep into the pockets of his white smock. "Bad business," he said. "Benjamin Myers and this woman, Sheila Thompson."

"Can you confirm from the autopsy that both victims were attacked with the same weapon?"

"No doubt whatsoever. Both Benjamin Myers and Sheila Thompson were both hit on the back of the head with the same hammer, probably a claw hammer. I can say with confidence that the perpetrator who inflicted the blows was powerfully built."

“So, you’re sure it was a man?”

“No question. Both skulls were crushed with one blow. To do that takes a lot of force.”

“Is there anything else you can tell me about the state of the bodies, Dr Carpenter?” Mason said. “I take it there was no sexual assault in either case?”

Carpenter shook his head. “No sign of anything like that,” he confirmed. “Apart from the crushed skull, the only thing they had in common was the state of their livers. If the blow hadn’t killed them, in a noticeably short time sclerosis of the liver most certainly would have.”

Mason frowned. “I know Sheila Thompson was a heavy drinker, but Benji Myers? Surely that can’t be right?”

Carpenter looked annoyed. “I assure you that my findings are beyond dispute,” he said. “Of course, if you wish for a further autopsy, please go ahead, but I assure you they will come to the same conclusion.”

“Dr Carpenter, I didn’t mean to question your findings. It’s just that… well Mrs Myers gave the impression that Benji rarely drank alcohol.”

“Then Mrs Myers is a liar, or her husband hid it from her.”

“I’ll look into it,” Mason scribbled a note. “Now, what can you tell me about Arthur Rhodes?”

“A savage attack,” the doctor said. “The person who inflicted those knife wounds was an extremely angry individual. All I can say with certainty is the killer was right-handed.”

“Again, you think the assault was carried out by a man?”

“My guess is yes, but of course there isn’t the same physical strength required as with the other two attacks.

The attack on Mr Rhodes was frenzied, barbaric. I believe the perpetrator to be an extremely disturbed individual."

"Can you pin-point the exact cause of his death?"

Dr Carpenter inhaled deeply. "There were over thirty stab wounds on the old man's body," he said, "but it was the wound penetrating the heart which caused his death."

"Can you say if the stabbing of his eyes was post-mortem?"

"Oh, yes. Most definitely. That was an evil after-thought I think."

"Thank you, Dr Carpenter. If you could arrange for a copy of your report to be sent to my office, I would be most grateful."

"No problem, Inspector. I'll get my secretary to do that right away."

25

It was almost ten o'clock when Mason left the mortuary. He was about to get into his car when his mobile rang. "Mason," he said.

"Sir, it's Leo Cutts."

"Yes, Leo. What have you got for me?"

"We managed to open the bag. The contents were interesting."

"Oh? Are we talking wads of cash?"

"If there had been money inside the bag it's been taken out. What I found were drugs. Pure Heroin. The haul must be worth thousands."

"Any fingerprints?"

"Yes, sir. That's where it gets interesting."

"Go on man, I'm listening."

"Freddie Roberts's fingerprints are all over the packages, but so are those of Benji Myers and Arthur Rhodes."

***

Mason got into his car and headed towards Redcar East where Freddie Roberts and his two sons lived. Their detached house on Oak Parade was well-maintained, with large Georgian-style windows and an impressive stone entrance porch.

Mason got out of his car and began to stride up the brick-red path towards the house. As he approached, the door flung open and a short, stocky man of about thirty appeared, his feet planted firmly in the doorway. Both his arms were heavily tattooed and his head was shaven.

"Yeah?" he challenged. "Who the fuck are you?"

Mason reached into his inside pocket and produced his warrant card. "I'm Inspector Jack Mason," he said. "I'm here to speak to Mr Roberts. Who are you?"

The man peered suspiciously at Mason. "I'm Billy," he claimed. "Billy Finlay. I work for Mr Roberts."

He snatched the warrant card from Mason's grasp and studied it carefully.

"What do you want with Freddie?"

Mason retrieved the warrant card and put it back into his pocket. "That's my business. Please let Mr Roberts know I'm here."

Scowling, the man closed the door shut. It was opened a few seconds later by a smartly dressed man of about thirty years of age.

"I'm Barry Roberts," he introduced himself. "I understand you wish to speak to my Father?"

"Yes. I have a few questions for him."

"You know my Father's not well?"

"I just want a few minutes of his time," Mason said. "Has he remembered anything about what happened?"

"No. He can't remember anything," Barry said, attempting to close the door. Jack stretched out his arm, pushing it open.

“I still need to speak with him. It won’t take long.”

Barry gave a defiant look, but stepped to the side. “All right but make it quick. Dad’s not well.”

Mason followed Barry into the spacious, well-furnished lounge. Freddie Roberts was reclining on a couch by the window. A red tartan blanket covered his legs. He looked inquisitively at his son, then at Mason.

“Dad, this gentleman is a policeman,” Barry said softly. “He wants to ask you some questions about the attack.”

Freddie squinted. “I can’t remember what happened,” he protested weakly. “I’ve already told the police that.”

Mason walked over to the couch and crouched down in front of Freddie. “We’ve retrieved your bag,” he said. “The one that got stolen.”

“What bag? I… I don’t remember any bag.” He turned to his son. “What’s he talking about, Barry? I don’t understand.”

“It’s all right, Dad. I’ll deal with this.” Barry turned to Mason. “Let’s go into the dining room,” he said, striding over to a door at the far side of the room. Mason followed and once inside the room, Barry closed the door. “My Dad doesn’t remember what happened to him,” he claimed, anger flaring in his eyes. “That bastard, Dyson, is responsible for that.”

“Dyson’s been dealt with by the court,” Mason said. “I need to know more about the bag your father was carrying.”

“It was his tote bag. All bookies have one.”

“There seems to be some discrepancy about the amount of cash that was in the bag at the time of the assault.”

"What do you mean, discrepancy? There were about five thousand quid, that's all. Hardly enough for ruining a man's life for, is it?"

"From what I've been told, there was much more than five thousand pounds in the bag. I understand it was over twenty thousand, possibly fifty."

"Bollocks. Who told you that? Redcar Races never brings in that sort of cash."

"When the bag was discovered, there was a significant amount of drugs inside."

"Drugs? That's nothing to do with my Dad. Speak to Dyson."

"Freddie's fingerprints were on the packages," Mason said. "Your dad must have handled them."

Barry began to pace the room. "That's nonsense. Dyson's responsible I tell you."

"Dyson's prints aren't on the packages," Mason said, "...but your dad's are."

Barry curled his lip, his face contorting with anger as he strode menacingly towards Mason. "Get the fuck out of this house," he said. "You don't talk to me or Dad without our solicitor present."

"This isn't going away, Barry. I'll be making further enquiries and..."

"Get out," Barry yelled, opening the door leading back into the lounge. "Don't come here again unless you have a warrant."

Mason made his way through the lounge towards the hall. "I'll see myself out," he said.

Barry watched through the window as Mason got into his car and drove away in the direction of town. "Bastard!" he muttered. "Interfering bastard."

Freddie flung the blanket onto the carpet and got off the couch, joining his son at the window.

"Dad, you should have let me loose on the thieving bastard after what he did to you."

"And who do you think would be top of the list if anything had happened to him? Besides, we didn't know where he had hidden the bag then, did we? We had to wait whilst he came out of the nick to get it back."

"Yeah, and what does the stupid bastard do? Bashes the brains out of the only two people who could lead him to it."

Barry sniffed loudly. "The man's a neanderthal. I still think me and Lee should..."

"Don't worry, son. Dyson hasn't got away with anything. I'm just biding my time, that's all. He'll get what's coming to him."

"So, what are we going to do? The cops have found the bag and your dabs are all over the gear. How are we going to explain that?"

"Pour me a drink," Freddie said, "a large one. Then I want you to get hold of your brother."

"Lee's still in Newcastle organising the next pick-up."

"I know where he is," Freddie said, "I sent him there. I need him to contact our friend at the nick. I have a little job for them." Freddie shuffled back to the couch. "Now, hurry up with that drink."

26

It was midday as Mason parked his car outside The Galleon, a micropub in the centre of Redcar. The owner, forty-year-old Judy Rice, was behind the bar chatting to the only two customers in the pub. Mason approached, taking out his warrant card.

"Good afternoon," he said. "I'm Detective Inspector Jack Mason. I wonder if I might have a word in private?"

Judy raised an eyebrow. "What's it about?" she asked. "I haven't been breaking any licensing laws, have I?"

Mason replaced his warrant card into his inside pocket. "No, it's nothing like that Ms Rice. It's about two of your customers."

James Waugh, who had been standing by the bar, banged his half-empty beer glass down on the bar. "Is this about them two who got murdered?" he said. "They were both regulars in here."

"Yes, I'm aware of that," Mason said. He turned to Judy. "Perhaps we could take a seat over there Ms Rice?" He indicated a small table near the window.

Judy shrugged. "All right, but there isn't much I can tell you," she said, walking over to the table, "and please, call me Judy. Everyone does."

When they were both seated, Mason took out his pocketbook. "I understand Benji Myers and Arthur Rhodes were regular customers of the Galleon," he began.

Judy sighed. "They were until they got barred."

"Oh, why was that?"

"Benji had always been... volatile. He was a heavy drinker and sometimes this led to him becoming violent." She pointed to the wall above the fireplace. "There was a mirror up there," she said, "until Benji threw a chair and smashed it. There was broken glass everywhere. Two of my customers sitting underneath it were covered with the shards."

"What caused him to throw the chair?"

"He'd been arguing with Arthur about something. These last couple of weeks they seemed to be arguing all the time. Anyway, I told the pair of them to get out and not come back."

"You say Benji was a heavy drinker?"

"Oh, yes. He could certainly knock the booze back. Buying that off-licence was the worst thing he could have done."

"Apart from the drinking, is there anything else you can tell me about either of them. I'm trying to build a picture of what they were like."

Judy sighed deeper. "I didn't know them really well," she said. "They were pleasant enough I suppose, but they tended to keep their own company. Usually, they weren't any bother. They'd sit over there playing dominos, not speaking to anyone, but this last couple of weeks they seemed to change."

"In what way?"

"It's difficult to explain really. They both looked anxious, and they started arguing... no, not arguing... more heated discussions."

"Did you hear what they were saying?"

Judy shook her head. “You can’t hear much when the pub’s full.”

James Waugh sauntered over to the table and plonked down on a stool opposite Mason. “If you want to know about Arthur, ask me. I’ve known him for years.”

The pub door opened and half a dozen people entered.

“I have to go,” Judy made he excuse as she rushed over to the bar. “Sorry I couldn’t be more help.” Smiling, she went behind the bar to attend to her customers.

Mason turned to Waugh. “You say you knew Arthur Rhodes well?”

“Me and Arthur worked together at the steelworks for years. My missus was big mates with Alice back in the early days.”

“I understand Mrs Rhodes died recently.”

“That’s right. Poor cow got MS. It broke Arthur’s heart seeing her fading away like that.”

“They were a close couple then?”

“He worshipped her. When Alice became ill, nothing was too much trouble for him. He was a good bloke was Arthur. Honest as the day was long.”

“What about Benji Myers? I take it you knew him too?”

“Benji and Arthur were chalk and cheese. I never understood why Arthur knocked around with that arsehole.”

“You didn’t like Benji?”

James looked furtively around before speaking. “Benji Myers was a drunk and he knocked his missus about. I can’t understand why Irene stayed with him all these years.”

"This is the first I've heard about that. Are you sure?"

"Ask Irene. Ask the neighbours. Benji Myers was a drunk and a bully. Mind you, a couple of weeks ago he got his comeuppance when his son-in-law knocked the shit out of him."

"You mean Giles Nixon?"

"Is that his name? I only know him as Sonja's husband. Poor Irene had bruises to her face one Sunday when they visited. She said she'd had a fall, but it was obvious what had happened. Anyway, words got to blows and… Not that it did any good. Irene would never leave Benji."

Mason had been making notes throughout the interview. He closed his notebook and placed it in his pocket. "Well, thanks, Mr Waugh. That's been most enlightening."

"Any time," Waugh said as standing up, he scraped back the stool. "Myers wasn't above a bit of pilfering either," he said. "When he was working at the plant, he often helped himself to stuff."

"Did you witness him stealing?"

Waugh shook his head. "No, not personally, but there were rumours."

Mason walked over to the door. "Thanks again," he said as he gave a cursory wave to Judy behind the bar. "I may be back in touch."

27

After a quick sandwich and a cup of tea in the police canteen, Mason returned to his office with Sergeant Brown in pursuit.

"I've sent Beaumont over to Queen Street on door-to-door enquiries, sir. There were a few people not at home when we went knocking the first time."

"Let's hope somebody saw something," Mason said. "So far we only have the one suspect, but no real evidence."

"Oh, Dyson's responsible. You can bet your pension on it. By the way, DCS Bainbridge was asking if you found anything on the CCTV from The Smuggler to corroborate Dyson's alibi."

Mason sat bolt upright. "Shit! I'd forgotten all about that." He bent down and unlocked the drawer where he had placed the disc. "I'll play it back now. Take a seat, sergeant. Two pair of eyes are better than one."

He placed the disc into his computer and the two men began to study the flickering images.

"There's Dyson," Sergeant Brown pointed. "He's behind that big bloke standing at the bar."

"And there's the delightful Leanne," Mason looked closer. "The timer says eleven-thirty. Rhodes was attacked sometime after midnight."

They moved the disc forward to twelve-thirty.

"Bloody hell, Dyson's still in the bar. He looks half cut," Sergeant Brown swore. "It looks like he didn't do for Arthur Rhodes after all."

Mason ran the disc for a second, then a third time.

"I suppose this puts him in the clear for the murder of Arthur Rhodes," he agreed at last.

"Yes, but it doesn't eliminate him from the murder of Benji Myers or Sheila Thompson. I don't suppose the pathologist could have got Rhodes's time of death wrong?"

"Highly unlikely. Dr Carpenter knows his stuff. No, if Dyson did kill Benji and Sheila, and we've identified a possible link between them and Arthur Rhodes, then it's a safe assumption that there's someone else involved."

Sergeant Brown rubbed his chin in concentration. "I've never known Dyson to work with an accomplice before. There's always a first time I suppose."

Suddenly Mason's posture stiffened and he pointed to the screen. "Is that who I think it is? Sitting at the table near the door?"

Sergeant Brown squinted at the flickering image for a few seconds. "That's Beaumont," he said at last, "and the woman he's with is definitely not Jodie."

"Do you recognise her?"

"Yes, I do. That's Denise Porter," he snarled. "PC Porter's wife."

28

It was an hour later when DC Beaumont arrived back at the station. His face was flushed with excitement as he made his way to Inspector Mason's office. He knocked lightly, before entering into the room.

"Inspector," he panted breathlessly. "I... I've found another witness in Primrose Avenue. He says he saw someone at Mr Rhodes's door the night he was murdered." Beaumont took several deep breaths before he continued. "The bloke's name is Frank Ellis and he gave me a description of the visitor. I took a brief statement in my pocketbook."

"What was Mr Ellis doing in Primrose Avenue at that time of night? Does he live there?"

"No, sir. He was taking a shortcut home. He works behind the bar at The Royal Hotel."

"You say he can describe the person he saw?"

"Yes, but his description bears no resemblance to what the neighbour, Pamela Reece said."

"What do you mean?"

"Ellis said the person he saw was well over six feet and a heavy build."

"Did he mention the person having an umbrella?"

"No, sir. He said the man was wearing a hoodie. It looks like Arthur had two visitors that night."

"Either that or one of them is lying," Mason thought for a moment. "Do you have an address for Mr Ellis?"

"Yes, sir," he took out his notebook. "He has a bedsit on Station Road. Do you want me to go along too, sir?"

Mason shook his head. "No, I want you to go and help with the door-to-door along Newcomen Terrace. We've only spoke to half the residents so far."

Beaumont looked disappointed. "I thought that was uniform's job, not CID."

"In a case like this, constable, it's everyone's job."

"Yes, sir," Beaumont moved towards the door. "By the way, sir, I understand Mrs Mason will be working alongside Jodie at the salon today."

Mason raised an eyebrow. "Oh, I didn't know that," he said.

"Jodie's been working there for almost a year now," Beaumont grinned. "She really enjoys it."

Mason gave a faint but dismissive smile as he pulled a pile of files towards him, watching as DC Beaumont left the room.

29

"You've informed the Drugs Squad?" Bainbridge asked, when conversing with Jack Mason in his office later that afternoon.

"They've been informed sir. They'll be picking up the drugs from our evidence room this evening."

"Good. This is the evidence they were looking for to prove Roberts is a key player in the drugs business. How did he seem to you when you met him?"

"Confused. I don't think he will be fit to plead."

"You don't think he's faking?"

"If he is, he's a damned good actor."

"He can afford to be. There's a lot at stake."

Bainbridge strode to the door. "It's six o'clock," he declared. "I'm going home. I think we've both done enough for one day, Jack."

DI Mason reached for his coat. "Yes, sir. I think you're right."

"By the way, I've been meaning to ask you, how's young Beaumont getting on? Has he settled in all right?"

Mason hesitated for a second. "I think so," his tone was neutral. "It's early days."

"Well, let me know if there's a problem," Bainbridge said, as he headed towards the door. "See you tomorrow, Jack."

It was six-thirty in the evening when Jack Mason arrived home. Annika was on the couch watching the local news on television.

"How did your first day go?" he asked, bending over and kissing her lightly on the cheek.

"It was all right," she huffed. "The salon's extremely busy. I haven't stopped all day."

"I hear you're working with the girlfriend of one of my detectives."

"You mean Jodie?"

"Yes. I didn't know she worked there until today. What's she like?"

Annika shrugged. "She's all right I suppose, but she thinks she knows a lot more than she actually does."

Jack poured two glasses of wine and handed one to his wife. "I hope it won't make things awkward for you, working with the girlfriend of one of my subordinates."

"Why should it?" she said, sipping the wine. "Jodie certainly isn't my boss."

"You do know you mustn't discuss any police business with her, don't you?"

Annika huffed theatrically. "Of course I do. Why should I want to speak to the likes of her about anything?"

"Well, you will be working closely together and women do tend to confide in one another."

Annika drained her glass, then got off the couch. "I'll ignore that remark," she teased. "I thought we could eat out tonight. There's an Italian just opened on Queen Street I'd like to try."

Jack sighed. "Okay, but I want an early night. I've another busy day tomorrow."

Annika walked into the hall. "Still haven't solved who killed the crinklies?" she laughed, as she began to climb the stairs to her bedroom.

"Annika, don't use that awful word. It's disrespectful, and no, I haven't found the killer of the three elderly victims but I will. I'm getting closer."

"What do you mean, you're getting closer? Do you know who's responsible?"

"The police have their suspicions," he said. "Now, hurry up and get changed if you want to eat out."

***

Detective Constable Wayne Beaumont was about to leave the station for the day when Sergeant Brown signalled him into his office.

"Yes, sarge," Beaumont said. "You wanted to see me?"

"Shut the door."

Beaumont looked anxious. "Is everything all right, sarge?"

"No, Beaumont. Everything is not all right."

Sergeant Brown placed the CCTV disk, recovered from the Smugglers Inn, into the computer and turned the screen to face Beaumont. "Can you explain to me what the fuck you are doing in The Smugglers with PC Porter's missus?"

Beaumont stared at the screen which showed a clear image of him and Denise Porter kissing.

"Sarge, I… I can explain," he said, the colour draining from his face. "Me and Denise… well… it's just a bit of fun that's all. No damage done."

"Does PC Porter know you've been seeing his wife?"

"Does he have to know, sarge? It was only a brief fling. It didn't last more than three months. Denise was feeling lonely, that's all. She needed a bit of company."

"And you fancy yourself as the go-to comforter, I suppose?"

"It's not like that. We were both at a bit of a loose end and… well, I'm sure I don't have to spell it out, but it's over. I won't be seeing Denise Porter again. I give you my word."

"You gave me your word after the incident with Maureen. Your word's shit, Beaumont."

"Are you going to tell PC Porter?"

Sergeant Brown rubbed his chin. "This is your last chance," he said. "I'll be watching you like a hawk. If I see you so much as smile at another man's wife, you'll be walking the beat along the cliffs at Whitby. Do you hear me?"

Beaumont exhaled deeply in relief. "Thanks, sarge," he said. "I won't let you down. You have my word."

***

Beaumont was in a foul move when he got home. He banged his car keys on the sideboard and threw his coat on the back of the chair. Jodie was in the kitchen cooking sausage, egg, and chips.

"Everything all right, love?" she said as he bounded into the room.

"That fucking sergeant," he said. "He's got it in for me. He always has had."

"Sergeant Brown? I thought you got on well with him."

"Well, I don't. Not anymore."

Wayne strode to the fridge and took out a can of lager, pulling back the tag. "Is tea going to be long?" he said. "I'm going out at seven."

"I thought we were staying in tonight to watch that film you've been wanting to see."

"Sorry, no can do. I've places to go, people to see," Wayne said as he put the can to his lips.

Jodie turned her attention to the chip fryer. "I met your bosses wife today," she said. "Proper bossy cow she is."

"What do you mean?"

Jodie shook the chip basket vigorously. "Thinks she knows everything. She tried to tell me I wasn't doing the foils right on Mrs Wilcher's hair, the cheeky cow. I soon told her where to get off."

Wayne bounded forward, grabbing Jodie's upper arm, spinning her round. "She might be a cheeky cow," he said, "but she's my bosses missus, so you make sure you get on with her, all right?"

Jodie shook free of his grasp. "Annika Mason is not my boss," she said. "I don't have to like her."

"Yes, you do, Jodie. This job's important to me and I don't want you jeopardising my prospects. I want you to be nice to her, do you hear me?"

Jodie sniffed. "I'll be civil," she said, "I can't promise more than that."

"Good girl," Wayne said, kissing the top of her head. "Now hurry up with my tea. I don't want to be late."

30

Detective Chief Superintendent Andrew Bainbridge arrived at The Mariners Restaurant at precisely seven forty-five. He was surprised to see his guest had already arrived. He looked admiringly at Sophie Barrett with her slim figure, shoulder-length auburn hair and flawless complexion with not a hint that she was in her mid-forties.

"Glad you could make it," he said as he walked over, kissing her gently on both cheeks.

"Thank you for inviting me," she smiled. "I was hoping we would meet up again. Holiday romances do have a habit of fizzling out quickly."

Andy smiled as he took his seat opposite and reached for the wine list. "What do you prefer, red or white?"

"Red every time," she said.

He glanced at the wine list. "Merlot, okay?"

"Perfect."

Andy signalled for the wine waiter and ordered a bottle of Merlot.

"I hear you've had quite a time of it in Redcar these last few days," she said. "Three suspicious deaths in as many days."

Andy put his elbows on the table and lacing his fingers, rested his chin and sighed. "I thought I'd seen the last of the mayhem after that last business."

Sophie reached out and gently stroked his arm. "Are you any closer to finding who's responsible?"

"We've established all three victims are connected in some way and we have a credible suspect for the first two. The trouble is the suspect has a cast iron alibi for the attack on Arthur Rhodes, the third. There's no way he could have carried out the assault."

Sophie furrowed her brow. "Tell me about your suspect," she said. "What sort of person is he?"

The waiter brought the wine to the table and began to uncork. "Leave it!" Andy said. "I'll do that."

"Very well, sir," the waiter said. "I'll bring the menus." He bustled away, returning a couple of minutes later with two leather-bound menus.

"Thanks," Andy said, handing one to Sophie. "I've heard the lamb is particularly good," he said, as he began to pour the wine.

Sophie took her glass and sipped at the wine. "Mm, that's good," she said. "Almost as good as the Xinomavro we had in Corfu."

Andy smiled. "The King's Wine," he said. "The Barolo of Greece."

"You were telling me about your suspect," she prodded for details.

Andy leant back in his chair and sipped his wine. "Sophie, I didn't ask you to dinner to talk about work. This is meant to be social. Relax."

"I'm a criminal psychologist. I'm always working, one way or another. Now, tell me."

"Okay, if you insist," he said. "His name is Shaun Dyson. He's been in trouble since the day he was born."

He proceeded to tell her about Dyson's antecedent history. "With his background I suppose you can't expect him to behave any differently."

Sophie listened intently. "The injury to his leg has not in any way immobilised him then?" she asked.

Andy shook his head. "Not at all. I think he could probably beat me in a hundred-yard dash."

The waiter hovered near the table waiting for their order.

"Ah, time to eat," Andy said. "I'm starving."

An hour later they were both relaxing in the hotel lounge sipping brandy.

"Thanks, Andy," Sophie said. "That was a lovely meal."

"A lovely meal for a lovely lady," he said, raising his glass.

Sophie opened her bag and took out her spectacles and a small notebook and pen. "Getting back to business," she said. "How's your new inspector working out? Inspector Mason, isn't it?"

"Oh, Jack's okay. This is the first murder investigation he's been involved with though. I think he's a bit out of his depth if I'm honest."

"He was based in Leeds, wasn't he?"

"That's right. He got promoted just before his transfer to Redcar. The poor sod's been thrown in at the deep end as SIO with not one, but three suspicious deaths."

"Don't you think the investigation should be given to someone more senior?"

"If we had someone available yes, but unfortunately, due to all the cuts, there isn't anyone. CID in particular have been cut to the bone. I'm overseeing the investigation and I'm helping where I can. It's difficult of course because I don't want to tread on his toes."

"I suppose not," she agreed. "Getting back to your suspect, have you ever considered the possibility that perhaps Dyson has an accomplice?"

"It's beginning to look like it, but I can't think who. Dyson's a loner. He's never worked with anyone before."

Whilst they had been talking, Sophie had been making notes.

"What are you writing?" Andy asked.

"Possibilities," she didn't look up. "Nothing worthy of discussion yet."

Andy sighed. "You will let me know if you come up with some genius plan to catch the bastard, won't you?"

Sophie drained her glass before putting the notebook back into her bag.

"Thank you for tonight," she said. "I've really enjoyed your company, but I'm afraid I have to go. My taxi will be waiting."

"We must do it again soon," Andy suggested as he helped her into her coat.

"I'd like that," she smiled, kissing him lightly on the cheek. "I'll be in touch soon, Andy. Good night."

31

It was eleven-forty-five when the telephone in DCS Bainbridge's bedroom gave out its shrill ring. Putting down his book, he reached out for the receiver.

"Bainbridge!"

"Sir, it's Sergeant Harris. I think it best if you come to the station right away."

"What's wrong? Whatever it is, can't Inspector Mason handle it?"

"Inspector Mason is here, sir. He's asked me to ring you."

"What's happened?"

"I'm sorry, sir, but I'd rather not say over the telephone, other than the matter is most urgent and needs your immediate attention."

Bainbridge sighed. "All right, I'll be there in twenty minutes."

On entering the station, Bainbridge saw two men pacing in Reception, along with Sergeant Harris, the night sergeant, and Inspector Mason. Mason rushed over to him.

"Sir, these officers are from the Drugs Squad. They came to collect the drugs recovered from the property store and..."

"And found the fucking things rendered useless," said a red-haired burly man as he pushed forward towards Bainbridge. "Someone in this nick has deliberately sabotaged them."

Bainbridge glared at the man. "And you are?"

"Detective Inspector Fielding," he said. "Drugs Squad."

"Well, DI Fielding, I am Detective Chief Superintendent Bainbridge. I'm in charge of this station, and I do not appreciate being spoken to in that manner. You will address me as sir, is that understood?"

Fielding inhaled deeply, anger flashing in his eyes. "Yes, sir," he said. "Sorry, sir, it's just... well like I said, the evidence has been compromised. Someone has poured an acidic substance over the bags. It's impossible to confirm fingerprints now."

Bainbridge turned to Mason. "Have you ascertained who had access to the property store in the last twelve hours?"

"It seems like half the station, sir. The officer in charge of the property store is off sick at the moment, so property has been placed inside the store by the officers dealing with the incident. All they had to do was sign the book at the front desk and take the key."

"Get me the book," Bainbridge said to Sergeant Harris, "then get onto Forensics. Let's see if they can retrieve any prints. It's a long shot I know, but it's worth a try." He turned to Fielding. "Leave it with me," he said. "I'll get back to you when we know more."

Fielding looked frustrated. "Very well, sir," he said. "Let's hope you get something we can use, otherwise its six month's work down the pan." He turned to his companion. "Come on Brad," he said. "There's nothing for us here. Let's get back to the office."

Bainbridge watched as both men left the building.

Bainbridge began to ascend the stairs leading to his office. "Inspector Mason," he said, "my office."

Carrying the Property Store Ledger, Jack Mason entered DCS Bainbridge's office. "I've got the record of everyone entering the storeroom," he said. "In the last twelve hours there have only been four constables and..."

"Sit down Jack," Bainbridge said. "I think we need to talk."

Mason perched on the edge of the chair, opposite Bainbridge's desk. He remained silent.

"Were you aware that the property store was unmanned?"

"I knew PC Bywater, the property store officer was on sick leave, but I didn't think it necessary to bring an officer off their duties to man the store."

"So, you left it to individual officers to record their evidence?"

"Yes, sir."

Bainbridge banged his fist down on the desk. "Damn it man. I told you that someone in this station could be in league with the Roberts' gang and you didn't think it appropriate to check who gained entry to the evidence?"

Mason looked shocked. "I… I realise now of course that I should have been more stringent about access, but..."

"Give me the log," Bainbridge said, snatching the black A4 book from Mason's grasp. He scanned the recent entries.

"I see there have been four officers depositing evidence in the store after the drugs were placed there. I want to interview each one of them."

"PCs Dewhurst and Renshaw have just finished their shift. They won't be back on duty until this afternoon. Walker and Porter are on the early shift. They'll be reporting for duty at six."

The veins on Bainbridge's neck began to pulsate. "Damn it man, I said now. Drag them out of bed if you have to."

"Yes… yes, sir. I'll do it right away."

32

Dressed casually in jeans and a sweater, PC Lisa Walker presented herself at the police station at one-fifteen that morning. Sergeant Harris was in Reception.

She strode up to the desk, a worried look on her face. "What's going on, sarge?" she asked.

"The boss wants a word," Harris replied. "There's nothing to be concerned about."

The sergeant picked up the internal phone. "PC Walker has just arrived, sir." He turned to the worried officer. "Go straight up. The DCS is in his office."

PC Walker swiftly climbed the stairs to Bainbridge's office. She knocked lightly on the closed door.

"Enter!" DCS Bainbridge was sitting behind his desk and DI Mason was standing by the window.

Bainbridge picked up a pen and prepared to take notes. "PC Walker, I see from the Stores Record Book that you logged in property yesterday afternoon."

Walker cast an anxious glance towards Inspector Mason.

"Don't look at the inspector," Bainbridge said. "Answer my question."

"Yes, sir. I arrested a shoplifter in Bon Marche and logged the stolen property into the storeroom."

"Was anyone with you during this transaction?"

"No, sir. I was alone. Graham… eh… PC Bywater usually fills in the log, but he's off sick at the moment."

"Did anyone enter the store whilst you were there?"

She shook her head. "What's… what's this about, sir? Have I done something wrong?"

Bainbridge ignored her question. "Do you know Freddie Roberts?"

"The bookie?"

"Yes, the bookie."

"Not really. I know his sons, Barry, and Lee. I was in the same class as Lee."

"Have you seen either of the Roberts brothers recently?"

"No, sir. Not for a long time."

Bainbridge stared hard at the young constable. After a few minutes he put down his pen.

"Very well, Constable Walker… you may go, but I don't want you speaking to anyone about what has taken place here this morning. Do you understand?"

"Yes, sir," she said.

When Walker left the room, Bainbridge turned to Mason. "Well, what do you think?"

"I think Lisa Walker is an honest, diligent young officer," he appraised. "We have no reason to doubt her story."

"Well, somebody tampered with the evidence," Bainbridge said. "If it wasn't her, it must have been one of the others."

His internal phone rang and Bainbridge could see it was Sergeant Harris. "Yes, sergeant… good, send him up."

PC Paul Porter looked nervous as he entered the chief superintendent's office. Porter looked younger than his twenty-eight years. He had fair skin and blue eyes and his blonde, unruly hair falling across his forehead gave him a boyish look. Porter was wearing grey jogging bottoms and a dark-blue hoodie.

"You wanted to see me, sir?" he quietly asked.

Beaumont picked up his pen. "I see from the property log that you were in the store yesterday."

"Yes, sir. I logged in two knives I'd confiscated from a lad I arrested on Victory Street."

"Was anyone else in the storeroom with you?"

Porter looked puzzled. "Not that I remember. PC Bywater is off sick so..."

"Yes, I'm aware of that," Bainbridge said, his irritation showing.

"Is something wrong, sir?"

"Yes, constable. Something is wrong. Were you aware a quantity of drugs had been placed in the storeroom?"

"Yes, sir. I understood they were going to be collected by the Drugs Squad."

"Did you see the drugs when you were in the storeroom?"

"I saw the evidence bag, sir."

"Did you touch the bag in any way?"

"No, sir. Why would I?"

"Do you know Freddie Roberts or either of his sons?"

"Freddie Roberts the bookie?"

"Yes, Freddie Roberts the bookie."

"I've heard of him, but we've never actually spoken. I've had dealings with Barry Roberts though. He likes to drive fast cars. I've issued three speeding tickets to him in as many months."

"Nothing else? No more communication with any of the family?"

"No, sir."

"I'll ask you again, constable, did you see anyone else near the property store when you were in there?"

"No. I entered the two knives into the property logbook, took the key from behind the desk and placed the knives inside evidence bags. I took them to the store, then I locked the door and replaced the key."

"And you never entered the store again?"

"No, sir. I did not."

Bainbridge exhaled his exasperation. "Very well, constable. You may go. Do not discuss this interview with any of your colleagues, all right?"

"Yes, sir. Er… may I ask what this is about?"

"No, you may not."

Inspector Mason walked to the door and opened it. "Go home and get some sleep, Porter," he said. "You have to be back here at six."

33

PC George Renshaw was in his late forties with only three months to his retirement from the Force. His attitude towards DCS Bainbridge's questions was much more defensive than the two younger constables had been.

"Sir, am I being accused of something, because if I am I want my union rep here. I won't say another word until he is."

"Nobody is accusing you of anything, PC Renshaw. I'm merely attempting to get to the facts."

"What facts? I put stolen property into the store, I filled out the appropriate paperwork and I locked the storeroom behind me. Those are the facts."

"Was anyone else in the store at the same time?"

"Are you saying I need a witness? I've been doing this job now for almost twenty-five years without a blemish on my character. To suggest that I would take property from the store is outrageous."

"No one is accusing you of taking anything from the store, Renshaw."

"Then what do you suspect me of doing?"

"I take it you know Freddie Roberts and his family?"

"Yes, of course. Everybody living in Redcar knows Freddie and his lads."

"What do you think of them?"

Renshaw huffed. “I wouldn’t trust one of them as far as I could throw them. Freddie’s bent. He always has been, and his two lads are going the same way.”

“Have you been involved with them personally?”

“I nicked the old man years ago for burglary. He broke into the old Beales’s shop up on Regent’s Walk. It’s closed down now. It’s one of those B&M places.”

“Anything else?”

“I cautioned Barry for fighting in The Galleon a couple of months back. The fight was over some girl.”

“And you’ve had no dealings with them since?”

“No, sir. Why should I?”

“Very well, constable. We’ll leave it there. Don’t speak of this interview to anyone. It is an extremely sensitive matter.”

“Very well, sir,” he said, as he strode towards the door.

Bainbridge turned to Mason. “Three down, one to go,” he said. “What do you think to Renshaw?”

Mason shrugged. “Like he said, he has a long and unblemished record.”

“You don’t think he could be taking back-handers, squirrelling away for his retirement?”

“I wouldn’t have thought so, but I’ll check his finances if you think it worthwhile.”

“Yes, I do. Check all of their finances. You can’t be too thorough. Somebody gained access into the storeroom and sabotaged those drugs, and as far as I can see, it could only be one of four people.”

There was a knock on the door.

“Ah, this will be Dewhurst.” The door opened and Sergeant Harris came into the room carrying a tray with two mugs of tea.

“I thought you could both do with a drink,” he said, placing the tray down on the desk.

“Thanks,” Bainbridge nodded his appreciation. “Any sign of PC Dewhurst yet?”

“No, sir. I spoke to his wife, but she said he hadn’t returned home after his shift.”

“Does she know where he can be at…” he looked at his watch, “… at two-thirty in the morning?”

“Mrs Dewhurst said that John… PC Dewhurst, sometimes goes to the casino in Middlesbrough when he’s on the late shift. He usually gets home about three.”

“PC Dewhurst likes the casino, does he? That can be an expensive hobby.”

“I wouldn’t know sir,” the sergeant said. “An occasional game of bingo down at the local and two lottery tickets every Saturday is about my limit.”

Bainbridge picked up the mug of tea. “We’ll give it another fifteen minutes,” he said. “If Dewhurst hasn’t made an appearance by then, we’ll call it a night. Tell his wife I want him in the office by nine o’clock tomorrow morning.”

“Yes, sir,” he said as he walked to the door.

34

It was after four o'clock in the morning before Jack Mason climbed into his bed. Annika was sleeping soundly, but Jack was too troubled to sleep. When the alarm by his bed finally rang at seven-thirty, Jack was wide awake.

"I'll make the tea," he said, as Annika began to stir. He got out of bed, and putting on his dressing gown, went downstairs to the kitchen. Annika followed him a few minutes later.

"What time did you get to bed last night?" she said, rubbing the sleep from her eyes. "I waited up until nearly midnight."

"Sorry, darling. I got called back to the station. There was an emergency situation I had to deal with and..."

Annika huffed. "You're not the only officer at the station," she said. "Why is it always you who has to deal with things? Can't someone else take responsibility?"

"I'm the officer in charge," Jack said as he placed a tea bag in each cup.

"No you're not. Bainbridge is."

"Actually, he was there too. We didn't get finished until four this morning."

"What was the emergency anyway? Not another body I hope."

The kettle began its shrill whistle and Jack poured the steaming hot water into the two cups. "No, nothing like that. It was evidence which had been tampered with."

"What evidence?"

"Drugs. Someone had poured acid over the packages."

"Do you know who?"

Mason shrugged. "We've narrowed it down to one of four constables."

"Who do you suspect?"

Mason sipped his tea. "We'll see," he said. "I have to be in the station early this morning so I won't have time for breakfast."

"I'm not hungry either," Annika said. "The junior at work brings in bacon sandwiches about eleven so I'll make do with that this morning."

Jack headed into the hall. "I'll have a quick shower, then I'd better be off," he said. "I don't want to keep the old man waiting."

"All right, Jack, but hurry up. I need to wash my hair this morning."

"Can't you do it at the salon?"

"You must be joking. I wouldn't use their products on next-door's dog."

Grinning, Jack ascended the stairs, showered, and dressed, and was behind the wheel of his car heading towards the police station in less than twenty minutes."

35

DCS Bainbridge was talking to Sergeant Brown in Reception when Inspector Mason arrived at the station.

"Good morning, sir."

"Good morning, Inspector. Let's go up to my office, shall we?"

Mason followed Bainbridge upstairs.

"I've just been talking to Sergeant Brown about the logbook," Bainbridge said. "He assures me that no one, other than the four constables we know about, had access to the store."

"Someone could have taken the key to the store. They needn't necessarily have gone into the store to place evidence."

"According to Sergeant Brown, the key is in the desk drawer in the front office. The desk where he works from. From the time the property was placed in the store to the time it was discovered to have been sabotaged, either Sergeant Brown or Sergeant Harris would have been on duty there. I spoke to Harris yesterday. He confirms no one could have taken the key without his knowledge."

"Has Dewhurst arrived yet, sir?"

"No, he hasn't. I'll interview him when he does arrive. In the meantime, I want you to go back and speak to Irene Myers and her son-in-law. There seems a lot those two have been keeping quiet about."

"Yes, sir. I'll do that this morning. Then I want to speak to Frank Ellis, the witness who claims to have seen someone at Arthur Rhodes's house the night he was killed."

"Good. Let me know how you get on."

The internal phone rang. "Yes, sergeant?... Send him up, will you?" Bainbridge turned to the inspector. "Dewhurst's just arrived. Let's see what he's got to say for himself."

Inspector Mason returned to his office. DC Beaumont was at his computer in the adjacent office. Mason rummaged through paperwork on his desk looking for the statement made by Frank Ellis. Beaumont, who had been watching, came to the office door.

"Anything I can help you with, sir?" he asked.

"I'm looking for Ellis's statement," Mason said. "I take it you had it typed up yesterday?"

"I dictated it for the typing pool. I don't think it's come back yet."

"Well chase it up man. I need it this morning before I interview him."

***

David Dewhurst was an ex-soldier and barely the minimum height to be in the police service. With a crop of bright ginger hair and a neat goatee beard, he was one of the most popular officers in the division. He marched into the DCS's office and stood to attention.

“I understand you’ve been trying to contact me, sir?” he said.

“That’s right Dewhurst, right up to two-thirty this morning.”

“I was in Middlesborough, sir.”

“So I hear. Do you spend a lot of time at the casino?”

Dewhurst’s posture stiffened. “Is how I choose to spend my spare time relevant, sir?”

Leaning back in his chair, Bainbridge narrowed his eyes. “I suppose not, but gambling in those places can be an expensive hobby.”

A faint grin appeared on Dewhurst’s face. “It can also be a lucrative one as well.”

“Oh, you consider yourself to be a lucky punter, eh?”

“I’ve had my successes. I’ve bought a villa in Spain from my winnings, as well as upgrading my car.”

Bainbridge was silent for a moment. “Good for you,” he said, “but we’re not here to discuss your gambling habits.”

“Why am I here, sir?”

“I see from the property logbook that you entered the storeroom yesterday afternoon. Can you tell me for what purpose?”

Dewhurst looked perplexed. “I needed to check something,” he said.

“Check what exactly?”

“I’d placed half a dozen stolen cameras in the store the day before. When I came to finish writing up my report yesterday, I realised I had only recorded five serial numbers. I went into the storeroom to get the last one."

"Whilst you were in the storeroom did you see anyone else in there?"

"No, sir. I was alone. It only took less than five minutes to write down the numbers."

"Were you aware that a quantity of drugs was being held in the store ready for collection by the Drugs Squad?"

"I'd heard something about it on the grapevine. Rumour is, Freddie Roberts was involved."

"How well do you know Roberts?"

"I haven't seen him about for a while. Before his accident, Roberts was an active thief. I was with PC Renshaw a few years back when we nabbed him for breaking into Beales."

"What about his sons? Do you know them?"

Dewhurst shook his head. "Never had the pleasure, sir," he said, "but if they're anything like their old man they're bound to come up on the radar soon enough."

Bainbridge had been making notes throughout the interview. He put his pen down and closed his notebook.

"This interview is to remain confidential, Renshaw. You must not disclose what we have discussed to anyone. Do you understand?"

"You can rely on my discretion, sir, but may I ask what exactly has happened?"

"I suppose it will come out eventually. The drugs that were to be collected by the Drugs Squad have been sabotaged. They have been rendered useless as evidence."

"And you think I'm responsible?"

"I think an officer from this station is responsible."

"I can give you my assurance that it has nothing to do with me, and I doubt it has anything to do with any of my colleagues."

"The drugs didn't pour acid over themselves, did they?"

Dewhurst remained silent.

"Very well, you're dismissed. Go home and get some sleep before your next shift."

"Yes, sir," he said and he turned and marched to the door.

36

In company with DC Beaumont, Inspector Mason arrived at Irene Myers's house just after ten o'clock that morning. He knocked briskly on the door, which after a couple of minutes, was opened by Irene's daughter, Sonja.

"Oh, you're the policeman who was here the other day," she said.

"That's right. I'm Inspector Jack Mason and this is my colleague, DC Wayne Beaumont. We would like a word with Mrs Myers and your husband, if possible."

"What on earth do you want to speak with Giles for? He doesn't know anything about what's been going on."

"Is that the nice young policeman?" Irene Myers, who had come into the hall, was standing behind her daughter. "Let them in, Sonja. I'll put the kettle on."

Sonja scowled as she stood to one side. "Very well, Mother," she said, "if, you're sure."

The two officers followed Sonja into the lounge. Through the window, Mason could see Giles Nixon crouching down, tending to the border plants in the garden.

"I'll pop outside and have a word with Mr Nixon," he said. "I won't be long."

Mason opened the French doors and strode out into the garden.

"Mr Nixon, I wonder if I could have a quick word?"

Nixon glared at the officer and huffed loudly. "What about?" he said, getting to his feet. "I don't know anything about what happened to Benji."

"I understand you had an altercation with him recently. Can you tell me what that was about?"

"Who's been telling you that? It was nothing, just a disagreement, that's all."

"That's not what I've heard. Why did you attack your father-in-law?"

Nixon looked uncomfortable, staring down at the grass and scuffing it with his toecap.

"Was it to do with Mr Myers assaulting his wife?"

"Oh, you know about that?"

"I've heard rumours. Tell me what happened."

Nixon inhaled deeply. "Benji wasn't the saint everyone thought he was, you know. What is that saying? 'House devil, street saint?' That sums up Benji Myers to a tea."

"I take it assaulting Irene was a regular occurrence?"

"Too bloody regular. Sonja will tell you. He used her as a punchbag when she was a kid. She couldn't wait to get out of this house."

"The police have no record of Irene making a complaint against her husband."

"She was too bloody scared of him, that's why. Me and Sonja begged her to leave him, but she wouldn't hear of it. She said she had made vows on her wedding day and she intended to keep them. That's bloody Catholics for you. More scared of the hereafter than of the present."

"Tell me about his drinking."

Nixon gave a harsh laugh. "I know he got through a bottle of whisky almost every night," he said, "as well as drinking in the pub."

"Yet he managed to run the off-licence without any trouble."

"Benji only worked in his shop a few hours a day, three days a week. He'd usually finish by five o'clock, but the week he was attacked the bloke who worked for him had gone on holiday, so Benji had to work till late."

"What made him buy an off-licence in the first place, do you know?"

Nixon shrugged. "After the steel plant closed, he got kept on as a part-time nightwatchman. Irene said it was to take him up to pension age. Anyway, about a year ago he announces he's leaving the plant and buying the off-licence."

"It can't have been cheap. Where did he get the money?"

"Me and Sonja thought he'd probably had a win on the horses or the lottery, something like that. It's the sort of thing he'd do… not tell anyone."

Mason turned to see Sonja stepping through the French doors and hurrying towards them.

"Mother's made tea," she said. "Hurry up, love. You know she doesn't like you being late."

Nixon put down the trowel he had been holding. "I'm coming," he said. "I'll be one minute, tell her."

Sonja hurried back towards the house.

"Promise you won't say anything to Irene about what I've been saying," he appealed. "She's still in denial. She won't have a bad word spoken about Benji."

Mason exhaled as he headed towards the house with Nixon. "Thank you for clearing that up. I don't think there's any need to bother Mrs Myers with any more questions."

"Good," Nixon said, stepping into the house. "Now, you must try some of Irene's home-made fruit cake. It's delicious."

37

DC Beaumont parked the car outside Frank Ellis's bedsit on Queen Street. "It looks a bit of a dump," he commented as he got out of the car.

Clutching Ellis's typed statement, Inspector Mason strode up to the green-painted door and pressed the button for flat four. There was silence. Mason pressed again. After a minute there was a crackling sound from the door intercom.

"Yeah? Who's that?"

"It's the police, Mr Ellis," Mason raised his voice to the scratched device. "Open the door please. We need to speak to you."

It was a further two minutes before the door bleeped and opened. Both officers entered the building and went straight to flat four. Ellis looked dishevelled as he stood in the open doorway dressed only in his boxer shorts and a dingey white tee-shirt.

"What time is it?" he yawned, rubbing his eyes with his knuckles.

"May we come in?" Mason asked as he pushed past Ellis and entered the room.

"What's this about?" Ellis said, closing the door and walking over to the couch. "I've been working till three. I'm knackered."

"I understand you work at the Royal Hotel. What is it you do there exactly?" Mason enquired.

"Whatever I'm told. Mostly bar work but sometimes I help out in the kitchen. Tonight, I was DJ for a wedding party. The bloke they'd booked didn't turn up."

"My, my, you are versatile," Mason scoffed.

"What the fuck is this about?" Ellis said, lighting a cigarette and flinging himself onto the couch. "If it's about seeing that bloke outside the old man's house, the one that got murdered, I've told your constable all about it. I've nothing more to add."

Mason took the typed statement from his pocket. "I have your statement here, Mr Ellis. Before I ask you to sign it there are a couple of points I want to go over with you."

"Such as what?"

"You claim you were in Primrose Gardens on your way home from work when you witnessed a man at Mr Rhodes's door."

"Yeah, that's right."

"But Primrose Gardens isn't on your route, surely? You would be heading away from your home if you took that route."

Ellis shrugged. "I… I felt like a walk. I wanted to clear my head. I do that sometimes when it's been a busy night. I'm never in a hurry to get back to this shitty dump. Would you be?"

"But it was raining heavily that night. I wouldn't have thought it was the kind of night to take a walk."

Ellis jumped to his feet. "What are you suggesting? That I'm lying? I've told you what I saw. A big bloke, wearing a hoodie. That's all I can tell you."

"And you say this was about midnight?"

"Yeah, that's right."

"Do you know Shaun Dyson?"

Ellis frowned, biting his lip. "No, I don't think so. Why?"

Mason handed the sheet of paper containing Ellis's statement to him. "If you wouldn't mind reading your statement through and then signing it, Mr Ellis," he said. "Here, I have a pen."

Ellis took the statement and pen and signed at the bottom of the page. "There," he said. "If that's everything, I'd like to get some kip."

The two officers headed back to the station.

"What do you think of Frank Ellis?" Mason asked as they pulled into the police car park.

"Rough as a bear's arse," Beaumont said, "but I don't see any reason to doubt what he says."

"So, you think there were two visitors that night? The one Pamela Reece described and the one Ellis claims to have seen?"

"No, sir. I think the old lady got it wrong. It was dark and the weather was atrocious. She couldn't have seen the visitor clearly at all. It's much more likely that it was the bloke Ellis saw."

As they entered the station, Sergeant Brown came over. "Inspector Mason, DCS Bainbridge would like a word, sir. He's in his office."

"Thanks, sergeant." He turned to Beaumont. "Start collating the reports, I won't be long."

"Yes, sir," Beaumont said as he headed towards the CID office.

When he had gone, Sergeant Brown turned to Mason. "I had a word with young Beaumont the other night," he said. "He tells me he won't be seeing Denise Porter again."

"And you believe him?"

The sergeant shrugged. "That young man couldn't keep it in his pants if he tried. If it's not Porter's wife he's chasing, it will be some other young woman. I doubt he'll try it on with one of his colleague's wives again though."

"Unless he does, there's not a lot we can do, is there, sergeant?" Mason said dismissively as he began to ascend the stairs to Bainbridge's office. "Keep me informed."

"Yes, sir," the sergeant said as he strode back to his desk.

38

DCS Bainbridge was seated behind his desk studying paperwork when Inspector Mason entered. "Come in, Inspector," he said, not bothering to raise his head. "How did it go with Mrs Myers and her son-in-law?"

"Much the same as I thought," Mason said. "According to Nixon, Benji Myers had been knocking Irene around for years."

"So, why did Nixon assault Myers that particular time? Was there a reason?"

Mason shrugged. "Who knows? He happened to be visiting that weekend and saw first-hand what had been going on. He was so outraged that he gave Benji a good hiding."

"Did Irene Myers confirm what Nixon had said?"

"Well…er…no, not exactly. I didn't think there was any point in upsetting her further. Her bully of a husband is dead. She wants to draw a line under it."

Bainbridge huffed. "Her bully of a husband was murdered, Inspector. Don't forget that. I want a statement from her confirming what Nixon claimed had been happening. Is that understood?"

"Yes, sir. If you think it necessary."

"I do. By the way, have you checked that Nixon was actually in Carlisle when the assault took place?"

Mason looked uneasy. "No, sir, but he came down the following day with his wife. You and I were at Mrs Myers's house when they arrived."

"When they said they arrived," Bainbridge corrected.

"I'll look into it," Mason promised as he shuffled uneasily in his chair.

"What about Ellis? Did he explain what he was doing in Primrose Gardens at that time of night?"

"He said he went for a walk before going home, something he often does after a gruelling shift at the hotel."

"And you believe him? It was raining heavily that night. Surely nobody goes for a walk in those conditions."

Mason shrugged. "That's what he said he did."

"Did you check Ellis's record before you visited him?"

"No, sir, I had no reason to. Ellis isn't a suspect."

"Everyone's a suspect until they're not," Bainbridge said. "If you had bothered to check, Inspector, you would have seen that for three months Frank Ellis shared the same cell as Shaun Dyson."

"Oh, I didn't know that."

"I want you to interview Ellis again at the station this time, and under caution."

Mason inhaled. "Very well, sir. I'll get Beaumont to bring him in."

Bainbridge leant forward, resting his elbows on the desk, steepling his fingers. "Jack, as SIO on these murder enquiries, you have to be more thorough with your investigations. Some of your work to date has been bordering on slipshod. I appreciate you don't have a great deal of experience, but I'm talking about basic police procedures not being followed. It simply isn't good enough."

"I… I'm doing my best, sir, but we desperately need more men, more resources. Sometimes it feels like I'm chasing round in circles and..."

"It's hard for everybody. We just have to manage with what we have. Now, how is the Sheila Thompson enquiry going? Have you managed to find any witnesses?"

"We received an anonymous call from a bloke who said he saw someone hanging around by the bridge over the lake in the early hours, but he couldn't see what he was doing."

"Was this person able to give a description?"

"No, sir. They were too far away. He said he saw the figure get into a car and drive away."

"Do they know what make of car? Was it an estate or a saloon? Did they see the colour?"

Mason shook his head. "All they could say was it was a small car with a noisy exhaust."

"Well, that's something I suppose."

"Yes, sir. By the way, have Forensics been able to come up with anything on the drugs packages?"

"They're still working on it, but they're not hopeful."

Mason got to his feet. "If that's all, sir, I'd better get back to work."

"Very well, Inspector, and pay heed to what I've said."

"Yes, sir," Mason said as he hurriedly left the room.

39

Maria's Hair & Beauty Salon was based on the seafront. Maria Crane, the owner, was in the back room checking stock when Annika came rushing over to her.

"Maria, I've asked Jodie to help me with Mrs Rushton's perm and she's refused."

"Why do you need help?"

"It's going to take for ever putting all those tiny rollers in. If Jodie helped, we could have it done in half the time."

"What is Jodie doing now?"

"She's reading a magazine. She said she has a client coming in in fifteen minutes for a shampoo and blow, but we could have Mrs Rushton's perm finished in that time."

Maria put down her clipboard and entered the salon. Mrs Rushton, a lady in her eighties with poor vision and even worse hearing, was sitting at Annika's workstation oblivious to the drama her perm was causing. Two stylists were drying their client's hair, whilst another was applying their client with foils. Jodie was behind the reception desk drinking coffee and scanning through a magazine.

Maria strode over to the desk. "Jodie, give Annika a hand with Mrs Rushton's perm, will you dear?"

Jodie snorted. "That's not fair. I've done two clients already this morning, and I've got Mrs Freeman coming in any time."

"Well, she isn't here yet, is she, so you can help Annika with the perm rollers until she gets here."

Jodie scowled as she strode over to Annika's workstation and began putting in the rollers. Annika gave a smirk of satisfaction. Ten minutes later, Mrs Rushton's perm was complete, just as Mrs Freeman entered the salon.

"Good morning, Gillian," Jodie said as she took Gillian Freeman's coat and handed her a salon gown. "The usual, is it?"

"Well dear, I was thinking I might have a change this week. I'm going on holiday at the weekend and I quite like the idea of going a nice shade of auburn. Do you think it would cover my grey roots?"

"I'm sure it would," Jodie said. "I'll bring you the colour chart and you can decide which shade you want."

For the next few minutes, Gillian and Jodie studied the colour chart and a suitable shade was decided upon. Jodie went into the back room to mix the colour whilst Gillian drank a coffee prepared by the trainee stylist, Hayley. Jodie had just about finished mixing the solution when Hayley came into the room. "Jodie, Wayne's on the phone. He says its urgent."

Jodie tutted in frustration as she left the solution and went to answer the phone.

"What is it, Wayne? I'm busy."

When Jodie put down the phone, she was angry. She marched over to Annika who was by the sink washing her client's hair.

"I think your husband expects too much of my Wayne," she said, pointing her finger. "He hardly ever gets home on time since he started this damned job in CID. We were supposed to be going to the Regent to see that new film with Chris Hemsworth, but he's got to work late."

Annika grinned mischievously. "What makes you think he's been working when he gets home late?"

Jodie stepped forward and pushed Annika against the wall. "What's that supposed to mean?"

Maria, who had been close by and witnessed the altercation, rushed over, and got in between the two women. "What the hell's going on?" she said, glaring at Jodie.

"Ask her," Jodie said. "She's the one that started it."

"And I'm finishing it," Maria said. "Now get on with Mrs Freeman's colour." Jodie huffed, then rushed into the back room to collect the solution. Maria turned sharply to face Annika. "I don't know what's going on between you two but it stops now. I won't have my business disrupted in this way. Do you understand, Annika?"

Annika shrugged. "I haven't done anything. Jodie's upset because her bloke is having to work late tonight. She carries on as if it's my fault."

Shaking her head, Maria walked back to her workstation, leaving Annika to carry on shampooing her client's hair.

Forty-five minutes later, Gillian Freeman was having the excess colour solution rinsed from her hair when Jodie stood back aghast.

"What on earth's the matter?" Gillian said as she went over to one of the wall mirrors. "Oh my god, what have you done, you stupid girl? My hair's turned purple."

Maria came hurrying over. "Oh, goodness, what's happened?" She glared at Jodie. "Please don't worry, Mrs Freeman," she said, "I can fix this."

Jodie burst into tears "It wasn't me," she said. "It's not my fault." She turned and ran out of the salon.

"Hayley, make Mrs Freeman a cup of tea. I'll just be a minute making up a mixture."

Gillian Freeman stared at her reflection in the mirror. "Maria, are you sure you can get this purple colour out of my hair? It looks terrible."

"Of course, Mrs Freeman. Don't worry. It will take about half an hour." Maria hurried into the back room and began mixing a solution. "Annika," she said, "can you come through here for a minute, please?"

Annika lightly sprayed Mrs Rushton's perm with lacquer. "That looks lovely," she said smiling. "It really suits you."

Mrs Rushton slowly got to her feet. "Thank you, dear," she said as she walked over to the reception desk to pay. "You've done a really good job."

Annika hurried into the back room where Maria was busy preparing the solution.

"Did you have anything to do with the colour mix-up?" Maria said.

"No, of course not. It was Jodie being careless."

"She's worked for me for two years and there's never been anything like this happen before. She's usually so careful. I can't understand it."

Annika shrugged. "All I know is she's been in a foul mood all morning. She probably wasn't concentrating."

Maria sighed as she made her way back into the salon carrying the mixture. "We'll have you looking perfect again in no time, Mrs Freeman," she said as she began applying the liquid to her hair. "Just relax and enjoy your tea."

Annika strode to the window and looked out. "Do you want me to find Jodie? She can't have gone far."

Maria shook her head. "No, I'll telephone her tonight and sort this out. Accidents do happen I suppose."

40

Frank Ellis flung himself onto the plastic chair in the interview room and folded his arms across his chest in a gesture of defiance. PC Beaumont sat across from him, placing a buff-coloured folder on the desk.

“How long is the inspector going to be then? I’ve got things to do.”

“Inspector Mason will be here shortly,” Beaumont said.

“Why am I here anyway? I’ve told you all I know. I’ve nothing more to add.”

The door opened and Inspector Mason stepped into the room.

“Thank you for coming in, Mr Ellis.”

“I didn’t have much choice, did I?”

“Mr Ellis, I need you to clarify a few things in the statement you made earlier.”

“What things? I’ve told you what I saw.”

“So you did,” Mason said as he picked up the folder and opened it. “When we spoke earlier, I asked you if you knew Shaun Dyson. Do you remember that?”

Ellis scowled, but said nothing.

“You told me that you didn’t know him. Do you remember saying that, Mr Ellis?”

Ellis began to fidget uneasily in his chair, he lowered his head, but still remained silent.

“I’ll ask you again, Mr Ellis. Do you know Shaun Dyson?”

Ellis leant forward, putting his elbows on the desk, and rested his chin in his hands. “All right! Yes, I know Shaun. We were banged up together a few months back.”

“You’re saying you shared a cell, is that right?”

“Look, I was doing a mate a favour, that’s all. Shaun said you were trying to fit him up for the murders, even though he had nothing to do with them.”

“So, you agreed to pretend to have seen someone at Mr Rhodes’s house, whose description was nothing like Shaun’s?”

“Yeah, like I said, he’s a mate.”

“But Shaun had an alibi for that night. He was at The Smugglers.”

“Shaun didn’t trust the landlord to give him an alibi. They had a fallout just before Shaun got sent down and he’d been barred. He’s only just been allowed back into the pub so he didn’t know CCTV had been installed. These days, CCTV is everywhere. It’s getting so you can’t go for a piss without it being on camera.”

Mason picked up the file and stood up. “Mr Ellis, you are going to be formally charged with wasting police time.” He turned to Beaumont. “Deal with that, constable,” he said as he turned to leave the room.

“Yes, sir,” Beaumont said.

Mason returned to his office and picking up the telephone, rang Irene Myers. The call went to answerphone. “Good afternoon, Mrs Myers,” he said. “I need to speak with you and Mr Nixon again at the station. Can you please ring to arrange an appointment. Thank you.”

There was a sharp rap on the door and Sergeant Brown came into the room. "Sir, I've just had Forensics on the line. The samples they took are useless, I'm afraid."

"Does the boss know?"

"Yes, sir. He was downstairs when the call came in."

"Very well, thank you for letting me know, sergeant."

***

It was almost five o'clock that evening when Giles Nixon telephoned Inspector Mason.

"We've just got your message," he said. "We've all been to Middlesbrough shopping today. Irene wanted a new coat for the funeral."

"You do know the Coroner won't be releasing the body for a while yet?"

"Yes, but Irene wants everything sorted for when she can bury Benji."

"Mr Nixon, I want you and Mrs Myers to come to the station tomorrow. There are one or two points I need to go over with you."

"Is that really necessary, Inspector? Can't we answer any questions over the telephone? It would be far more convenient."

"No, I'm sorry. I need to speak to you both personally. Shall we say ten o'clock tomorrow morning?"

"Very well, but it really is most tiresome," Nixon said as he put down the receiver.

41

Annika was in the kitchen when Jack got home at six-thirty. He strode over to the drinks cupboard and poured himself a large whisky before joining her.

"Hello, darling," she said as she began straining the pasta. "How's your day?"

Jack kissed her lightly on the cheek. "Bloody awful. Bainbridge is driving me up the wall."

"Oh, I thought Supercop could do no wrong."

Jack huffed. "The man's a stickler for the tiniest detail. I think he'll be wanting to know what they had for breakfast next."

"What details exactly? I thought you had taken statements from all the witnesses."

"I had, then this bloke turns up claiming to have seen someone at Rhodes's door about the time of the killing. It turns out he was a mate of Shaun Dyson and gave a description that couldn't possibly be him. The whole thing's a bloody mess."

"So, what was Bainbridge kicking off about? You sorted it, didn't you?"

"Yes, but only after a second interview. The bloke's being charged with wasting police time." Throwing back his head, Jack drank the contents of his glass and headed back to the lounge. "Want one?" he asked as he poured a generous amount of whisky into his glass.

“I’ll have a vodka,” she said as she began assembling the food on the plate. “A large one. You’re not the only one who’s had a shit day.”

Jack carried both drinks into the kitchen. “Back on the vodka again I see,” he said, a wide grin on his face. “The gin phase didn’t last long.”

Annika banged the dish of chicken and vegetables onto the table. “For fuck’s sake, Jack, vodka, gin, what does it matter?” She reached out and taking her drink from Jack, took a large gulp. “I needed that,” she said.

“What’s the matter, love. Has something happened at work?”

Annika snorted. “You could say that. That bitch, Jodie is trying to cause trouble for me.”

“Why, what’s she done?”

“Her client’s hair turned bright purple and she tried to blame me, that’s what.”

Jack began to chuckle.

“It’s not funny, Jack. She tried to get me sacked.”

“Surely Maria didn’t believe you were responsible?”

Annika shrugged. “I’m not sure. She’s friendly with Jodie.”

“I’m sure everything will sort itself out,” Jack said, as he took his place at the table. “Oh, by the way, don’t forget we’re going to Superintendent Barraclough’s do tomorrow night at The Grey Horse.”

Annika served up the food and handed a plate to Jack. “I would have thought you’d see enough of that lot at the station without giving up your spare time to be with them.”

"Needs must," he said, reaching for the salt. "By the way, we might have a breakthrough with Sheila Thompson. A witness claims to have seen a car by the boating lake."

Annika plonked down onto her chair. "What witness? Who?"

"They refused to give a name," he said. "They didn't want to get involved I suppose."

"Did the person give a description of who was driving the car?"

"No, not really. A local plod took the call. It's probably nothing important. Attention seeking, maybe."

"You still don't have any real suspects other than Shaun Dyson?"

"Enquiries are continuing, as they say, but Bainbridge is convinced it's him. He hasn't considered anyone else."

"That seems a bit short-sighted, don't you think?"

"We'll see. I'm interviewing Benji Myers's widow again tomorrow, and his son-in-law."

"Surely you don't suspect them of being involved?"

"They've both lied to my face. I intend to find out why." Jack ate the last piece of chicken from his plate. "That was delicious. I don't suppose there's any more is there, love?"

Jodie was watching television when Wayne Beaumont got home.

"What's for tea," he asked, plonking down heavily into an armchair. "I'm starving!"

Jodie jumped to her feet. "Get your own bloody tea," she said, rushing up the stairs to the bedroom and slamming the door shut.

Wayne followed her. "What's the matter, you moody cow," he said as he entered the bedroom.

Jodie charged towards him and began pounding his chest with her fists. "Is it true you've been having an affair? Is that why you're always home late?"

Wayne grabbed her wrists and pushed her away. "What are you talking about, you mad bitch? Who's been saying that?"

"Your bosses wife, that's who."

Wayne grabbed Jodie by the arms and pulled her to him. "It's not true. I wouldn't cheat on you, love. You know that."

"What about that optician's wife? You were cheating with her."

"She was a nympho, I told you that. She was stalking me, but that's all over now, Jodie. I haven't seen her in weeks."

"Then why are you always going out without me?"

"It's the job, love. Sometimes the only way you can interview a witness is at night. That's mostly what working in CID's about, speaking to witnesses."

"Then why would Annika say what she did if it isn't true?"

"Maybe she's just winding you up. Some people are like that."

Tears began to trickle down Jodie's face. "I'm sure it was her that deliberately messed with the solution for Mrs

Freeman's colour. Her hair should have been auburn but it came out bright purple."

"Purple? What happened?"

Jodie sniffed loudly. "I was so upset I… I ran out of the salon."

"You mean you've packed your job in?"

"I thought I'd get the sack, but Maria rang me about an hour ago. She said she'd managed to put the damage right, and that I should go back to the salon tomorrow and she'll forget all about it. But it wasn't my fault, Wayne. It was Annika. I'm sure of it."

"Why would she do that?"

"She doesn't like me. She's out to cause trouble for me, that's why."

"Look, I've told you before, you have to get along with her. She can make life difficult for me too if she starts blabbing to her old man."

"I can't believe you're taking her side."

"Of course I'm not taking her side. It was probably an accident. You misread the label or something."

"Are you saying I'm stupid?"

"Jodie, you're becoming paranoid." He turned and went back down the stairs. "Set the table," he said. "I'll call at the fish shop, then we can go to the pub for an hour."

42

The following morning, Chief Superintendent Bainbridge was in his office studying four confidential files regarding financial information when Inspector Mason entered.

"You wanted to see me, sir?"

"Yes, inspector. Close the door and take a seat."

When he was seated across the desk, Bainbridge opened one of the files.

"I've just received these," he said. "They're the financials of the four officers who had access to the property store."

Mason raised an eyebrow. "Anything interesting?"

Bainbridge inhaled. "It seems PC Walker is living beyond her means. All three of her credit cards are maxed out."

"That surprises me. I always thought she was a sensible young woman."

"It seems she's been surviving by robbing Peter to pay Paul."

"I'll have a quiet word with her, sir," he said. "I'll find out exactly what's going on."

"You do that, but discreetly mind. She's a good officer. Whatever she's been up to we should try to help her."

"Yes, sir. I'll have a quiet word tomorrow."

Bainbridge turned to another file. "PC Renshaw seems to have his affairs in order. It looks like he's going to have a comfortable retirement."

"He deserves it after twenty-five years' service."

He opened the third file. "Dewhurst was right about being a lucky gambler. There are some extremely large deposits in his account from gambling casinos and from betting online."

"Lucky sod. He'll probably go on to win the lottery."

Bainbridge opened the last file, which relating to PC Paul Porter. "This young man's finances look the dodgiest," he said.

"In what way, sir?"

"Looking back over the months, it seems there is a good deal of money being spent on spa treatments, luxury hotels, expensive restaurants, not to mention female clothing from some of the more affluent boutiques. I would say young Porter is living way beyond a police constable's salary."

"What about deposits?"

"There are several large cash deposits paid into his account. Three thousand last month, two thousand the month before, and two days ago, ten thousand pounds." Mason pursed his lips and blew.

"No indication as to where the money has come from?"

"Apparently they were all cash deposits so there's no way of tracing them."

Bainbridge picked up the internal phone. "Sergeant Brown, ask PC Porter to come up to my office straightaway, will you? What? When?" He placed the receiver back onto its cradle. "It appears that PC Porter has rang in sick this morning."

Mason sprang to his feet. "I'll fetch him in myself," he said.

"I suggest you send Beaumont, but don't tell him what's going on. You've got Irene Myers and her son-in-law coming in at ten, don't forget."

"Of course. I'd better go down to the interview room. They'll be here any time."

"I intend to join you later," Bainbridge said. "I think Nixon knows a lot more about what was going on between Benji and Arthur Rhodes."

43

Irene Myers was sitting in Reception engrossed in a copy of 'Woman's Weekly' when Mason descended the stairs. Giles Nixon was getting a cup of water from the fountain dispenser. On sight of Mason, Giles strode purposely over to him.

"What the hell is this about? Irene has told you everything she knows and I have no knowledge of the assault on my father-in-law."

"Take a seat, Mr Nixon," Mason said. "I need to speak to Mrs Myers alone."

"I insist on being present," Nixon said. "Irene is in mourning. She's fragile. Anyone can see that."

Mason walked over to Irene. "Good morning, Irene. Will you come with me, please? I have a few more questions for you I'm afraid."

"Of course, dear," she said, placing the magazines back on the table. "Ask as many questions as you like."

"This way," Mason said, heading towards Interview Room One. "Can I get you anything, Irene? Tea, coffee?"

Irene shook her head. "No thank you dear," she said. "I had some tea before I set off."

Mason led the way to the interview room and Irene sat where he indicated.

"I'm going to record our conversation. It's just procedure. I'm also going to have to caution you."

Irene shrieked and wrung her hands. "Oh, this is so exciting," she said. "It's just like on the telly."

Mason administered the caution and gave the usual introductions for the benefit of the tape. “Irene, since I last spoke to you, certain anomalies have arisen.”

Irene tilted her head to the side. “Anomalies? What sort of anomalies?”

“You claimed that Benji was a kind and loving husband who rarely drank alcohol.”

Irene smiled. “Yes, that’s exactly what he was.”

“No, Irene, he was not. We have several reports of Benji Myers being violent towards you. We know he drank excessively and..."

“No,” Irene said, clenching her hands into fists. “I don’t know who’s been saying these things. It just isn’t true. Benji was a good husband.”

“Do you deny he hit you on a regular basis?”

“Of course I do.”

“We have witnesses,” Mason said. “They all say the same, that Benji frequently used his fists on you.”

Irene’s breathing became erratic and beads of sweat began forming on her brow. “They’re lying,” she said. “They’re all lying.”

“No they are not lying, Irene. We know your husband was a brute towards you. What I don’t understand is why are you still defending him?”

Irene’s posture stiffened in a steely defiance.

Mason leant forward across the desk and took her hands in his. “Benji’s gone now. He can’t hurt you anymore.”

Irene began to rock gently. “You… you don’t understand what he was like,” she whispered. “Nobody does.”

"No I don't," Mason said, "so tell me. Tell me what living with Benji was really like."

Irene's eyes brimmed with tears. "It doesn't matter now," she said. "He's dead, Rotting in some wooden box waiting for the fires of hell to devour him."

"Why didn't you leave him? I understand your daughter offered you refuge at her house."

Irene looked puzzled. "Live at Sonja's?" she said. "No dear, I could never do that."

"Why not?"

"Giles wouldn't allow it for one thing. And then there was Benji. He threatened to kill me if I ever tried to leave him."

"You could have reported him to the police."

Irene snorted. "I threatened to once," she said, "about ten years ago now. That's when he did this." She pulled up the coat sleeve on her right arm revealing a large burn mark. "He did that with the iron," she said. "He held it on my arm until I passed out. I couldn't use my arm properly for weeks."

"But you could have got help."

"Not when I was locked in the cellar. He used to lock me in the cellar for days at a time."

"You say Giles Nixon wouldn't allow you to stay with him?"

Irene sniffed. "Giles and Benji were close. Giles would never go against him."

"Why did Giles give Benji a black eye the other week? What had they fallen out about?"

"I… I've no idea. They'd been down to the shed and something must have happened there."

"Tell me about the bag that was hidden in the shed," Mason said. "Did you know what was inside it?"

Irene shook her head. "How could I? I wasn't allowed in the shed."

"But surely Benji must have spoken to you about it? Given you some indication where it had come from?"

"All I know is that he and Arthur found a bag some time ago. I'd almost forgotten about it until I heard what had happened to poor Arthur."

"Irene, can you tell me where Benji got the money from to buy the lease for the off-licence? I understand he paid cash."

Irene shook her head. "I've no idea," she said. "Benji kept all money matters to himself. All I know is that one day he suddenly announced that he had bought an off-licence."

"What did you think to that?"

"It was nothing to do with me, dear. I just hoped he would drink himself to death."

"I still don't understand why you never reported what was happening. You could have got help."

"What, and have everyone knowing my business? No, dear. Some things are best kept private. That's the way it's always been."

"Is there anything else you want to tell me, Irene?"

"I don't think so," she said. "Are we done now? I should be getting home."

"I need to speak to Giles first," Mason said. "If you wait outside, I shouldn't be long."

44

Mason escorted Irene to Reception where Giles Nixon was anxiously pacing.

"There you are, Irene. I was beginning to think you'd been locked up."

"Of course not, dear," Irene said. "I've just been having a chat about Benji to this nice policeman."

Mason escorted Irene to a chair, then turned to Giles Nixon. "If you could come with me, please Mr Nixon."

Nixon huffed loudly but followed Mason to the interview room.

"I hope this isn't going to take long. I'm going back to Carlisle later today."

"Oh? I thought you and your wife would be staying a little longer with Irene."

"I'll be back for the funeral, but I have to get back to work. Sonja is staying on with her mother for a few more days."

"What is it you do?" Mason asked.

"I drive for a haulage firm," Nixon said. "'Here & There' Haulage."

Nixon followed the inspector into the interview room and flung himself into the chair. Before Mason could close the door, DCS Bainbridge entered the room carrying a buff-coloured file.

"I thought I'd sit in on this one. I've got a couple of questions for Mr Nixon myself."

"Of course, sir," Mason said as they both took a seat at the table. He continued to administer the caution as he turned on the tape.

Bainbridge leant forward, steepling his fingers in front of him. "Mr Nixon," he began, "where were you the day before your father-in-law got attacked?"

Throwing back his head, Nixon crossed his arms. "Why do you want to know that?"

"Please answer the question," Bainbridge said.

Nixon leant forward. "I was at home all day on the Sunday. I played a round of golf in the morning, then came home for lunch and potted about in the garden for most of the afternoon."

Bainbridge raised an eyebrow. "You didn't come over to Redcar at all that day?"

"No, I've told you. I was in Carlisle."

Bainbridge opened the file and produced a sheet of paper. "In that case," he said, pushing the document towards Nixon, "perhaps you can explain to me how your credit card was used to buy petrol at Morrison's garage in Redcar that day?"

"There… there must be some mistake. I was nowhere near Redcar that Sunday."

"Mr Nixon, I suggest you stop pissing about and start telling the truth. What were you doing in Redcar, and why are you lying about it?"

Nixon lowered his head, staring at the floor. His breathing became shallow as the colour drained from his face. "If you must know, I was meeting someone."

"Someone?"

"A woman. We've been having a bit of a fling for a couple of months now."

"What's her name?"

"She's nothing to do with anything. I don't want her getting involved."

"I won't ask you again," Bainbridge said, thumping the desk with his fist. "What is the woman's name?"

Nixon looked startled. "Her name's Kathy," he said. "Kathy Blackburn."

"And where can I find Ms Blackburn?"

Looking nervous, Nixon licked his lips. "She's married. Her husband will kill her if he finds out about us. He'll probably kill me too."

"Don't worry, we'll be discreet," Bainbridge said, picking up his pen. "What's her address?"

"She lives in Fountain Estate, number seventeen, but Kathy works at the Arcade on the seafront. She's there most days."

"I take it Mrs Nixon isn't aware of your... your liaisons with this woman?"

Nixon gasped. "Christ no. You're not going to tell her, are you?"

"The police are not in the business of wrecking marriages, Mr Nixon. I'm sure you don't need any help in that department."

Nixon scraped the chair back and began to stand. "Well, if there's nothing else," he said.

"Sit down," Bainbridge said. "We haven't finished yet." He turned to Mason. "Perhaps you can speak to Ms Blackburn and see if she corroborates Mr Nixon's statement."

"Yes, sir!"

"Tell me about the fight you had with your father-in-law," Bainbridge said, turning to face Nixon. "What exactly was that about?"

Nixon huffed. "I've told you people already. I saw what Benji had done to Irene and I just saw red."

"But you knew he was violent towards his wife. You never intervened before. What made you this time?"

Nixon shrugged. "I don't know. It was one step too far, I suppose. Benji really was a nasty individual."

"I've heard that you and he were quite close."

"Rubbish. Who told you that?"

"Did you know about the bag Benji had found at the plant?"

"No I did not."

"You had no idea what was inside the bag?"

"I'd never seen the bloody bag until you brought it out of the shed."

"Benji never discussed it with you?"

"I've already told you, no."

"Irene tells me the argument you had with Benji started in the shed. What was that about?"

Nixon inhaled; his posture stiffened. "I've nothing more to say. Benji hit Irene so I hit him. That's all there was to it."

"Why didn't you offer sanctuary to Irene when you knew what was happening?"

"I don't believe in interfering in other people's marriage."

"Even though you knew she was in danger?"

"I've said all I intend to say," Nixon said as he got to his feet. "If you want to question me again, do it with my solicitor present." He walked to the door, "If there's nothing further, I'd like to leave."

"Very well, Mr Nixon," Bainbridge said, "but I may need to speak to you again."

"Whatever," Nixon said as he went through to Reception where Irene was sitting on a chair reading a magazine.

"Come on Irene," he reached for her arm. "Let's get out of here."

***

"Well, what do you think to those two?" Bainbridge asked Mason, as they walked into Reception. "Personally, I think they're both hiding something."

"Their statements are certainly contradictory," Mason said. "According to Irene, Nixon and Benji had a good relationship up until the fight."

"I think Nixon's in it up to his neck. Go and interview this woman, Kathy Blackburn. See what she has to say for herself. And Mason, make sure you're discreet."

"Yes, sir," Mason said. "I'll do it now."

"I have to go over to Middlesbrough this morning for a meeting, so I'll see you this evening at The Grey Horse."

"Yes, sir. My wife and I are looking forward to it."

DC Beaumont came hurrying over to Inspector Mason. "Sir," he said, "I've been to PC Porter's house, but there was no-one in. A neighbour said he saw him driving away early this morning. He had a couple of suitcases with him."

Mason turned to Bainbridge. "Should I organise a search for his vehicle?"

"Yes, but keep it low key. Say he's wanted in connection with some missing paperwork or something like that. I don't want him panicked."

"Very well, sir. I'll get a search started right away."

45

Freddie Roberts was nervously pacing his lounge. Sitting on the couch were both his sons, Lee and Barry, with Paul Porter in between.

"You shouldn't have come here," Freddie said, pointing his finger at Porter. "This is the first place they'll look."

"Where else could I go? I didn't have any choice."

"Are you sure Bainbridge's onto you?"

"Yes, of course I am. One of my mates in Personnel rang me first thing to say Bainbridge had requested my financials."

"I can't believe you were so fucking stupid as to pay the cash into the bank leaving a paper trail."

"I had no choice. There were standing orders to meet and credit cards to pay off."

"Does anyone at the station know we're related?"

"No, but it won't take Bainbridge long to find out."

Freddie huffed. "You're my nephew on my wife's side, that's all. He can't know that."

"Don't underestimate Bainbridge. He knows everything."

"Pity he didn't know about Myers and Rhodes before..."

Porter gasped. "Christ, Uncle Fred, you'd nothing to do with them getting murdered, had you?"

Freddie shook his head. "Some bastard got to them first unfortunately."

"Well at least the police can't touch you now about the drugs. They have no evidence to produce in court."

"Yeah, but we got rid of one problem only to be faced with another. What to do about you?"

"I can drive him up to Sunderland, Dad," Barry said. "Terry will be able to put him up until we can figure out what to do."

Porter jumped to his feet. "I'm not going anywhere without Denise."

"It's that bloody wife of yours that's put you under the spotlight," Barry said. "She spends money like water. Where is she anyway?"

"She's at The Spa Hotel in Harrogate. She'll be back tomorrow."

Freddie turned to Lee. "I want you to find her and take her to Terry's today. Barry, you drive Paul up to Sunderland now."

"He could always try to bluff it out," Barry said. "Tell them he won the money on the horses or something."

"I gave him ten grand for that last job," Freddie said. "Do you have any idea what the stake would have to be to recoup that amount?"

"We could speak to one of the touts and get him to confirm a large win."

Freddie shook his head. "Nah, too risky. Besides, that lot down at the track would ask too many questions and they'd want a cut."

Barry shrugged. "Just an idea, By the way, when's Billy due back from Newcastle?"

"Later today," Freddie said. "He's still sorting out the next pick-up. I'll get him to get rid of Paul's car when he gets back."

"What do you mean, get rid of my car? It's almost brand new."

"Once your pals at the station realise you've done a runner, they'll be looking for the bloody thing."

Paul lowered his head into his hands. "I wish to God I'd never got involved with you. My life's ruined."

"Don't blame me. You came to me remember? Worried out of your skin about the debt that wife of yours was running up."

Paul sighed. "I never realised when I passed on bits of information that it would end like this. We're talking serious jail time if I'm caught."

"Do what I say and that won't happen," Freddie said. "We'll have you out of the country in less than a week."

"Out of the country? I never agreed to that."

"You can't stay round here, Paul. Use your head for fuck's sake."

"But..."

"If we're going to Sunderland we'd best get moving," Barry said, grabbing Paul's arm "It won't take the cops long to figure out our involvement."

"What about Denise? I'm not going anywhere without my wife."

"I'm going to collect her now," Lee said, striding towards the door.

Barry and Paul followed.

Left alone, Freddie picked up the telephone and dialled a number. "Terry? Barry's on his way with Paul. Lee's gone to fetch Denise so he should be with you in a couple of hours. You know what to do? I want them both silenced for good. Understand?"

46

Kathy Blackburn was an attractive thirty-something with blonde, short-cropped hair and a slim figure. She was dismantling one of the gaming machines in the 'Summertime Fun' Arcade when Inspector Mason entered the building.

"Ms Blackburn?" he said, noting the identity badge fastened to her pink tabard.

Kathy continued with her work, not bothering to look up. "Yeah, that's right," she said. "What can I do for you?"

"I'm Detective Inspector Mason. I wonder if I could have a word with you in private?"

"Giles said you'd be coming round. What is it you want to know?"

"It's rather a delicate matter Ms Blackburn. Perhaps we could go to the office?"

Kathy closed the glass door on the machine and gave a satisfied sigh. "Sorted," she said as she began to refix the screws she had previously taken out. "These bloody machines they bring in from China are nothing but trouble. That's twice this week this one has malfunctioned."

"Ms Blackburn, I..."

"All right, Mr Policeman. Keep your hair on," she said, wiping her hands on the cloth she had tucked in her pocket. "Through here."

Mason followed her into a small, untidy room at the back of the arcade which served as an office. Papers were strewn over the two desks and boxes were piled high against the walls.

"Well, what is it you want to know?" she said, closing the door.

"Last Sunday, where were you?" Mason said, "between six and seven o'clock?"

Kathy grinned. "I was getting fucked in the back seat of Giles Nixon's car," she said.

"What time did you meet Mr Nixon?"

Kathy shrugged. "I finished here at five. Giles was waiting for me in the car park. We went for a drink and a bite to eat at The Beacon Lounge and then we drove down the coast to The Stray and parked up."

"Did anyone see you?"

"Christ, I hope not."

"So I just have your word that you were with Mr Nixon at the time in question?"

"That's right. Giles and I have… have an arrangement. He comes over to Redcar every two weeks, always on a Sunday. That's when Gary, my husband, visits his mother. She's in a Care Home in Whitby."

"And what about Mrs Nixon? What is she doing when these liaisons take place?"

"I've no idea. All I know is that every other Sunday, Giles and I meet up and have the most amazing sex."

"Where did you meet Mr Nixon?"

"Online," she said. "I wanted some excitement in my life, excitement in the bedroom that is. Gary's a decent bloke but once every couple of months just doesn't do it for me, if you know what I mean."

"Does Mr Nixon ever talk to you about his family? His father-in-law for instance?"

"That bloke who got murdered?"

"Yes, that's him."

Kathy pouted for a moment. "I think they'd had a fallout over something."

"What about, do you know?"

"I've no idea. I know Giles thought his father-in-law was a bit of a twat, but I don't know the details. To be honest, Inspector, I was more interested in getting a good shag than listening to stories about his family."

"Very well, Ms Blackburn. I'll need you to come down to the station and make an official statement about what you've told me."

"A statement? I don't think so."

"But you're providing an alibi for someone who could be deemed a suspect in a murder enquiry. You have to make a statement."

Kathy stormed to the door. "I'm not getting involved in no murder investigation. Giles Nixon and I were shagging buddies, that's all."

"But Ms Blackburn, you..."

"Do you have any idea what Gary will do to me if he finds out? You can't ask me to get involved. It isn't right."

"I give you my assurance the matter will be handled discreetly," Mason said. "There's no reason your husband need ever know, but you must make a statement. You have no choice. I will take your statement personally."

Kathy snorted. "Bastard," she said. "Fucking bastard."

47

Wearing a dark-green silk dress, Annika Mason entered The Grey Horse Restaurant arm in arm with Jack, at exactly seven-thirty. A dozen or so people were already congregated.

"Ah, there's Bainbridge," Jack said, steering her towards a middle-aged man standing close to the bar. "Come on darling, I'll introduce you."

Annika glanced at the tall, muscular man dressed in a light-grey suit. "So that's Supercop," she said. "I thought he'd be older. And who's that woman with him? I thought you said he was single?"

"No idea," he said, striding over to Andy Bainbridge. "Good evening, sir," Jack said, "I'd like you to meet my wife, Annika."

Annika smiled, holding out her hand. "It's lovely to meet you, Chief Superintendent," she said. "Jack speaks highly of you."

Bainbridge reached out and shook her hand. "He speaks highly of you too and tonight it's Andy. Forget about the rank." He turned to his companion. "I'd like to introduce you to my dear friend, Sophie Barrett."

"It's nice to meet you both," Sophie said. "How are you settling in, Jack? Redcar must be a big change from Leeds."

Jack grinned and put his arm protectively around Annika's shoulders. "It's certainly a lot busier that I thought it would be," he said. He turned and walked towards the bar. "Can I get anyone a drink? Annika?"

"Vodka and tonic, please," she requested.

"And you, Sophie? Andy?"

"I think I'll have the same," Sophie said.

"Me too," Andy said.

Jack stood at the bar waiting to be served leaving Annika with Andy and Sophie.

"Jack was telling me you work at a hair salon?" Andy said.

"Hair and beauty," Annika corrected. "I'm a fully-trained beautician as well as a hairdresser." She turned to Sophie. "What about you, Sophie? What do you do?"

"Nothing so glamorous I'm afraid," Sophie said. "I'm a criminal psychologist."

Annika arched an eyebrow. "How interesting. Does that mean you can spot a psychopath at a hundred yards?"

Sophie shrugged. "Life would be a lot easier if I could," she said. "Unfortunately, that only happens on television dramas I'm afraid."

"So, how do you detect a dangerous criminal? Are there giveaway signs?"

Before Sophie could respond, Jack arrived carrying the drinks. He handed them round. "Oh, I think we've been summoned into the dining room."

"Good," Annika said. "I'm starving."

After the meal and presentation, the party returned to the main lounge where they split into small groups. Sophie and Annika shuffled into one of the booths, leaving the two men standing.

"Barraclough's in good spirits," Andy said. "He was telling me he's bought a small place in Scotland. He intends to spend his days fishing, the lucky sod."

"I think I'd like to do something like that when the time comes," Jack said. "A place away from the hustle and bustle, somewhere tranquil where you can appreciate nature in all its beauty."

Annika huffed. "If you do that you'll be going on your own," she said.

"Doesn't a quiet life appeal to you, Annika?" Sophie said.

"It most certainly does not. I hate the countryside. It's full of old people with queer customs, not to mention animals and their horrible smells."

Jack looked slightly uncomfortable. "I'm afraid my wife is a towny through and through," he said. "Isn't that right, darling?"

"Where were you brought up, Annika?" Sophie said.

"Torquay," she said. "To be honest I couldn't wait to get away."

"Really? I think Torquay is one of the most beautiful parts of the country."

Annika huffed but remained silent.

"What's everybody drinking?" Andy said. "One for the road, eh?"

Andy and Jack went to the bar leaving Sophie and Annika together.

"How did you and Jack meet?" Sophie said, as she began to reapply her lipstick. "I only ask because you seem so… so very different."

"We met in a bar in Leeds," Annika said. "I was out on a night out with the girls from the salon I was with at the time. Jack was on a stag do with some of his colleagues from the nick. He was only a sergeant then of course, but I could tell he was destined for bigger things." She turned sharply to face Sophie. "What about you? Where did you meet Andy?"

"We met on holiday a few weeks ago," she said, returning the lipstick to her handbag. "We were both staying at the same hotel in Corfu."

"I've never been to Corfu. They say it's a beautiful island."

"It is. I try to visit at least once a year."

"My parents owned a villa in Valencia. I holidayed there every year as a child. They're both dead now though so the villa got sold."

"I'm sorry to hear that," Sophie said.

"Oh don't be. I was sick of Spain anyway. I much prefer Italy."

"Actually, I meant about your parents. You must miss them."

Annika shrugged. "No, not really. They weren't my real parents. They adopted me when I was a baby. They couldn't have kids of their own."

Andy and Jack returned to the table carrying drinks.

"How are you getting home, Jack?" Andy said. "I've got a taxi booked in half-an-hour. We can drop you off. It's on our way home."

"Thanks, but I've booked a taxi too, in fact it should be here in ten minutes." He turned to Annika. "Drink up, darling. We don't want to keep the taxi driver waiting."

Annika chuckled. “If he doesn’t wait, he doesn’t get paid,” she said.

“And if he doesn’t wait, we don’t get home.” Jack said.

Annika shrugged as lifting the glass to her lips, she threw back her head and gulped down the vodka.

Andy and Sophie were in the taxi heading towards Andy’s house.

“Jack’s wife is a pretty girl,” he said. “What did you think to her?”

“I thought she was interesting.”

“Interesting?”

“Mm, I think there’s a lot more to Annika Mason than meets the eye.”

“Does that mean that you like her?”

Sophie was quiet for a moment. “Do you know something, Andy? I don’t think I do.”

48

When Mason got to the station the following morning, Sergeant Brown was at his post behind the reception desk.

"Inspector, there's a message for you."

Mason joined Brown at the desk.

"Moira Winstanley telephoned earlier," he said, handing him a piece of paper with a telephone number on it. "She wants you to give her a call."

"Did she say what it was about?"

"Something to do with Sheila Thompson. She wouldn't say more than that, I'm afraid."

Mason made his way to his office and immediately dialled the number.

"Hello?" said a female voice. "Who's that?"

"Ms Winstanley? I'm Inspector Mason from Redcar and Cleveland Police. I understand you have some information regarding Sheila Thompson?"

"Is there a reward? I'm not saying anything unless I get paid."

"If you know anything concerning what happened to Sheila… Where are you, Moira? Perhaps we could meet and discuss the matter face-to-face?"

"All right but bring some cash with you. I'm not a bleeding charity."

"Where do you want to meet?"

"Do you know Fisherman's Square?"

"Yes."

There was silence.

"Moira, are you still there?"

"Yes, I'm here," she said. "Meet me in one hour and come alone. What I've got to say is for your ears only. Understand?"

Mason put down the receiver just as Sergeant Brown entered his office. "Sir, there's still no sign of PC Porter or his wife. You don't think he's decided to take a holiday or something?"

"I don't think so, sergeant. Keep up the search."

"Very well, sir," the sergeant said as he began to slowly meander back to Reception. "It's not like young Porter to go off like that without a word. It's not like him at all."

"Before you go, sergeant," Mason said, "do you know this woman, Moira Winstanley?"

"Yes, sir. Moira's a rough sleeper. She usually hangs around Redcar East. I believe she uses a squat there sometimes."

"Was she a friend of Sheila Thompson?"

"They both like the bottle. I wouldn't be surprised if they knew one another."

"She wants me to meet her at Fisherman's Square."

"Should I get Walker to go with you, sir? Moira's a feisty character, especially when she's had a drink."

Mason shook his head. "No, not this time sergeant. I'm sure I can handle a feisty woman, even a drunken one."

It was only a ten-minute drive to Fishermen's Square, a large car park on the way to Marske. Several small boats and towing tractors were parked along one half of the area, whilst cars were parked on the other. Mason parked his vehicle, got out of the car and looked around. The area looked deserted. He was about to get back into his car when a middle-aged woman, wearing a bright orange cardigan and shabby denim jeans, emerged from behind one of the boats. She gestured for him to join her.

"Where's Bainbridge?" she asked, nervously looking around. "He's the one I need to talk to."

"DCS Bainbridge is in overall charge of the investigation," Mason said, "but I deal with the day-to-day business. So, what is it you want to tell me about Sheila? I must warn you that if you're withholding information about Sheila Thompson, you can be arrested."

Moira sniffed and shuffled uneasily. "I just want a few quid for some fags, that's all," she said, "after all I'm not a bleeding charity."

Mason put his hand in his trouser pocket and produced two ten-pound notes. Moira attempted to grab them from his hand.

"Not so fast," he said. "Information first."

Moira gave a defiant glare at Mason before she spoke. "Sheila came to the squat the day she died. She didn't want to stay at home because a copper was going to come round that morning to take a statement about what she had seen."

"Did she say why she didn't want to make a statement?"

"She told me she had seen who robbed Benji. She rang them and said she would keep her gob shut if they paid her fifty quid."

"So, what happened?"

"She told me she was going to get the money later that day, but then she heard Benji had died."

"Why didn't she come to the police?"

Moira snorted. "Don't be daft. Sheila would never do that. She's a lot of things but she's not a grass."

"So, what did she do?"

"She rang someone and said it was going to cost a lot more than fifty quid to keep her quiet."

"Did she say who the person was?"

Moira shook her head. "Nah, she just said they were meeting at the boating lake that night. I offered to go with her, but she insisted on going alone."

"And you're sure you've no idea who she was meeting?"

Moira shook her head. "Sheila became secretive and made the phone call from outside, but I could tell she knew the person well. She seemed really excited though. She said all her money troubles would be over soon."

"Sheila didn't have her phone when she was found. Did she take it with her?"

Moira lowered her head. "No, she left it with me."

"Where is it now?"

Moira put her hand into her pocket and pulled out a mobile phone. "She found it in the long grass on The Stray, a few days ago," she said. "It's a pay-as-you-go one."

Mason took the phone from Moira's grasp. "I need to take this," he said.

"But why? It's mine. Sheila would want me to have it."

"It's evidence," Mason said, placing the phone in a plastic evidence bag. "You'll get it back when we're finished with it. All right?"

Moira shrugged. "I suppose so," she suddenly darted forward, grabbed the money from Mason's hand and scuttled back through the car park.

49

Inspector Mason called in at the Forensics office and handed over the phone to Leo Cutts. "I want to know every call made on this in the last week," he said.

Cutts grinned. "Where did you find this?" he said, taking the evidence bag from Mason. "It's ancient."

"This is the phone Sheila Thompson used to speak to her killer. I want to know everyone she spoke to. Understand?"

Cutts nodded, appreciating the seriousness of the task. "Leave it with me, sir. It shouldn't take long to trace the numbers. I'll get on it straight away."

***

Wayne Beaumont was at his desk when Mason returned to the station. "Any word yet on PC Porter?" he said.

"No, sir," Beaumont said. "He seems to have disappeared off the face of the earth."

"What about the crew? Don't they know anything?"

Beaumont shook his head. "Porter was a quiet bloke. He didn't mix much so nobody really knows much about his private life."

"Talking of private lives, come into my office, Beaumont," Mason said. "I want a word."

DC Beaumont followed the inspector through into his office and at Mason's invitation, sat on the chair opposite the desk. "Is everything all right, sir?" he said.

"No, Beaumont. Everything is not all right. When you joined CID, we had a little chat about your private life. Do you remember?"

Beaumont looked puzzled. "Yes, sir, but..."

"Tell me about Denise Porter," Mason said.

"Denise? I... I don't understand."

"Then I'll spell it out for you, constable. You were seen on CCTV in The Smugglers, canoodling with Denise Porter a few nights ago."

"Sir, I can explain. Denise and I are just friends. She..."

"You were more than just friends, Beaumont. You were lovers."

Beaumont inhaled deeply. "Denise was… she was lonely. Paul wasn't the most attentive of blokes."

"So, you thought you'd comfort her in her hour of need, is that it?"

"It wasn't like that, sir."

"I understand Mrs Porter has some extremely expensive tastes," Mason said.

"I know she likes nice things, but..."

"And how do you think those things are paid for? She doesn't work, does she?"

"No, sir. She said Paul didn't want her to work."

"When was the last time you saw her?"

Beaumont began to shuffle uneasily in his chair, the colour rising in his cheeks. "We were supposed to meet last night, but she didn't turn up. She'd been to a spa in Harrogate and was coming home a day early to meet up."

"Have you been in contact by telephone?"

"I tried, but her phone has been switched off."

"I want you to tell me everything you know about her," Mason said.

Beaumont shrugged. "What can I say? She's an attractive, intelligent woman who has a taste for the nicer things in life."

"Things that cost money. Lots of money. Money a police constable simply doesn't have."

"I don't know about that, sir. Like I said, me and Denise just liked to go out for a drink together sometimes, that's all."

"What about her relationship with her husband? Did she discuss that?"

"No, not really. She did mention Paul was close to his uncle. From what Denise said, the uncle was loaded."

"Who is his uncle, do you know?"

"No idea."

"Then perhaps we'd better find out and if Denise does ring you, I want to know at once. Understand?"

"Yes, sir," Beaumont said, hurrying towards the door.

"Ask PC Walker to pop into my office, will you? I need a word."

"Yes, sir," he said, closing the door.

"You wanted to see me, sir?" Walker said, entering Mason's office.

"Sit down, Walker," Mason said.

Looking perplexed, she perched on the chair across from the inspector.

"PC Walker, I received a telephone call earlier today from Mr Parker."

"Parker? I don't think I know anyone called Parker," she said.

"Mr Parker is from a debt collection agency. He telephoned me as a courtesy. Apparently, you've been contacted before about your debts and you've ignored it. According to Mr Parker, the next step is to send in the bailiffs."

Walker's cheeks flushed as she fidgeted on the chair.

"It would appear you've got yourself into a bit of a financial mess, Walker."

"I... I have a cashflow problem at the moment," Walker explained. "It's nothing I can't sort out."

"How did this cashflow problem arise?"

Walker remained silent as she lowered her head, lacing her fingers on her lap.

"Walker, you're a serving police officer. You can't have bailiffs knocking on your door. You could lose your job over this. I suggest you tell me exactly what's been happening. There may be something I can do to help."

Walker shook her head as tears began to trickle slowly down her cheeks. "You can't help," she said. "Nobody can. It's... it's all too late."

"Crying isn't going to help," Mason said. "You have three years' service in, don't you? You should be on a decent wage. Where is your money going?"

Walker remained silent.

"Well?"

"On stuff," she said. "Lots and lots of stuff."

"What do you mean stuff? What sort of stuff?"

She sniffed loudly. "Clothes, shoes, handbags," she said. "I have dozens of outfits still with their tickets on. The same with shoes. I counted thirty-six pairs, all still in their box." She took out a tissue from her pocket and blew her nose. "Then there are the cosmetics and the perfume, again untouched. I see them and I just have to have them. I can't help myself."

"So, you're saying you're a compulsive shopper?"

"Yes, sir. I suppose I am. I'm ashamed of myself. I know I can't afford the stuff, but when I see something I like, I have to have it."

"How long has this been going on?" Mason said. "Weeks? Months?"

"I suppose it started last year," Walker said, dabbing her eyes, "after my fiancé and I broke up. He'd been cheating with another woman and they got married a couple of months after we split."

Mason inhaled. "I'm going to telephone the Force Welfare Department and make you an appointment," he said. "They can advise you on the best route forward."

"Will… will everyone know?" Walker said. "I'd hate for my crew to know what I've done."

"Don't worry. They are discreet. Now, what I need you to do is telephone Mr Parker," he handed her a slip of paper containing a telephone number. "Tell him you are addressing the problem with our FWD and they will be in touch soon. Do you think you can do that?"

"Yes, sir," she said quietly.

"Let me know how you get on."

Walker got up to leave. "Thank you, sir," she said.

"You can thank me by getting yourself out of debt. Do you think you can manage that?"

"I can try, sir," she said. "I can try."

50

Maria entered the salon carrying an enormous bouquet of pink and white roses. She went into the back room and prepared a bucket of water to place them in.

"Oh, Maria, they're lovely," Jodie said. "Are they from an admirer?"

Maria grinned. "No, they're for Mum. I'm taking them round to her nursing home. It's her birthday tomorrow. Mum always did love roses."

Jodie sighed. "They're gorgeous. You're so lucky having your mother around to buy flowers for."

"Oh, I'm sorry love. I didn't realise your mother was dead."

"She probably is for all I know. I was adopted when I was a baby, and my adoptive parents died in a car crash a couple of years back."

"You poor kid," Maria said, placing an arm around Jodie's shoulder, "that's awful."

Jodie smiled weakly as she returned to the salon where Annika was putting foils in Mrs Armitage's hair.

"Those flowers Maria brought in must have cost a fortune," Annika said.

"Probably. They're for her mother."

Annika huffed. "I don't see the point. Maria was telling me her mother has dementia. Why spend all that money when the old woman doesn't even know what day it is?"

"That's a terrible thing to say," Jodie said. "You really can be quite heartless at times."

"I'm just being truthful. It seems a total waste of money to me. She's probably braindead so what does she want with a bunch of flowers?"

"Receiving flowers always makes me feel better," Jodie says. "My Wayne brings me flowers every week."

"When men do that, it usually means they've been up to something they shouldn't," Annika said, smiling maliciously. "I'd keep a close eye on him if I were you."

Jodie huffed as she walked over to the reception desk as two extremely plump young women entered the salon.

"Good morning," Jodie said smiling. "How may I help you?"

"Hello, love. My names Samantha," said the first woman. "Me and my friend want an appointment for a full colour. I want to go blonde like Holly Willoughby, and Tracey wants to go darker." Both women began to giggle.

"The same colour as Julia Roberts," Tracey said. "I think her hair's lovely."

Smiling, Jodie studied the appointment book. She turned to Samantha. "I can do yours tomorrow at two," she said. "My colleague, Annika, can do Tracey's hair at three, if that's okay?"

"That's perfect," Tracey said, heading towards the door. "I can't wait."

When the women left the salon, Annika joined Jodie at the reception desk. "Holly Willoughby and Julia Roberts?" she scoffed. "You have to be joking. They both have the face of a gargoyle."

"Maybe, but that doesn't mean we can't give them the hairstyle they want. After all, that's what we're here for."

Maria came out of the back room and walked over to Reception.

"Annika, stop gossiping and attend to Mrs Armitage. You've only done half the foils."

Annika sniffed loudly as she returned to her workstation leaving Jodie chatting to Maria.

It was half-past one when Annika got back to the salon after buying a ham and cheese sandwich from Greggs.

"Your husband called whilst you were out," Maria said. "He asked me to tell you he will be late home tonight so don't make him anything to eat."

Annika scowled. "Did he say why he's going to be late?"

Maria shook her head. "No, just that he would be tied up with work."

Carrying a mug of tea, Jodie came into the salon from the back room. "Wayne rang me," she said. "He said they've arrested a suspect for the murder of that woman found by the boating lake the other day."

"Did he say who they've arrested?"

"His name's Shaun Dyson."

51

"I want my solicitor," Dyson yelled as he was frogmarched by two constables through the police station reception towards the interview room. "I'm not saying a bloody word till he gets here. You've no right arresting me. It's harassment, that's what it is. I'll sue the lot of you."

Leanne raced after her husband. "Don't worry, Shaun," she said. "Mr Kendall is on his way. He'll sort this out."

PC Walker stepped in front of Leanne. "You can't go through there, Mrs Dyson," she said. "You must wait here in reception."

"Fuck you," Leanne said, attempting to push the constable to one side. "I'm going with Shaun and you can't stop me."

PC Walker grabbed Leanne's arm and held fast. "Take a seat," she said, "or you'll have to wait outside."

Leanne brought back her fist as if to strike the officer, then grunted and lowered her arm. "My Shaun's done nothing," she said. "Nothing, do you hear? This is a fit up." She turned and strode over to a row of plastic chairs lined up against the reception wall. "If he's not out in half an hour…" she said, pointing her finger aggressively.

Shaun Dyson was in handcuffs as he glared across the desk at Inspector Mason. "You'd better have a good reason for this, or my brief's gonna sue the arse off the police."

Mason placed a buff-coloured file on the desk. "Firstly, Mr Dyson, I will remind you that you are still under caution. You do understand that anything you say will be..."

“I’m saying nowt,” Dyson stated angrily, “…not until my brief gets here. You’ve got nothing on me. Nothing.”

“For the benefit of the tape, present is Shaun Dyson, Detective Chief Superintendent Bainbridge, DC Beaumont and Inspector Jack Mason.”

“The whole bloody circus,” Dyson scoffed.

There was a sharp rap on the door and PC Walker entered the room. “Sir,” she said addressing Mason, “Mr Kendall has arrived.”

“About fucking time,” Dyson said. “Fetch him in here. Let’s get this cleared up once and for all.”

Mason nodded to Walker who left the room, returning a few seconds later accompanied by a plump, middle-aged man wearing a smart grey suit and horn-rimmed spectacles.

“I’m Melvyn Kendall,” he said, placing his briefcase on the table and drawing up a chair next to Dyson. “I’m Mr Dyson’s legal representative. I would like a few moments alone with my client.”

Mason turned off the tape. “Fifteen minutes,” he said as he made his way to the door, followed by Bainbridge and Beaumont.

Kendall smiled weakly. “I don’t suppose there’s any chance of a cup of tea, Inspector? I’m parched. I’ve been in court all morning.”

“I’ll see what I can do,” Mason said as he left the room.

Leaving Beaumont to sort out the drinks from the canteen, Mason followed Bainbridge up to his office.

"Dyson's right of course," Bainbridge said once they were both seated at his desk. "You don't have enough evidence for a conviction."

"There's the phone used by Sheila Thompson," Mason said. "It clearly shows she rang Dyson several times that day, the last call just before midnight."

"Does it? It shows that someone used the phone to ring him, but can you prove it was Sheila?"

"Moira said..."

"Moira is a homeless drunk. No jury is going to believe anything that woman says." Bainbridge rubbed his chin. "I think you've come in a bit early on this one, Jack. You need more evidence, concrete evidence that the slimy little bastard can't wriggle out of."

"But, sir..."

"Were Sheila's fingerprints found on the phone?"

"No, sir. None that could be identified. The only clear fingerprints were those of Moira."

"What about the SIM card? Did you check that for prints?"

"No, sir. I… I'll get Cutts onto it right away."

Bainbridge shook his head. "Take my advice, Jack and let Dyson go for now. Bring him in when you can prove without doubt that he's the killer."

Mason sighed. "If you think that's best, sir."

"I do," Bainbridge said. "How's the investigation into Arthur Rhodes's death going? Any more witnesses?"

Mason shook his head. "No, sir. Only that nutcase Ellis and of course he withdrew his statement."

"Have you interviewed the neighbour again, Mrs…"

"Reece. Pamela Reece."

"She's had a couple of days to think about things. She might have remembered something else; you never know."

"I was planning to visit her again tomorrow," Mason said. "I'll take Beaumont with me."

"You might be better taking PC Walker," Bainbridge suggested. "She's much better at that sort of thing."

Desperately trying to hide his annoyance at Bainbridge's interference, Mason nodded his agreement. "Very well, sir," he said, as he headed towards the door. "I'll cut Dyson free for now."

"Good man," Bainbridge said, picking up the desk phone. "We'll get the little bastard, don't worry about that. We just need more evidence."

52

Annika was varnishing her nails when Jack arrived home at six-thirty.

"Oh, I wasn't expecting you so early," she said, putting down the bottle of pink nail polish. "Jodie said you and Wayne would be working late tonight."

"I should have been," Jack said, "but that bloody Bainbridge stuck his nose in and made me release Dyson without charge."

"Why did he do that?"

"Bainbridge thinks I don't have enough evidence for a conviction."

"Do you?"

"I think so, but you can't argue with the boss, can you?"

"What made you arrest Dyson in the first place if there was no evidence?"

"That's just it. There was evidence. I checked the phone Sheila Thompson had been using. She telephoned Dyson a couple of times the day she died. The last call was just before midnight which to me proves she was arranging to meet him."

"You can't know that, Jack."

Jack huffed as he strode over to the drinks cabinet and poured himself a whisky. He turned to Annika. "Want one?"

Annika shook her head. "No thanks. I want to finish my nails and then I'll start dinner."

“Don’t worry about that,” Jack said. “We can eat out tonight.”

“No, darling. I have some pork chops in the fridge which need eating today.”

Jack shrugged. “Suit yourself,” he said plonking in an armchair and turning on the television.

“I didn’t know Sheila had a phone. You never said.”

“She left it with a friend she was visiting that day.”

“Did this friend actually hear Sheila speaking with Shaun?”

“Nah. Sheila became secretive when she made the calls.”

“Well then, I don’t see how you can prove it was Shaun she spoke to.”

“Of course we can. It was his number she dialled.”

“But you can’t prove...”

“For fuck’s sake Annika, you’re starting to sound like Bainbridge. Just leave it, will you? I’m tired and I’m hungry.” He got up and strode towards the hall. “I’m going for a shower.”

Annika shrugged. “All right, darling,” she said. “I’ll start dinner.”

***

Wayne Beaumont got home about the same time as Jack Mason. Jodie was in the kitchen peeling potatoes. “I’m glad you’re not working late,” she said, walking over and kissing him on the cheek. “There’s a group on at The Galleon I wouldn’t mind watching.”

"Sorry, love. I'm not in the mood tonight."

Jodie huffed. "Suit yourself, but I'm going. I haven't been out in ages."

Wayne opened the fridge door and took out a can of lager. "Do what you want," he said, pulling back the tab. "I've had a lousy day. All I want to do is have something to eat, a couple of drinks and watch the footie."

Jodie moved over to Wayne and placed her hand gently on his arm. "What's wrong, love?" she asked. "You look like shit."

Wayne threw back his head and gulped at the lager, wiping his mouth with the back of his hand. "It looks like Mason's in trouble with the boss. The old man had a right go at him today."

"Why? What happened?"

"Bainbridge made him release that prisoner he'd brought in. He said Mason didn't have enough evidence to get a conviction."

"Did he?"

Wayne shrugged. "I don't know, but I could tell Mason was annoyed."

"If you ask me, you're best keeping well out of it. Just do what you're asked, then walk away."

"Don't worry, I will. This is what happens when they pull someone through the ranks just because they happen to have a degree."

"Ah, I wondered why he got to be an inspector at his age."

"I think the case is just getting too much for him. He doesn't seem to be making any progress."

"So apart from Shaun Dyson, there are no suspects at all?"

Wayne shook his head. "None. Nobody saw anything, nobody heard anything, or if they did come forward, the information they gave proved to be worthless. The press is having a field day at our expense."

"Still no sign of Paul and Denise Porter?"

"Nope. They've vanished from the face of the earth. The lads think they've gone abroad."

"What do you think?"

Wayne shrugged. "Could be. I know his uncle has the contacts."

"Does Mason know about him?"

"No. Paul told me about Freddie Roberts in strictest confidence, and that's the way it's going to stay."

"But if Freddie knows where Paul is..."

"Like I said before, I'm not getting involved. If Porter's got himself in the shit, he can get himself out of it. It's nothing to do with me." He gulped at the lager. "Hurry up with the tea, will you? The footie's on in half-an-hour."

53

Arm-in-arm, Shaun and Leanne left the police station and went straight to The Galleon.

“That bastard’s certainly got it in for you,” Leanne said, picking up a pint of lager and holding it to her lips. “If it wasn’t for Bainbridge, he’d have had you locked up.”

“Don’t worry, love. Mason can’t prove anything.”

“It’s not going to stop him trying though, is it?”

Shaun winked. “Don’t forget our ace in the hole. Mason can’t touch me I tell you.”

“I hope you’re right, but what if...”

There was a shrill ringing tone. Shaun removed his mobile from his pocket. “Who the fuck is that?” he said, pressing the green button. “Yeah?... Yeah, I’m Shaun Dyson… What? Where?... I’m on my way.” He replaced the phone in his pocket and picking up his glass, drained the contents. “It’s Arron,” he said panicking. “He’s at the hospital. He’s been in an accident.”

“What sort of accident?”

“He’s been hit by a motor vehicle,” he said, rushing towards the door, followed closely by Leanne.

“What did they say, Shaun? Is he badly hurt?” she said, racing to keep up with him.

“He’s in surgery. He has a head injury and broken bones. When I get my hands on the bastard who hurt my boy… I’ll...”

"Calm down, love. Let's make sure he's all right before you start with that."

They hurried along to their car which was parked a few yards away from the pub and were soon driving at speed in the direction of James Cook Hospital.

"How's my boy?" Dyson said as he charged towards the A&E reception desk. "I want to see him now."

The receptionist peered over the top of her steel-rimmed spectacles. "What name?" she asked calmly.

"Arron. Arron Dyson. He's ten years old and he's been knocked down by some drunken bastard."

The receptionist studied her computer screen for a few seconds. "If you take a seat Mr Dyson, I'll get a nurse to come and explain the situation."

Dyson banged his fist on the counter. "I don't want to talk to some pipsqueak, I want to speak to the doctor treating my son."

The receptionist inhaled deeply, leaning slightly forward across the desk. "Please calm down, Mr Dyson. I assure you your son is in good hands. Mr Davidson, one of our top surgeons, is in theatre dealing with your son's injuries right now."

"How bad are his injuries? Is he going to be all right?"

"Like I said, I'll arrange for one of the nurses to speak to you in a moment. Now, perhaps you wouldn't mind taking a seat? There are other patients."

"Come on, Shaun," Leanne said, taking his arm and gently guiding him to the row of seats. "Let's do as she says."

Dyson snorted and turned to face the receptionist. "I want to speak to someone now," he said, jabbing his finger towards her.

A nurse came hurrying into reception and after a brief word with the receptionist, walked briskly over to Dyson. "Good evening, Mr Dyson," she said. "I'm Nurse Cartwright."

"How's my boy?" Dyson said, jumping to his feet. "Where is he? I want to see him."

"If you'll follow me," the nurse said, as she turned and walked down the corridor, Shaun and Leanne in close pursuit. Nurse Cartwright opened a door on the right of the corridor and all three entered the room.

"Please, take a seat," she said, a sympathetic look on her pretty oval face. "I'm afraid Arron is in an extremely serious condition. He has sustained life-threatening injuries."

"What do you mean, life-threatening? Are you saying my boy is going to die?"

"We're doing all we can," the nurse said, "but you should be aware, his injuries are severe."

Dyson's body trembled violently, and Leanne began to sob uncontrollably.

"What… what happened?" she said through her sobs. "Was it a drunken driver who hit my boy?"

"I don't know all the details, I'm afraid. All I know is he was hit by a lorry. The police are on their way. They'll need to speak to you both."

"The police? What the hell for?"

"It's procedure I'm afraid. They have to get involved when there has been a fatality."

"Fatality? But Arron's not dead."

"No, but the lad who was with him is."

"What lad?"

"Like I said, Mr Dyson, I don't know all the details yet but…" There was a sharp rap on the door and PC Walker and PC Jones entered the room. "Ah, the police are here. I'll leave you to talk." Nurse Cartwright left the room.

PC Walker handed Leanne a tissue from her bag and put her arm around her shoulder to comfort her. Leanne grabbed the tissue before pushing Walker away.

Dyson began to pace the room. "Do you know what happened? I swear to God, when I get my hands on who's responsible, I'll..."

"Mr Dyson, I'm sorry about what's happened to your son, but I must ask you some questions."

"What the fuck for? My lad's done nothing. It's that bastard drunken driver you should be questioning, not me."

"I assure you the driver has been questioned. He's also been breathalysed and it was a negative reading."

"So what happened? Why did he knock down my lad?"

"Arron is ten years old, is that right?" Walker said.

"Yeah. He's only ten but he's a bright lad."

"Did you know he's been riding around Redcar on a stolen quad bike?"

"Don't be daft. He wouldn't do that."

"Arron and his friend, Micky Clark, were seen driving recklessly around the streets of Redcar East this afternoon. Neighbours reported them to the police."

"I don't believe it," Leanne said, wiping her eyes. "Arron wouldn't do that. He's a good boy. It must have been the other lad who led him on."

"No, Mrs Dyson. Arron was driving the quad. Micky was on the back. Apparently, Arron rode straight across a junction into the path of an on-coming lorry. The impact caused Micky to soar forward over the handlebars colliding with a lamppost. The poor lad died at the scene."

Dyson punched at the wall, tears streaming down his face. "So, you're saying the police were chasing them? They're responsible for what happened?"

"That's not what happened, Mr Dyson. The squad car was dealing with an incident in the town centre when the accident happened."

Dyson stood menacingly in front of Walker, stabbing his finger into her arm. "I don't believe you," he said. "You lot have always had it in for me. You couldn't get me so you got my lad instead."

PC Jones stepped forward and pushed Dyson's hand away from his colleague. "That's enough," he said. "Calm down. PC Walker and I are only doing our duty. You need to concentrate on your son."

Dyson snorted as he plonked down on one of the chairs. "Well, you've done your duty," he said, "now piss off and leave us alone."

The door opened and a middle-aged man wearing theatre scrubs entered the room. He turned to Dyson. "You're the boy's father?" he said.

"Yeah, that's right. Is Arron going to be all right, doc?"

"I'm sorry to have to tell you, but I'm afraid your son died on the operating table. There was nothing I could do to save him. His injuries were too severe."

There was a shrill, piercing scream from Leanne as holding her head in her hands, she sank to her knees screaming hysterically.

54

It was nine o'clock the following morning. Sergeant Brown had just informed Inspector Mason of the double fatality the night before concerning Micky Clark and Arron Dyson.

"I met the Dyson lad briefly when I visited the house," Mason said. "He seemed a cheeky little bugger to me."

"He was, but the poor lad had literally brought himself up. According to the school records he was hardly ever there. Those two would never get any award for good parenting."

"It's a shame. The poor kid didn't have much of a chance at life. What about the other boy who got killed, Micky Clark?"

"Micky was fifteen, but with a mental age of about eight, apparently," the sergeant said. "He has been in a care home since he was three and had a habit of absconding whenever he could."

Mason shook his head and sighed. "Does he have any family?"

"An uncle, I believe, but he's in Durham nick doing time for burglary and assault."

"Great! So that poor kid's got nobody."

"Another job for Social Services, sir," the sergeant said.

"I'm going to speak with Arthur Rhodes's neighbour again. You never know, she might have remembered something now she's had a chance to have got over the shock of finding him."

Red-faced and panting, DC Beaumont hurried into reception. "Sorry I'm late, sir," he apologised. "The alarm didn't go off this morning."

Sergeant Brown glared at the constable and snorted his indignation. "I suggest you invest in a more reliable alarm then," he said, "and don't keep the inspector waiting."

"Yes, sarge. Sorry, sarge," he spluttered. "It won't happen again."

Inspector Mason strode over to the door. "Come on then, Beaumont. I don't have all day."

They arrived at Pamela Reece's bungalow twenty minutes later. Pamela was in the garden pruning roses. On sight of the two officers, she put down the secateurs and smiling, opened the small gate.

"Hello again," she said. "I was hoping you'd pop by. It saves me coming to see you." She led the way through the hall and into the lounge. Bernard Reece was in his armchair, a copy of The Gazette in his hands.

"You haven't caught the bugger yet then?" he said, letting the newspaper fall into his lap.

"There, Bernard," Pamela cooed. "They're doing everything they can." She indicated for the officers to sit on the couch. "I'll put the kettle on," she said, hurrying into the kitchen. "It won't take a minute. Tea or coffee?"

It was ten minutes later when all the coffee had been drunk, the ginger biscuits eaten and the empty cups returned to the kitchen, that Pamela picked up her handbag and removed a small notebook. "I've been making notes of things I remembered from that night," she said. "I was so upset at finding Arthur that I couldn't think straight at the time."

Mason sat bolt upright. "What more have you remembered, Mrs Reece? Anything, the smallest detail, could be of the greatest value."

Assuming an air of importance, Pamela opened the notebook. "Well, for a start, like I said at the time, it was dark that night and raining heavily. It had been raining most of the day as a matter of fact."

"Yes, we know that," Mason said. "Was there something else you saw that could help us?"

Pamela turned a page in her notebook. "As a matter of fact, Inspector, I think there is." She readjusted the cushion supporting her back. "It was the person standing at the door. The more I think about it, the more I'm convinced I was wrong."

"I don't understand. Wrong about what?"

"Well, dear, it was the umbrella."

"The umbrella?"

"Yes. I was saying to Bernard only yesterday, how many men do you know in Redcar that carry an umbrella? None, dear. That's how many. I know it's popular down in London and such, but not up here. It's usually only women who have an umbrella. Don't you agree?"

Mason ran his tongue over his dry lips. "So, you think the figure you saw at Arthur's door that night was a woman, not a man?"

"I can't say for certain of course. I didn't get a good enough look at them, it was too dark, but I think it most probably was a woman. Thinking about it, I don't think Arthur would have opened the door to a man, do you?"

Mason was deep in thought as he returned to his car. The thought of a woman inflicting such horrific injuries on the old man had unsettled him more than he realised.

"What do you think, Beaumont? Is a woman capable of such violence?"

"I think it's a big leap to assume it was a woman just because the attacker was carrying an umbrella. I'm sure lots of men use them."

"Do you own one or have ever owned one?"

"Well, no. My jacket has a hood, but that doesn't mean all blokes do that."

The police radio crackled into life. "Control to Inspector Mason."

Mason picked up the radio. "Mason!" he answered.

"Inspector, please make your way to the station immediately."

Mason knew that no further information would be given as to why his presence was needed so urgently in case there were radio hackers listening.

"On my way," he said. "ETA fifteen minutes." He accelerated, sensing the urgency of the request. "I wonder what that's about," he said, as he headed towards the police station. "Whatever it is you can bet it's not good news."

55

You could not comprehend how
I feel towards the man
responsible for killing the boy.

The maelstrom of emotions swirling around
my head like an angry sea crashing
against the rocks.

Revenge, it demands.
An eye for an eye.
Tonight.
It has to be tonight.

56

Andy Bainbridge had arrived at The Ship in Marske at precisely twelve-thirty. Sophie was already seated at a table by the window when he arrived.

"Thanks for meeting me," she said smiling. "I know you're busy but..."

"It was a pleasant surprise," Andy said. "I don't get asked out that often these days, especially by a beautiful woman."

"Well, it's going to be a working lunch, I'm afraid," Sophie said.

Andy shrugged. "Okay, but let's order first. I'm hungry."

After making their choice from the menu, Andy went to the bar to place their order, returning with two glasses of coke. "Now tell me, what's so important?"

Sophie sipped at her drink before she spoke. "It's this business of Dyson having an accomplice," she said. "I'm convinced there is some other person involved."

"If there is someone helping him, we can't find him. We've checked all his known friends and acquaintances, but there's absolutely nothing to connect any of them with the murder of Arthur Rhodes."

"You told me Dyson has a vicious temper, the same as his dad."

"That's right. I've witnessed him losing it. When he does, it's as if the devil himself takes hold. His father was just the same."

"Have you given any consideration to Dyson's sibling, the baby whose life he saved from the fire?"

"No, not really. I know the kid was adopted. He must be into his twenties by now."

"Twenty-three as a matter of fact," Sophie said, "and it's not he. Dyson has a younger sister."

"A sister? You're not suggesting that his sister killed Arthur Rhodes?"

Sophie shrugged. "Think about it, Andy. They both had the same DNA as that monster of a father. What's to say that the girl doesn't have the same evil tendencies as her big brother?" Sophie sipped her drink once more. "You know what they say," she said smiling. "It might be the cock that crows, but it's the hen that lays the eggs."

Andy slowly stroked his chin in concentration. "I'll look into it," he said at last. "See if I can trace her through the adoption agency."

"I've already tried that," Sophie said. "After her adoption, the family moved abroad. The trail goes cold after that."

"I'll use every resource at my disposal to trace her," Andy said. "I'm sure we can find her."

"I'm sure you can but do be careful. If I'm right, she will be just as dangerous as Shaun. Probably more so."

57

Inspector Mason arrived back at the station and hurried to the coms room, followed by DC Beaumont.

"What's so urgent?" Mason said, addressing Sergeant Brown.

"It's PC Porter, sir," the sergeant said. "His car has been found burnt out. Inside were two bodies, believed to be those of Paul and Denise Porter."

"Oh my God. Where did this happen?"

"Sunderland, sir. Newlandside Quarry near Stanhope to be exact. A routine patrol found them about an hour ago."

"What the hell were they doing in Sunderland?"

"Are… are they sure it was Denise's body in the car?" Beaumont said, the colour visibly draining from his face. "There… there couldn't be a mistake?"

"No mistake, son," the sergeant said. "I think you'd better go to the canteen and get yourself a cup of tea with plenty of sugar."

Beaumont hurried from the room.

"He's taking it badly," the sergeant said. "It looks like Mrs Porter was more to him than a bit on the side."

"Who's dealing with the enquiry?" Mason asked.

"Inspector Palmer from the Durham Constabulary," the sergeant said. "I've put his contact details on your desk."

"What about DCS Bainbridge? Has he been informed?"

"Yes, sir. He's on his way."

Mason returned to his office and dialled Inspector Palmer's number. The phone was answered immediately. "Inspector Palmer?" he said. "I'm Inspector Jack Mason from Redcar and Cleveland Police. I understand you have discovered the bodies of one of my constables and his wife?"

"Yes, that's right, Jack. Thanks for getting back to me so soon. I'm Bryan by the way."

"What can you tell me about the fire, Bryan? Do you think it was an accident?"

"The car is with our vehicle examiner's people. The bodies are with the pathologist, but one thing I can tell you with certainty. This was no accident. Both bodies had been shot through the head."

Mason gasped. "I'm coming up to Durham straight away. Can you arrange accommodation for me for a couple of nights?"

"Of course. I'll get you a room at The Three Bells."

"Thanks. I'll see you later today." Mason hung up the phone just as DC Beaumont came into his office.

"Are you all right, Beaumont?" Mason said. "You look like you've seen a ghost."

"Sir," he said, "I have something to tell you about Paul and Denise. Things I should have told you earlier."

"Sit down man," he said, "before you fall down."

Beaumont perched on the edge of the chair across the desk from Mason. He nervously laced and unlaced his fingers.

"What is it, Beaumont?" Mason urged. "What haven't you been telling me?"

58

Briefed on recent events, Bainbridge strode into Mason's office just as DC Beaumont was leaving.

"What's the matter with Beaumont?" he said. "He looks like he's about to faint."

"Beaumont was fond of Mrs Porter," Mason said. "He's taking all this hard."

"What the hell's going on, Jack? It's like this whole business is getting out of control."

"I'm going up to Durham later today," Mason said. "Inspector Palmer is in charge of the case. He said both PC Porter and his wife had been shot through the head."

"Shot? Are you sure?"

"That's what Palmer said. The bodies are undergoing postmortem now."

Bainbridge sighed deeply. "Do we have any suspects?"

"Yes, sir. I think we do. DC Beaumont has just informed me that PC Porter has an uncle here in Redcar. A wealthy uncle."

"And who might that be?"

"Freddie Roberts. Denise told Beaumont that's where her husband got a lot of his money from."

"Mm, that makes sense. Porter's bank account had plenty of regular cash payments."

"Probably bribed by his uncle to destroy the fingerprints on the drugs packages amongst other things."

"But why would Freddie kill him?"

"Porter must have got wind of us suspecting his involvement in sabotaging the drugs and decided to make a run for it. I don't think Freddie would be too happy about Porter leading a trail right to his back door."

Bainbridge huffed. "You go to Durham and assist there," he said. "I have another line of enquiry to pursue."

Mason raised an eyebrow. "Oh, what's that?"

"I've just found out Dyson's sibling, the baby he saved from the fire, was a girl."

Mason frowned. "I'm sorry, I don't see..."

"She'd be in her twenties by now. What if she is his accomplice? What if she's the one that stabbed Arthur Rhodes? The girl was adopted and moved abroad years ago, but we've got to find her, if only to eliminate her."

"But you can't honestly think a woman would be capable of such a frenzied attack?"

Bainbridge shrugged. "If I'm right and she's inherited the same DNA as her brother and father, I think she would be more than capable."

Mason leant forward, steepling his fingers on his desk. "I interviewed Pamela Reece earlier," he said. "She said something interesting."

"Oh?"

"She thought the figure she saw outside Arthur's house was most probably a woman."

"What made her think that?"

"The umbrella, sir. She said men around here don't usually carry an umbrella. It's beginning to look like she could be right."

Mason drove home, packed an overnight bag and left Annika a note informing her that he would be away on enquiries for a couple of days and promising to ring her later that night. He then got back into his car and headed along the A19 towards Durham.

59

Inspector Mason presented himself at the Mortuary in Durham at five o'clock that evening. Inspector Palmer was already there. He held out his hand in greeting.

"Glad you could get here so quickly, Jack. The pathologist has just finished examining the second body. He's waiting for us in his office."

Mason followed Palmer into a small room down the corridor. A large oak desk was in the middle of the room. Mason noted how neat the desk was with paperwork filed in one of three baskets down one side. A grey telephone was to the right of the desk, and a computer monitor was in the centre. The pathologist, Dr Stanley Glover, was seated behind the desk in a large, red-leather chair. Wearing a paisley waistcoat beneath a dark blue suit, his appearance was as impressive as his desk.

"Come in, gentlemen," he said, "so good of you to come up to Durham at such short notice, Inspector Mason. May I ask my secretary to get you both a cup of tea?"

Both men shook their head.

"No thanks, Doc," Palmer said. "We just need you to confirm how the two victims died."

"They were both shot in the head," Glover stated. "I suppose one could take comfort from the fact that death would have been instantaneous."

"So, just to confirm, they were dead before the car was set alight?" Palmer said, writing furiously in his pocketbook.

"Oh yes. There was no smoke inhalation, I can assure you of that."

"If they were already dead, why bother to set fire to the car?"

Dr Glover shook his head and sighed. "One can only presume they intended to get rid of the evidence to make our job as difficult as they could," he said opening his desk drawer and removing a packet of cigarettes. He put one in his mouth, lit it and inhaled deeply. "What a lot of people don't realise is that it's far more difficult to burn bodies than you're led to believe in television programmes."

Palmer got to his feet. "Well thanks, Doc," he said. "If you can let me have your full report, I'd be grateful."

"Before you go Inspector, there's something else you should know."

"Oh?"

"The lady in the vehicle, Mrs Denise Porter, was two months pregnant."

60

Charlie Bull drained his glass and put on his topcoat. "I'm glad you talked me into coming out, Joey," he said. "It's driving me mad looking at the same four walls. Nothing to do but remember."

Joey Kemp huffed. "You've got to stop blaming yourself, mate," he said. "The accident wasn't your fault."

"I didn't have a chance to stop," Charlie said. "The quad bike pulled straight out in front of me. They were only kids."

"They shouldn't have been on the bloody thing in the first place," Joey said. "I heard the driver was only ten. What were his parents thinking of, letting a young 'un like that out on the road in the first place?"

The two men left The Galleon and began walking along the promenade. It was dark and deserted.

"Best get a shuffle on," Joey said, "it looks like it's going to rain." Their pace quickened.

"I was thinking of writing a letter to the lads' parents, but what could I say? 'I'm sorry' doesn't seem adequate somehow."

"If you take my advice Charlie, you'll leave it alone. Nobody blames you for what happened."

"Mm, I suppose you're right," Charlie sighed as they reached the bottom of Henry Street.

"See you tomorrow," Joey said, turning into the street, "and stop beating yourself up about it. You've been driving for near on forty years without so much as a parking ticket. Remember, this wasn't your fault."

"Thanks for the company," he said. "It felt good to get out again."

Deep in thought, Charlie made his way along Majuba towards his home in Newcomen Terrace. He began to cross over the common, a shortcut to his house. It was poor lighting here but he knew the common like the back of his hand as he made his way closer to home. Five more minutes and he would be tucking into his supper with a can of lager to wash it down.

"Are you Charlie Bull?" a voice asked in the darkness.

Charlie squinted to see, as the figure drew closer.

"Yes, I'm Charlie Bull. Who are you?"

The figure darted towards him. The last thing Charlie saw was the glint of the knife in the moonlight as it was thrust deep into his chest… once… twice… Then everything went black.

61

DCS Bainbridge was already at the scene when Leo Cutts arrived. It was six o'clock in the morning.

"No Inspector Mason this morning?" Cutts said, putting on his forensic suit.

"He's away on enquiries," Bainbridge said. "I'm SIO on this one."

"Has the body been identified yet?"

"His name's Charles Daniel Bull. He lives just over there on Newcomen Terrace."

Cutts inhaled. "Poor bugger. He was just a few hundred yards from home."

Bainbridge signalled for PC Jones to join him.

"Yes, sir?" Jones said.

"The woman that found the body, have you taken her statement?"

"Yes, sir. Mrs Wendy Grimes lives a couple of doors away from Mr Bull. She was walking her dog when she found him."

"It's a bit early to go dog-walking, isn't it?"

"She works in Middlesbrough at a care home. Her shift starts at half-seven."

"I see. Okay, you can let her go about her business."

"Yes, sir," Jones said.

A cordon had been erected with the familiar blue and white 'Police Line – Do Not Cross' tape. A white forensic tent was in the centre covering the blood-stained body of Charlie Bull.

Cutts began his examination, leaving Bainbridge to organise the officers in attendance.

"I want the common thoroughly searched," he said. "Every square inch of it." He turned to PC Walker. "Speak to his wife. Find out where Mr Bull was this evening and who he was with."

"Yes, sir," she said, turning and hurrying towards Newcomen Terrace.

Cutts stepped out of the forensic tent. "Stabbed… just like Arthur Rhodes."

"Are you saying it's the same person responsible?"

"I'm saying the injuries appear to be the same, even down to gouging the eyes. The pathologist is on his way. He'll be able to give you more details, but in my opinion, we're dealing with the same killer who did for Arthur Rhodes."

"I'm going to wait in my car," Bainbridge said. "I have a couple of calls to make. You carry on here and let me know the minute Dr Carpenter arrives."

"Okay," Cutts said, opening his bag containing his scientific paraphernalia.

Once inside his car, Bainbridge took out his mobile and rang Sophie. "It's happened again," he said as soon as she answered. "The same devil that killed Arthur Rhodes has done it again."

The front door of Mr Bull's house was slightly open with several of the neighbours hovering around, talking in hushed voices. PC Lisa Walker knocked briskly on the door and entered. Two women were busy making tea in the kitchen, whilst another was on the settee hugging a woman who was sobbing loudly.

"Mrs Bull?" Walker said, walking over to the distressed woman. "I'm PC Walker."

The woman lifted her head slightly. "Have you caught the bastard who killed my Charlie?" she said between her sobs. "Why haven't you arrested him?"

Walker crouched down in front of her. "We will," she said, "but first I need to ask you some questions if you're up to it."

Mrs Bull pulled away from her companion, sat upright and reaching for a tissue, began dabbing at her eyes. "It was that Shaun Dyson who did this," she said. "He's been telephoning, threatening my Charlie for what happened to his lad, but it wasn't Charlie's fault. Everybody said so."

"Your husband was driving the lorry that the quad bike ran into the other day?"

"Charlie didn't have a chance to stop. The lad pulled out straight in front of his lorry. My Charlie wasn't to blame."

"You say Dyson has been making threatening phone calls?"

"Yes, all the time," she said. "That wife of his too. They both threatened to kill my Charlie for what he'd done."

"Didn't you report this?"

"I wanted to, but Charlie said no. He thought it was their grief talking."

"Mrs Bull, can you tell me where your husband was last night? Who he was with?"

She sniffed loudly. "He went for a couple of pints with his mate, Joey Kemp. Charlie hadn't been through the door since the accident. He couldn't sleep, he didn't eat. He kept blaming himself for what happened."

"Do you have Mr Kemp's address?"

"He lives somewhere in Henry Street. I don't know the number."

"Don't worry, I'll find it."

Walker stood up and headed for the door. "I'll come along later and take your statement," she said.

One of the women who had been working in the kitchen came into the lounge with a mug of tea. "Drink this, Nora," she said, handing the mug to Mrs Bull. "I've put plenty of sugar in." The woman plonked down on the couch next to her. "She'll be all right," she said. "We'll look after her. You need to get out there and get that bastard off the streets."

PC Walker left the house and joined DCS Bainbridge, who was standing by his car. She relayed the conversation she had had with Nora Bull.

"Do you want me to bring the Dysons in?" she said. "According to her, they've both been threatening to kill her husband."

"DC Beaumont is doing that right now," Bainbridge said. "I need to get back to the station, but I want you to get a statement from his friend, Joey Kemp. Take PC Jones with you."

“Yes, sir,” Walker said.

A dark-red Mercedes pulled up nearby. “Ah, Dr Carpenter at last,” Bainbridge said, walking towards the vehicle. “I’ll have a quick word with the pathologist before I interview the Dysons.”

62

PC Jones knocked several times on Joey Kemp's door before it was eventually opened. Wearing a blue woollen dressing gown over striped pyjamas, a short chubby man with thinning grey hair appeared in the doorway rubbing his eyes with his knuckles.

Kemp squinted at the two officers before reaching into his dressing gown pocket and taking out his spectacles. "Police?" he said, placing them on his nose. "What's happened? Has something happened to our Daisy? I never wanted her to go to work in London. It's a dangerous place. I warned her..."

"No, it's not your daughter, Mr Kemp," PC Walker said. "May we come in?"

Kemp led the way into the lounge, followed by the two officers.

"If it's not our Daisy, then what is it?

"Mr Kemp, we understand you were out last night with Charlie Bull. Is that right?"

"Yeah, we had a couple in The Nags Head, then went up to The Galleon. There was supposed to be a darts match on but it was cancelled." He plonked into an armchair. "What's this about?" he asked. "Has something happened to Charlie?"

"I'm afraid Mr Bull is dead," Walker said.

Kemp grabbed the arm of the chair for support. "Dead? What do you mean dead? He was all right when he left me last night."

"His body was found early this morning on the common close to his house. First indications are that he was murdered."

Kemp gasped, screwing his hands into fists. "Murdered? No, not Charlie. That can't be right."

"Did Mr Bull have any altercation with anyone last night?" Walker said.

"Altercation? What do you mean, altercation?"

"Did he get into an argument, a disagreement with anyone?"

Kemp shook his head. "No, everyone was sympathetic towards him over the accident. Everyone knew it wasn't Charlie's fault. I take it you heard about that?"

"Yes, we are aware, sir," Jones said respectfully.

"Charlie had got himself into a right state about it at first. Nora, his missus, rang me and said he was depressed and would I come round and cheer him up."

"And did Charlie cheer up?"

"Yeah, he seemed a lot more like his old self by the end of the night. We walked back along the front about eleven o'clock, then I left him at the bottom of the street and he went home."

"You weren't aware of anyone following you?"

"Of course not. Why would anyone want to follow two blokes?"

"Did Charlie seem anxious or scared about anything?"

"You mean the threats from Shaun Dyson?"

"He told you about that?"

"Yeah, but Charlie didn't believe he'd carry out the threats. He thought Shaun was just grieving for his lad."

Walker took out her notebook. "Mr Kemp, I need you to make a statement about last night. Do you think you could do that?"

The lounge door opened and a middle-aged woman came into the room. "What's going on Joey?" she said. "What are the police doing here. Is it about our Daisy?"

"No love, it's not Daisy. It's Charlie Bull."

"What about him?"

"It seems the poor sod's been murdered."

63

Inspector Mason put down the telephone after speaking to DCS Bainbridge.

"Everything all right, Jack?" asked Inspector Palmer. "You look like you've seen a ghost."

The two men were in Inspector Palmer's office in Sunderland.

"That was the boss," Mason replied. "There's been another murder."

"Another one? What the fuck is going on in Redcar!" Palmer exclaimed. "How many stiffs does that make in the last two weeks?"

"Four," Mason said, "plus PC Porter and his wife."

"And you've still got nobody in the frame?"

"Shaun Dyson is favourite, but we just don't have enough proof. This latest victim, Charlie Bull, is the bloke who killed Dyson's ten-year old son in a motor accident."

"And you think Dyson's responsible?"

"It's too much of a coincidence not to be him, don't you think? Bainbridge is interviewing Dyson now."

"I've heard Bainbridge is a good bloke. The guys are still talking about the way he cleared up that business a few months back."

"Yeah, he's hard to keep up with sometimes."

Palmer poured himself a coffee from the machine. "Want one?" he offered.

"No thanks," Mason said, perusing papers on his desk. "I'm just reading up on this bloke, Terry Roberts."

"Another slippery bastard," Palmer said. "He dabbles in anything bent. Rumour is, he's into drug distribution."

"It's beginning to look like the whole family are involved," Mason said. "His brother, Freddie, is suspected of distributing drugs at the racetracks."

"Didn't he get attacked a while back? I heard he was little more than a cabbage."

"No, that's an exaggeration," Mason sneered. "Freddie Roberts is still very much on the ball, although he doesn't want people to know that."

"What I don't understand is how they manage to distribute the drugs all over the country," said Palmer. "Terry's been under surveillance for weeks now and we've come up with nothing."

"Terry's not been travelling around the country?"

Palmer shook his head. "An occasional visit up to Carlisle, that's all. I still don't understand why they would kill young Porter. After all, he was part of their family."

"Only on Freddie's wife's side," Mason said. "She buggered off a few years ago and left them. I don't think the Roberts family had any loyalty towards Porter once they'd got him to do their dirty work."

"Porter's car was picked up on camera not five miles from Terry's house just two days ago. The house is being raided in about half-an-hour. Are you coming along?"

"I wouldn't miss it for the world," Mason grinned. "Let's hope we find something. We could do with some luck."

64

It was nine-thirty in the morning when Chief Superintendent Bainbridge, together with DC Beaumont, entered Interview Room One at Redcar Police Station. Kendall rose to his feet as Bainbridge entered the room.

"This is most irregular, Chief Superintendent. Mr Dyson and his wife are in mourning. Their child is dead. You have no right to treat them like this."

Bainbridge banged the file of papers down hard on the desk and looked directly at the solicitor. "Sit down, Mr Kendall," he said. "Your client is here because he made threats to kill Mr Charles Bull. Mr Bull's mutilated body was found this morning just yards from his home."

"I… I need to confer with my client," Kendall stammered. "I thought he was here about the other matter."

"Mr Dyson will be questioned about that too, in due course," Bainbridge replied briskly.

Shaun Dyson sat motionless, his shoulders drooped, a faraway look in his eyes.

"You have been cautioned," Bainbridge said, "so anything you say..."

"My client is aware of that," Kendall said, resuming his seat and scraping his chair closer to the desk.

Bainbridge switched on the tape. "The time is nine-thirty am.," he began. "Present in Interview Room One is a person of interest, Mr Shaun Dyson, along with his solicitor, Mr Melvyn Kendall. Also present is Detective Constable Wayne Beaumont and Detective Chief Superintendent Andrew Bainbridge."

Dyson attempted to suppress a yawn, then placed both hands behind his head. "Is this going to take long?" he said. "I've got a funeral to arrange for my kid."

"Do you know Mr Charles Bull?" Bainbridge said.

"I know he's the bastard that killed my boy."

"That was an accident as well you know," Bainbridge said. "Have you ever had any contact with Mr Bull?"

"I might have rung him a couple of times to let him know what I thought of him," Dyson leered.

"According to Mr Bull's phone records you rang him twenty-six times in a two-day period," Bainbridge said. "That's a little more than a couple of times."

"I was angry, upset. My lad was only ten. He had his whole life ahead of him."

"That's true and I'm sorry for your loss, but your son had stolen a quad bike and had been driving it recklessly around the town. We should be thankful that not more people were killed."

Dyson banged his fist on the desk, his body shaking with rage. "I don't give a fuck about other people! I only care about my lad."

"Mr Dyson, where were you last evening between eleven o'clock and midnight?"

"Can't remember," Dyson said.

"Were you anywhere in the vicinity of Newcomen Terrace?"

"Is that where the bastard got done?"

"Answer the question, Mr Dyson," Bainbridge said.

"I was at home with Leanne," he said.

Bainbridge scoffed. "Ah, the same alibi as last time and the time before. Was anyone else present?"

A wry smile crept across Dyson's face. "As a matter of fact, there was. Plenty of people as it happens. Leanne's lot had come over from Middlesbrough and a couple of pals of mine. We had a bit of a party, a sort of wake, you might say."

"And you were present the whole time?"

"I was too pissed to go anywhere."

Melvyn Kendall sniffed loudly as he collected his papers together and placed them in his briefcase. "If there's nothing further," he said, "I want my client released."

Bainbridge got to his feet. "Your client's going nowhere until I've checked his alibi thoroughly," he said. He turned to Beaumont. "Take Mr Dyson back to his cell."

65

Leanne Dyson was pacing Interview Room Two. PC Walker was standing by the door. Leanne sprang forward when Bainbridge and Beaumont entered. They were closely followed by Melvyn Kendall.

“You’ve no right bringing me and Shaun in here,” she said, prodding Bainbridge in the chest with her finger. “It’s victimisation, that’s what it is.”

Bainbridge grabbed Leanne’s wrist. “Sit down, Mrs Dyson,” he said. “The sooner we get this over with the sooner you can leave.”

PC Walker took hold of Leanne’s arm and led her to a chair at the table.

“Now,” said Bainbridge, once Leanne was seated, “tell me where you were last night between eleven and midnight.”

“Partying,” she said. “We had family over to ours and we had a party to remember our Arron.”

“You had a wake?” Bainbridge said. “I’ll need the names of everyone who attended.”

“Why? What’s this about anyway? Why are we here?”

“Charles Bull was murdered last night,” Bainbridge said.

A broad smile crept over Leanne’s face. “You mean that murdering bastard is dead? He’s really dead?” She jumped up from her chair and began dancing around the room, clapping her hands. “I’m glad. He deserved it.”

“Sit down, Mrs Dyson,” Bainbridge said.

Still smiling, Leanne returned to her seat.

"Did you or Shaun leave the house at any time last night?" Bainbridge asked.

She began to chuckle. "Shaun was pissed as a newt by nine o'clock. He was flat out on the couch. Never stirred 'til this morning."

"What about you? Did you leave the house?"

"Why would I? Me and our Fi were drinking vodka and talking over old times till the early hours."

"Fi?"

"Fiona. She's my older sister. We haven't seen each other for years, so there was lots to talk about."

"What about Shaun's sister? Was she there?"

Leanne's posture stiffened. "What are you talking about? Shaun doesn't have a sister. What makes you think he has?"

"Have you met her?"

"He's never mentioned a sister to me," she said.

"Is this line of questioning relevant?" Kendall interjected. "Mrs Dyson has told you she doesn't know about any sister."

"Perhaps she can have a think about it in the cells," Bainbridge said as he walked towards the door, leaving Leanne glaring at him intensely.

66

Bainbridge returned to his office followed closely by Beaumont.

"What's this about Dyson having a sister?" asked Beaumont. "I thought Dyson didn't have any family."

"Shaun saved the kid's life in a house fire. She was a baby then and was soon adopted and moved abroad with her new family. I'm trying to trace her."

"Sir, I don't understand. Are you saying this sister is somehow involved in the murders?"

"It's beginning to look like that. Sophie thinks it's highly likely."

"Sophie?"

"She's a friend of mine. A criminal psychologist."

Beaumont flopped down heavily on a chair. "Bloody hell, this is getting crazier by the minute."

Bainbridge picked up the internal phone. "Sergeant Brown? Has Mason rung in this morning?"

"Yes, sir. About ten minutes ago. He asks if you could please ring him back."

"Is Inspector Mason still in Sunderland?" Beaumont asked.

"Yes, he's liaising with the Durham Police. PC Porter's murder, and that of his wife, are his priority at the moment."

Beaumont supressed a yawn. "Sorry, sir," he said. "I haven't been to bed yet. I've been interviewing neighbours of Charlie Bull most of the night."

“You’d better get yourself off for a few hours,” Bainbridge advised, as he took out his mobile. “I’ll give Inspector Mason a call and see what progress he’s making.”

Beaumont took his jacket from the stand. “Thanks, sir. I’ll be back in a couple of hours.”

Left alone, Bainbridge dialled Inspector Mason’s phone. It was answered almost immediately.

“Good morning, sir.”

“Good morning, Jack. How’s it going up there?”

“Terry Roberts’s house was raided early this morning. We’ve found some pretty damning stuff in there hidden beneath the floorboards.”

“Such as?”

“For a start there’s a paper trail leading to a haulage company, ‘Here to There.’ That’s the company Giles Nixon works for.”

“Nixon? You think he’s involved with the Roberts family?”

“It’s beginning to look like it. We’ve found a journal giving particulars of deliveries and payments. It seems Terry likes to keep a record of transactions. The analysts are going through it now. It details meetings with known suppliers in Newcastle and the names of distributors and dealers. The Drugs Squad are wetting themselves with excitement. This thing is going to be huge.”

“Have you found anything linking Terry to the murder of PC Porter and his wife?”

"No, not yet, but we're sifting through tons of paperwork. Then there's his computer to be analysed. That's with the lab boys, but it's all going to take time I'm afraid."

"All right. Keep me informed."

"How's it going in Redcar, sir? Has there been any progress?"

"I've got Shaun and Leanne in custody," Bainbridge said. "They've got solicitored up so they're not saying much at the moment. We may have a breakthrough though. It's beginning to look like Dyson did have an accomplice after all."

"An accomplice? Who?"

"I'm looking into the possibility that Dyson's sister could be involved."

"I… I don't understand. What makes you think that? Do we know who she is, or where she is?"

"No, not yet, but enquiries are continuing as they say. Ring me as soon as you hear back from the lab."

Bainbridge put down the phone as PC Walker entered the room carrying a cup of tea.

"I thought you might need this," she said.

"Thanks. You're a lifesaver. How's Leanne doing?"

"She's been demanding to speak with Shaun."

"Make sure you keep them apart. I don't want them conferring."

"Yes, sir," Walker said as she quietly closed the door behind her.

67

It was almost ten o'clock that morning when DC Wayne Beaumont arrived home. As he entered the kitchen, he was surprised to see Jodie sitting at the table drinking coffee.

"Shouldn't you be at work?" he asked gently, kissing her lightly on the cheek.

"I'm on lates today," she said. "I start at one and work through until eight."

"How come? I thought your job was a nine till five."

"It is usually, but Maria has decided to open the salon late one day a week."

"What about your mate? Is she working late too?"

"What mate?"

"Annika."

Jodie huffed. "She's no mate of mine! I can't stand the arrogant cow."

Beaumont took off his jacket and flung it on the back of a chair. "I'm knackered. I didn't get to bed last night," he said, flinging himself onto the couch. "There's been another murder."

Jodie put down her mug. "Who is it this time?"

"That bloke who killed Dyson's kid. He was found in the early hours on the common. He'd been stabbed." Beaumont lay down on the couch, placing a couple of cushions behind his head. "Wake me up before you go will you, love? I have to get back to work later."

Jodie strode over to her husband. "Do you think it was Shaun or Leanne who did for him?"

Beaumont yawned. "I've no idea. Bainbridge seems to think there's some woman involved."

"What woman?"

"He's got it into his head that Dyson has a sister somewhere and she's helping him."

"Leanne's never mentioned Shaun had a sister."

"When have you been talking to Leanne?"

Jodie shrugged. "She comes into the salon sometimes. Maria used to go drinking with her at The Smugglers when Shaun was inside. I've been out with them a few times after work."

"You've been out drinking with Leanne Dyson? Are you mad woman?"

"Leanne's a bit of a rough diamond, I suppose, but she's all right once you get to know her. In fact, I like her."

"I don't want you mixing with the likes of the Dysons," Wayne warned, wagging his finger. "They're criminals. The whole bloody lot of them." He leant back onto the couch and closed his eyes. "I need to sleep for a couple of hours, so piss off. and don't forget to wake me before you leave."

68

Inspectors Palmer and Mason were seated in the interview room at Durham Police Station when Terry Roberts was brought in, escorted by two constables. Roberts was in handcuffs. A constable roughly steered him to a plastic chair across from the two officers and Roberts dutifully sat down.

"You're wasting your time. I've done nothing and you can't prove I have."

Inspector Palmer turned on the tape and made the necessary introductions. "Can I remind you, Mr Roberts, that you are still under caution. I will ask you once again, do you wish to call on the services of a solicitor?"

"No. Why should I? I've done nothing."

"If you should change your mind at any point," Palmer said, "I can..."

"How many times have you people got to be told, I don't want a bleeding solicitor."

"Very well, as you wish. I understand you're employed as a market trader. Is that correct?"

"Yeah. I've worked the markets for years."

"What is it you sell?"

"Pet supplies," he said. "Dry food, pet treats, collar and leads, dog beds, that sort of thing." He began to chuckle. "I'm a bit like Mothercare," he grinned. "I supply everything, but the puppy."

"Can you tell me the last time you spoke to your brother, Freddie Roberts?"

Terry shrugged. "I can't remember. It must be a couple of months."

"What about Barry and Lee? Have you seen or spoken to either of them?"

"What's it got to do with you if I have?" Terry said. "They're family."

"Paul Porter is family too, isn't he? When did you last see him?"

Roberts banged his fist down on the desk. "What's this about? Why do you want to know about our Paul? He's one of your lot, isn't he?"

"Paul and Denise Porter were found dead in a burnt-out car," he stated calmly. "They had both been shot through the head."

Roberts inhaled deeply. "That's a shame. Paul was a nice lad despite being a copper. Do you know who killed him?"

"I was hoping you could tell me," Palmer said. "How well did you know him?"

Roberts shrugged. "Not well," he said. "He more or less cut himself off from the family when he joined the police."

"Do you own a gun?" Mason asked.

"No, I don't. What would I want with a gun?"

"You've been convicted previously for firearms offences," Palmer said.

"That was years ago. I was young and foolish. I got caught and I did my time. Believe me, I've learnt my lesson."

Mason leant forward. "Do you know Giles Nixon?"

Roberts shook his head. "No, I don't think so."

"He drives for a haulage firm 'Here to There'."

"Still don't know him."

"We found reference in your journal regarding the firm," Palmer said. "It would seem you do regular business with Mr Nixon."

Roberts became agitated. "I do business with a lot of people," he said. "I can't be expected to know all their names."

"What exactly was your business with Nixon?"

"He sometimes moves stock around for me if I get a glut of stuff from my supplier. I sell it on to other traders and Nixon transports it for me. It's not a crime, is it?"

"Using the company's transport to carry unauthorised stock might be seen by the owners as a crime."

"What're you talking about? It's not like it takes up much space."

"How did you meet Mr Nixon?"

"I don't remember."

"Mr Roberts, this is going to turn out to be an extremely long day if you don't start answering my questions," Palmer said. "Now, I'll ask you again, how did you meet Giles Nixon?"

There was a sharp rap on the door and a young constable stepped nervously into the interview room.

"Yes, Wallace. What is it?" asked Palmer.

"May I have a word outside, sir?"

"Spit it out man, I don't have all day."

The constable inhaled deeply. “We’ve just had confirmation from the search party at Mr Roberts’ house that they have found a gun concealed in the attic.”

Roberts sprang to his feet and raced towards the door. Mason barred his path.

“Not so fast,” he said, grabbing Roberts’s upper arms and leading him back to his seat.

Colour had drained from Roberts’s face and he began to visibly tremble.

“I… I think I will have that solicitor after all,” he said.

69

On receiving the phone call from Mason about developments, DCS Bainbridge telephoned the Carlisle Police and instructed them to arrest Giles Nixon. Twenty minutes later Sergeant Thomas from the Carlisle Police telephoned Bainbridge.

"Sorry, sir. Nixon's gone. We've brought Mrs Nixon into custody, but she says she has no idea where her husband is."

"Thanks, sergeant," Bainbridge said. "I'll send someone over to Carlisle to bring her to the station."

Sonja Nixon had remained silent throughout the journey from Carlisle to Redcar. She sat motionless in the interview room across from Bainbridge and Sergeant Brown.

Having gone through the formalities of the caution and introduction on the tape, Bainbridge opened the file on the desk in front of him. "Mrs Nixon, where is your husband?"

Nixon shrugged. "No idea," she replied.

"It's important I speak with him, if only to eliminate him from our enquiries."

"What enquiries? Giles knows nothing about the attack on my Father."

"Do you know a man called Terry Roberts?"

"Of course I do. He's a mate of Giles."

"A good mate?"

"They spend a lot of time together I suppose. Why are you asking about Terry? What's he done?"

"Terry Roberts is helping with our enquiries," Bainbridge said.

"Surely you can't suspect Terry of attacking my Dad?"

"I need to find your husband as a matter of urgency. Are you sure you have no idea where he is?"

"No, I don't. This is so out of character of Giles."

"When did you last see him?"

"This morning, about eleven o'clock. He got a phone call then he dashed upstairs and a few minutes later came down carrying a suitcase."

"Who was the call from?"

"He didn't say."

"Didn't you ask where he was going?"

"Of course I did. He said he would call me later and explain. Before I could do anything, he was through the door and zooming off in his car in the direction of the M6."

"And you haven't heard from him since?"

"No. About an hour after he left, one of you lot came to the house looking for him and then took me to the police station."

"Mrs Nixon, does your husband own, or has ever owned a gun?"

She sniffed her indignation. "Of course he hasn't. What a ridiculous thing to ask. What on earth would he want with a gun?"

"Do you know if Terry owned a gun?"

She shrugged. “I have no idea. I wouldn’t have thought so. He sells pet supplies, for goodness sake.”

“Have you ever met any of Terry’s family?”

“I’ve met his nephew Lee a couple of times when he’s been in Carlisle.”

“Oh? When was this?”

“He came just a few days ago, actually.”

“Did he want anything in particular?”

“If he did, he didn’t tell me. Giles and Terry met him in The Three Bells. I think they had some business on.”

“What sort of business?”

“I don’t know. All I know is that Giles wasn’t happy when he got back. He said something about having to make a diversion to his normal route the following day. Giles drives a lorry you know.”

“Tell me more about this diversion he had been asked to make.”

Nixon took a deep breath and clasped her hands in front of her. “It’s nothing illegal,” she said. “From time to time, Giles earns a few extra quid for transporting stuff for Terry. Like I said, Terry runs a pet supplies business and occasionally he gets more stock than he can handle. That’s when Giles helps out by taking some of the stock to other traders around the country. He gets to keep a percentage of what he takes.”

“How long has this… this arrangement been going?”

“Not long. A few months maybe.”

“Who else knows about this?”

"Nobody, only Terry's family."

"Tell me about the day your husband hit Benji. I want to know everything that happened."

Her persona stiffened as she clenched both hands into fists. "That was a family matter," she said. "It has absolutely nothing to do with the police."

"On the contrary," Bainbridge pressed. "I think it has everything to do with the police. Now, I'll ask you again, what caused your husband to fight with your Father? And please don't try and tell me it was because he'd given your mother a beating. I know Eileen had suffered much worse injuries inflicted by your father in the past."

Nixon sighed heavily. "All right," she said. "If you must know it was over the bag."

"The bag I recovered from Benji's shed?"

She nodded. "Dad told Giles about it and Giles was furious. He wanted dad to give it back to Freddie Roberts, but dad refused. That's when the fists started flying."

"Do you know what was in the bag?"

"No, but I could make a good guess. Giles said the bag had to be returned or else there would be trouble from the Roberts family."

"So, what happened?"

"There was an argument, then Giles struck dad. That's how he got a black eye. But dad was the much better fighter and he overpowered Giles. He told him to get Freddie to make him an offer to return the bag."

"And did he?"

Nixon shook her head. "No. Giles said he didn't want to get involved and if dad wanted to make a deal with Freddie, he had to do it himself."

"So, Freddie Roberts was not aware that your father had the bag."

"If he did, he certainly didn't hear it from Giles. That I do know."

"Do you know where your father found the bag?"

"He told Giles he had found it at the plant one night. Him and Arthur Rhodes."

"I take it they divided the cash in the bag?"

"Yes. That's how dad could afford the lease for the off-licence."

"Why didn't Benji and Arthur try to sell the drugs?"

"Arthur wouldn't. He said he didn't want it on his conscience putting that filth on the street. Besides, who could they sell them to? Dad said it was pure heroin. It needed to be diluted down."

"What about Shaun Dyson? How does he fit into all of this?"

"Dad said it was Shaun who hid it in the steel plant. That's when dad and Arthur took the bag."

"Did Shaun come looking for the bag when he came out of prison?"

Nixon shrugged. "I've no idea. Dad never said anything." Her posture suddenly stiffened. "You… you don't think it was Shaun Dyson who killed my dad?"

"The possibility is under investigation. I can say no more than that at the moment."

Nixon began trembling, the colour draining from her face. "Could I have some water, please?" she asked politely.

"Of course. Sergeant…?"

Sergeant Brown left the room, returning a few minutes later with a paper cup of water from the dispenser.

"Thank you," she said as she gulped at the liquid.

"Is there anything else you can tell me, Mrs Nixon? Anything that will help me find your husband?"

"I've no idea where Giles is," she said. "He's probably with that blonde slut he sees every couple of weeks."

"Your husband's having an affair?"

"I wouldn't call it an affair exactly. There's no secret texts or mysterious phone calls in the middle of the night or anything like that. But Giles goes somewhere every other Sunday and comes home smelling of cheap perfume with blonde hairs on his jacket."

"That's not really a police matter, I'm afraid," Bainbridge said. "You must take that up with your husband."

Sergeant Brown had been writing furiously in his pocketbook. Bainbridge got to his feet and walked towards the door. "Will you be staying at you mothers until this is cleared up?" he asked. "I may want to speak to you again."

Nixon nodded as she strode to the open door. "You will find Giles, won't you?" she asked. "He's not really a bad man, he just…"

"Don't worry, we'll find him," Bainbridge said, indicating for a constable to show Mrs Nixon out of the building.

70

“Well, what do you think, Sergeant?” Bainbridge said as they entered his office. “Does Sonja Nixon know where her husband is?”

“I wouldn’t think so, sir. I’ll go down to the arcade and see if she’s right about him being with Kathy Blackburn.”

“You can try,” Bainbridge said, “but I doubt you’ll find him there. I think Giles Nixon is in this mess right up to his neck and is making a run for it.”

“I’ve released details of his car and informed the Port Authority and the airports,” Brown said, “just in case he tries to skip the country.”

“Good. Let’s hope it brings results. By the way, it might be an idea to keep an eye on Mrs Nixon, just in case.”

“I’ll get PC Jones onto it, sir. He likes a bit of cloak and dagger.” Grinning, Sergeant Brown left Bainbridge’s office and went down to reception.

PC Walker arrived at Redcar Police Station and went straight to Sergeant Brown in reception.

“Sarge,” she said, “I’ve checked with everyone who was at the Dyson’s the night Charlie Bull was murdered and they all say Shaun and Leanne never left the house all night. Apparently, Shaun was so drunk he spent most of the evening sprawled on the couch asleep.”

“Most of the guests were Leanne’s family, weren’t they?”

"Yes, sarge, but I checked with Shaun's neighbours and they confirmed the noise from their house until the early hours."

Sergeant Brown huffed. "All right, constable. I'll let Chief Superintendent Bainbridge know."

He picked up the internal phone. "Walker's confirmed the Dyson's alibi," he said. "Do you want me to release them, sir?"

"We don't have much choice. Bail them to return to the station in a week."

"Very well, sir. I'll do it right away."

Sergeant Brown was busy in the evidence room when the visitor's buzzer rang in the main reception. He made his way through to see a nervous-looking middle-aged man standing in front of the counter. "Yes, sir," the sergeant said, "how can I help?"

"My name is Giles Nixon," the man said. "I… I believe the police are looking for me."

71

It was early afternoon when Jodie arrived at the salon. Annika was in the back room making herself a cup of tea.

"Part-timer," she scoffed, as Jodie removed her coat. "We could have done with you here this morning. It's been manic."

Jodie ignored her as she reached for a teabag to make herself a drink.

"Mrs Burton rang," Annika said. "She's cancelled her six o'clock appointment so I gave the appointment to that girl from the fish shop, the one with the pink hair."

Jodie huffed. "Oh, that girl has a mouth like a sewer. She does nothing but complain. I wish she'd find somewhere else to go for her hair."

Annika grinned. "I hear she got banned from the salon on Sycamore Street because of her behaviour."

"Wayne said your husband's in Durham, looking into Paul Porter's murder. Has he arrested anyone yet?"

"I've no idea," Annika said. "Jack doesn't discuss his work with me, and Wayne shouldn't talk to you about police matters either."

Jodie snorted as she headed into the salon carrying her cup. "Wayne said Shaun Dyson has a sister. They think she could be mixed up in the murders."

"That's rubbish. Who's been saying that?"

"That friend of Bainbridge, Sophie something. She's some sort of psychologist so she knows about these things. She says it's likely that the sister is involved."

Annika grabbed Jodie's arm, spinning her round causing the hot tea to splash onto her chest. "What do you mean, involved? How do they know that? Jack's never mentioned Shaun Dyson having a sister."

Jodie flinched in pain as she pulled away from Annika. "Careful," she said, grabbing a cloth and dabbing at the damp patch on her tabard. "Why are you so interested anyway? I thought you didn't get involved with Jack's work."

Maria came into the back room and clapped her hands sharply. "Come on ladies, enough chatting for today. There are customers waiting."

Both women went back into the salon and began work.

72

Inspector Palmer was standing outside Durham police station smoking a cigarette, together with Jack Mason.

Jack grinned. "The wife would throw a fit if she saw me doing this," he said as he slowly exhaled, "but I do enjoy a crafty smoke now and then."

"That's one thing I don't have to worry about," Palmer said, a wry smile on his lips. "A nagging wife."

"Aren't you married?"

"Not anymore. It's been two years now since the divorce."

"Oh, I'm sorry, mate."

"Don't be. I'm well shut. What about you, Jack? How long have you been hitched?"

"Three years," Jack said. "Her name's Annika."

"That's a pretty name. What's she like?"

Jack shrugged. "Annika's... well, she's Annika. She's pretty, intelligent and self-confident, too much so sometimes. She's a hairdresser, no, I stand corrected, a beauty therapist. She's most particular about her title."

"Kids?"

"No. Well, not yet anyway. I'm too career focused at the moment to think about starting a family. I'm on this fast-track scheme. I've been told I'll be a superintendent before I'm forty."

"Is that what you want, to be a superintendent?"

Jack shrugged. "It's what Annika wants. She's the ambitious one. Personally, I would prefer to lecture law in some university somewhere. I think I'd be much more comfortable doing that." He inhaled deeply on the cigarette.

"Will you be going back to Redcar tonight?" Palmer enquired. "If not, I thought you might like to join me for a pint at my local. They do a mean tandoori."

"Sounds good," Jack said. "I think I will stay over one more night. I'll ring Annika and..."

There was a sharp cough from the open door of the building. Palmer turned to see a constable standing in the doorway. "Yes, Wallace. What is it?"

"Mr Roberts's solicitor has finished his meeting with his client, sir," he said. "He wonders if he might have a word?"

Inspector Palmer threw down the half-smoked cigarette and bore it into the ground with the toe of his shoe. "Tell him I'll be there in a few minutes," he said, winking at Mason. "I'll keep the bastard waiting. I'm going for a piss first."

***

The heating system at Durham police station had been on the blink for days. That afternoon it had decided to give up completely. Palmer rubbed his hands together for warmth before he entered the interview room with Mason.

Terry Roberts was seated at the table, his head lowered. William Carter-Bloom, his twenty-something duty solicitor, was sitting next to him. Palmer had never met the solicitor before and guessed he was newly qualified. Before either of the policemen could take their seat, Carter-Bloom handed Palmer a handwritten, one-page statement.

"My client has made this statement voluntarily," he said. "As you can see, he has confessed to owning the gun which you found in his house, but refutes your allegation that he shot that policeman and his wife with it."

Palmer plonked down on a chair opposite the solicitor. "The gun has been sent to Forensics," he said. "They will determine if it was the weapon used to kill Paul and Denise Porter."

"It wasn't me who shot them," Roberts said, raising his head. "I was told to provide the gun, that's all. I didn't know the mad bastards were going to kill a copper."

"Who shot PC Porter?" Palmer said. "If it wasn't you, then who?"

Roberts turned to Carter-Bloom, roughly grabbing his arm. "You make the deal like I told you," he said, "then I'll tell everything."

Carter-Bloom removed Roberts's hand and brushed his jacket sleeve with his hand. "My client has certain information," he said. "Information which could prove extremely valuable to the police. In return for this information my client requires charges against him to be dropped, or at least reduced."

"The police are not in the business of making deals," Palmer said, "as both you and your client are aware."

Roberts turned to Palmer, a look of desperation on his face. "They're planning to kill somebody else," he said. "You'll be responsible for their death if you don't help me."

Palmer scowled. “I’ll have to speak to a more senior officer before I can agree to anything,” he said as he got up and walked towards the door where Inspector Mason had been standing.

“Whilst you’re about it,” Carter-Bloom said, “perhaps you could arrange to have the heating turned higher. It’s freezing in here.”

73

Bainbridge turned on the tape. "You do fully understand the caution I've just given, Mr Nixon?" he said.

Nixon nodded slowly.

"For the benefit of the tape, I need you to speak up," Bainbridge said. "Do you fully understand the caution?"

"Yes," Nixon said. "I'm not stupid."

"No-one is suggesting you are. Now, Sergeant Brown over there, will be making notes of this interview, but before we begin, I would strongly urge you to have legal representation. If you don't have your own solicitor, I can arrange for the duty solicitor to come and represent you."

Nixon inhaled deeply. "No solicitor," he said. "I have stuff to get off my chest, bad stuff I've done that I'm not proud of. I don't need a solicitor for that, do I?"

"If you should change your mind at any time…"

"I won't. Now can we just get on with it?"

"As you wish," Bainbridge said. "Let's start with your relationship with Terry Roberts."

"Terry's a mate," Nixon said. "He has a market stall selling pet supplies."

"Do you ever use your haulage van to transport goods for him?"

"Sometimes," he said. "Terry's supplier would send too much stock over, so Terry would arrange to sell it to other traders. I would deliver the boxes to them and Terry would give me my share of the profit."

"Did you ever question what was in the boxes?"

"I was told it was dog biscuits, that sort of stuff."

"And did you believe that?"

"The first couple of times I thought it was legit, but then I realised it was more than dog biscuits I was carrying."

"What do you think was in the boxes?"

Nixon ran his tongue over his lips. "I asked him outright if it was drugs."

"And what did Terry say."

"What could he say? I told him I wanted a bigger cut. He wasn't chuffed, but he eventually agreed."

"So, how exactly did it work?"

"Freddie Roberts was in charge, that's Terry's brother. His two lads, Barry and Lee, would fetch the stuff from Newcastle for Terry to distribute around the country. I was just one of his couriers, there are others. Freddie would take some with him to the racetracks and supply dealers from there. I don't know all the details, but it's a big operation they've got going."

"So how did your father-in-law get involved?"

"Bad luck really. Him and his mate, Arthur Rhodes, came across Freddie's tote bag hidden at the plant where they were working. The pair of them managed to get the bag open and saw the cash. Benji said there was nearly sixty-thousand quid."

"I take it they spent the money?"

"Yeah. Benji used part of his share leasing the off-licence, and his mate spent his on medical supplies for his wife.

Benji said it didn't do much good though because the poor cow died anyway."

"So, what about the drugs?"

"Benji said there were a couple of dozen sealed packages at the bottom of the bag. He knew it was heroin. His mate wanted to dump it somewhere, but Benji said it was worth a lot of money."

"Has the bag been in Benji's shed all this time?"

Nixon shook his head. "No, he left it with Arthur Rhodes for a while. Arthur's missus had died by this time, so there was no-one to poke about and find it at his house."

"So, what changed? Why was it moved to the shed?"

"When they heard Shaun Dyson was being released from prison, they knew he would come looking for the bag. Arthur got scared, really scared. He said he didn't want it in his house anymore. He told Benji that he must hide it. That's why they fell out."

"And that's how the bag ended up in the shed? How come you knew about the drugs?"

"I didn't at first. I mean, I know my father-in-law was no saint, but I would never have put him down for drug dealing."

"How did you find out?"

"Benji asked me if I knew anyone who would buy the drugs off him. I'd heard Freddie Roberts had been robbed, so, I knew straight away where they had come from. I told Benji it was a bad idea to fuck with the Roberts family, but he wouldn't be told. He asked me to speak with Freddie about buying back the drugs."

"And did you?"

"No, I did not. I told him I wanted nothing to do with it. I warned him not to get mixed up with Freddie Roberts and his lot."

"Did he listen?"

Nixon shrugged. "Benji was a stubborn old bastard. He said he could find someone else to take the drugs. I warned him it was dangerous but..."

"Let's go back to your relationship with Terry Roberts. According to your wife, you two were good friends. Is that right?"

"My wife? Have you been talking to Sonja?"

"Mrs Nixon was interviewed earlier today," Bainbridge said.

"You'd no right," Nixon said, banging his fist on the table. "Sonja has nothing to do with this. She knows nothing."

"Tell me about the meeting you had with Terry and Lee Roberts."

Nixon huffed. "We went for a pint, that's all."

"I understand you were annoyed at having to make a diversion from your usual route. Where were you asked to go?"

Nixon shuffled uncomfortably on his chair. "I… I don't know what you mean," he said.

"Your wife has told me all about it. Now I want to hear it from you."

"All right. Terry said he had a new dealer. I was asked to go to Runswick Bay. I wasn't happy because it was miles off my route."

"And did you go to Runswick Bay?"

"I didn't have much choice, did I? Once you're in with these people, there's no getting out."

"I take it you were paid an extra bonus?"

"Of course I was. It's going to pay for my holiday in Lanzarote."

"I don't think you'll be going to Lanzarote or anywhere else for quite some time," Bainbridge said.

"Did you know if Terry owned or had access to a gun?"

Nixon inhaled deeply, beads of sweat forming on his brow. "I don't know anything about a gun," he said, shuffling again in his chair. "Why would Terry want a gun?"

"Did you know Paul and Denise Porter?"

"No."

"You never met them?"

"No."

"PC Porter and his wife were shot. Porter was related to the Roberts family. Did you know that?"

Nixon shrugged. "Terry told me once there was a copper in the family. He thought it was funny, but I never met him."

"What about Barry and Lee Roberts? How close were you to them?"

"I hardly knew them. The last time I met up with Terry at the pub, Lee was there too, but once he had given the instructions for the drop, he left."

Bainbridge turned to Sergeant Brown. "Take Mr Nixon back to the cells, sergeant," he said. "I will continue this interview later."

"Later? Why don't you charge me and release me on bail? I've told you everything I know."

"Until I'm satisfied that is the case, Mr Nixon, you will remain in police custody," Bainbridge said. "Sergeant?"

Sergeant Brown took hold of Nixon's upper-arm and got him to his feet. "This way, sir," he said, guiding him towards the door. Nixon tried to pull away. "I want a solicitor," he said. "I'm not saying another word until I have a solicitor."

"Very well, Mr Nixon," Bainbridge said. "I'll arrange for a duty solicitor to be present at our next interview."

74

Annika arrived home at six-thirty that evening to see the answerphone flashing. She pressed the button.

"Sorry, love," Jack's voice said. "I'm not going to be home until sometime tomorrow I'm afraid. I'll call you later tonight. Love you." She played the message through twice, becoming more and more irritated.

"Damn you, Jack," she said, pouring herself a vodka.

Opening the fridge, she took out a ready-meal and put it in the microwave before turning on the television. The local news was all about the murder of Charlie Bull. Bainbridge was seen giving a brief interview to reporters outside the police station. Annika turned up the volume to hear him say… *'I can personally assure residents that the police are closing in on those responsible for not just the murder of Mr Bull, but that of Benji Myers, Sheila Thompson and Arthur Rhodes. We are confident arrests will be made shortly.'*

The microwave gave its familiar 'ping' indicating that the Thai Green Curry was ready to eat. Removing the container from the microwave, Annika carefully peeled back the lid and tipped the contents onto a plate. Before she could begin her meal, her phone rang. It was Jack.

"Hello, love," he said. "I'm sorry I have to stay up at Durham tonight, but I'll be back first thing tomorrow."

"What's going on, Jack?" she said. "Bainbridge has just been on the telly saying he's about to make an arrest."

"Things are moving at a pace, love. I'll tell you all about it tomorrow."

"What's this about Shaun Dyson's sister?"

"Where did you hear about her?"

"It doesn't matter. Do you know who she is?"

"Bainbridge is looking into that, but it's not public knowledge so, please don't discuss it with anyone."

"What makes you think she's involved?"

"It's only a theory we're working on at the moment. Sophie suggested it as a possibility."

"Sophie? That friend of Bainbridge? How is she involved?"

"She isn't, well not directly, but she is a criminal psychologist so her theories can't be ignored."

Annika huffed. "It seems a stupid theory to me. The idea that a woman could inflict such horrific injuries. Stabbing someone through the eyes is pure barbaric."

"You'd be surprised what some people are capable of," Jack said. "PC Porter and his wife for instance, both shot in the head and set on fire, and it looks like it was his own family who are responsible."

"Surely not. Families stick together, they don't kill each other. After all, blood is thicker than water."

"You'd think so, wouldn't you? But the truth is, a lot of families have serious rifts, rifts that are magnified simply because they are family. You'd be surprised at the statistics for murders committed by family members."

"Jack, this is all too horrible," Annika said. "I'm probably going to have nightmares tonight."

"Sorry, darling. I'll be home tomorrow, so stop worrying. I'm going to the pub for a bite to eat."

"I wish I was coming with you," she said. "I'm having a microwave curry."

"I promise when I get back, I'll treat you to a slap-up meal."

"I'll hold you to that. Can we go to the Mariners? I've heard it's the best in the area."

"Well, we could, but…"

"But what?"

"The Mariners is Bainbridge's favourite restaurant. I don't really want to see him at work and in my free time. As a matter of fact, I've just been talking to him about the case and he's going there tonight with Sophie."

"I'll have to think of somewhere else then, I suppose. I'd better go before my meal gets cold," she said. "See you tomorrow."

"Okay," Jack said. "Love you."

75

Andy Bainbridge and Sophie Barrett had finished their meal at The Mariners and were reclining in the lounge, each with a glass of brandy.

"That was a wonderful meal," Sophie said, "but next time you must let me pay the bill."

"Absolutely not," Andy said smiling. "I won't hear of it. You're my guest. If it makes you feel any better, you can regard it as payment for services rendered."

"Services rendered?"

"Advice," Andy said. "If it hadn't been for you, no-one would be looking for this Dyson girl."

"How are you getting on tracing her?"

Bainbridge shrugged. "It's not easy. She was adopted by a school teacher and his wife, who was also a teacher. They worked in Dubai for a few years, taking the child with them, then they moved back to Europe. I've traced them to Italy, but the trail's gone cold. The Italian authorities are going to contact me when they know more." He handed Sophie a buff-coloured file. "All I do know is her name was Joanne Connolly."

Sophie reached out and took the file. "Thanks, Andy," she said. "I'll read this tomorrow. By the way, do you have any other suspects? If I've got this wrong and this girl has nothing to do with what's happened… I don't want to mislead your enquiries."

"Do you think you are wrong about her?"

"Theoretically no. The profile fits, but these things are never black and white."

Andy drained his glass. "Well, lovely as this is, I'm afraid I have to leave. I've a busy day tomorrow."

"What's on your agenda?"

"I'm interviewing Freddie Roberts and his two lads. The Drugs Squad arrested them earlier today on another matter, but I'm convinced they're involved in Paul and Denise Porter's murder."

"I thought Jack was the lead on that enquiry?"

"He's assisting the Durham police. They've arrested Terry Roberts, Freddie's brother. They suspect he supplied the gun used to kill Porter and his wife."

"It sounds like you've got your hands full," Sophie said getting up from the table. "I'll phone for a taxi."

"There's no need to do that," Andy said. "I can drop you off. It's no trouble."

"No, Andy. I insist. You go home. You look tired." She slipped into her coat and picked up her bag. "Thanks for a lovely dinner. I'll call you tomorrow."

It was almost ten o'clock when Jodie rang Redcar Police Station. Sergeant Harris, the night sergeant, pushed his bag of fish and chips to one side as he answered the phone.

"I'm sorry love," he said, in answer to Jodie's enquiry. "Wayne isn't here. He left just after eight."

"Do you know where he went?"

"I've no idea. Maybe he's in the pub."

Jodie huffed. "I've tried there. Is DCS Bainbridge about? He might know."

"Mr Bainbridge is off duty," the sergeant said. "I believe he's having dinner with his young lady at the Mariner Hotel."

Jodie sniffed purposefully. "All right for some," she said. "If you do hear from Wayne, tell him to ring me straight away, will you?"

"Very well, Jodie. I'll do that."

The sergeant put down the phone, then turned to his companion. "Is everything all right between you two?" he said, placing a large piece of battered cod in his mouth. "Jodie sounded upset."

"Jodie's always upset about something," grumbled Beaumont. "I'm thinking of jacking it in with her to be honest."

"Why lad? What's gone wrong?"

"Oh, you know what women are like. Nag, nag, nag."

"I always thought Jodie was a nice girl, always smart and well turned-out."

Beaumont grunted. "She's a feather-brain. She told me today she's been out drinking regularly with Leanne Dyson. Can you believe it? Bainbridge would throw a fit if he knew."

Sergeant Harris frowned. "Why would Jodie want to go drinking with a woman like that?"

"You tell me. I've told her to keep away but... well, knowing Jodie, I bet she does the exact opposite. She doesn't give a shit about my career."

Having devoured the fish and most of the chips, Sergeant Harris screwed up the paper they had been wrapped in and threw it into the wastebin beneath the desk. "What was it the boss wanted you to do tonight?" he said, draining the last of the tea from the mug.

"He wants me to go through Nixon's log and check his routes. Bloody boring, I can tell you."

Harris shrugged. "Part of the job, old son. You can't be out chasing villains all the time."

"I wouldn't mind, but whilst I'm getting square eyes going through this lot, the boss is out wining and dining. It doesn't seem fair."

Harris grinned. "If that's how you feel lad, I'll tell you what you can do," he said as if imparting a great secret. "Get your head down and pass all the promotion exams until you get to be Chief Superintendent. Then you can sit back and enjoy the good life whilst the underlings do all the work." He began to chuckle. "No rest for the wicked," he said, drawing a wire tray containing a dozen statements towards him. He turned to Beaumont. "You'd better get on with what you've been tasked. The boss has a sneaky habit of calling into the station late at night."

76

Bainbridge returned home after his meal with Sophie. He would usually go to the police station for a couple of hours at the end of the day, but tonight he needed to be alone to think. It was almost midnight when his mobile phone rang. "Bainbridge!" he said.

"Andy, it's Sophie. Something terrible has happened."

"What's wrong? Are you alright?"

"Someone has broken into my apartment and ransacked my desk."

"Stay where you are. Make sure your door is locked and I'll come round straight away. Are you sure you're alright? You're not hurt?"

"I'm fine," she said. "Whoever it was took off over the balcony before I got into the room."

"I'll get Cutts to come over and..."

"I think he got what he came for."

"What do you mean?"

"The file you gave me tonight about Dyson's missing sister. It's gone."

"Don't worry about that," Andy said, "I can easily make you another one. Now lock the door. I won't be long."

Sophie Barrett's modern apartment was on the first floor of a three-storey building just outside Marske. Andy parked his car and satisfied that the area around the block was deserted, made his way to the fall pipe outside of Sophie's balcony window. On the soft ground he could see the unmistakable impression of a footprint. He went into the building and up the one flight of stairs to apartment three. He rang the doorbell.

"It's me, Sophie," he said quietly. "Open the door and let me in."

There was the sound of a key being turned and a bolt being drawn back before the door opened. Sophie flung herself at him, throwing her arms around his neck. "Thank god you've come," she said, tears trickling down her cheeks. Andy hugged her tightly.

"It's all right, love. You're safe now."

He followed her through the apartment and into the study.

"He was in here," she said. "He got out of that window onto the balcony and climbed down the fall pipe."

"Did you get a look at them?"

Sophie shook her head. "No. I was sleeping. I became aware of a noise so I got up and went into the study. The lamp on my desk was lit and I saw the silhouette of someone bending over my desk." She began to tremble. "I was so scared. I screamed and the figure grabbed the file and went out through the balcony window." She grabbed Andy's arm. "How did they know where I lived, Andy?"

Andy put his arm around her shoulders, drawing her close. "I don't know, love. I think the best thing to do is for you to come and stay at mine tonight."

The sound of the doorbell ringing startled Sophie.

"Don't worry," Andy said. "That'll be Leo Cutts." He went over to the door and opened it. "Come in, Leo."

"Good evening, sir." He gave a faint nod by way of acknowledgement to Sophie.

"It looks like whoever it was got in and made their escape through here," Andy said, leading the way into the study. "There's a good shoeprint on the ground directly below the balcony."

Cutts grinned. "It looks like my jobs half done already." He put on latex gloves and opened his box of equipment. He turned to Sophie. "I will need a set of your fingerprints for elimination purposes."

"Yes, of course," she said.

After taking Sophie's fingerprints, Cutts began dusting for prints on the desk whilst Sophie went into her bedroom to pack. Bainbridge put his hand on Cutts' arm. "The shoeprint outside," he said, "it's small. Probably a size five or six at the most."

"That sounds like it could belong to a woman."

"I think it probably is," Bainbridge said. "I don't want you mentioning that in front of Sophie. She's worried enough."

"If you think that's best, sir," he said. "I've just about finished here. It looks like whoever it was wore gloves. I'll check the balcony for prints then go and make an impression of the shoeprint."

"Good man," Bainbridge said. Cutts stepped out onto the balcony.

77

It was four o'clock in the morning. Shaun Dyson was in his bedroom, hurriedly bungling clothes into a suitcase.

"You're not thinking of doing a runner?" Leanne asked, pulling her dressing gown around her. "That'll be admitting you're guilty. If you just keep your nerve, they can't prove a thing."

Shaun pushed her to one side as he opened the dressing table drawer. "They've got the Roberts lot down at the nick," he said. "How long do you think it will be before they dob me in?"

"Who's going to believe anything those lying bastards say? They're just trying to save their own skin."

Shaun grabbed Leanne by her arm. "Stop yapping and help me pack," he said. "Where's my brown trousers?"

"They're in the wash, along with most of your gear. I've been too upset about Arron to do the washing."

Shaun huffed as he pushed a pair of jeans into his bag. "I'm going to London. I'll be safe there."

"Where in London? We don't have any money for London."

"She's given me a couple of grand to tide me over," he said, "and the keys to a bedsit she owns down there."

Leanne sniffed. "This is all her fault. If she hadn't killed Rhodes, the police wouldn't be that interested. I wish she'd never come into our lives."

Shaun grunted, and raising his arm, struck Leanne hard across the face with the back of his hand. "Don't you ever let me hear you speaking about her like that," he said. "She's my sister. My flesh and blood."

Leanne cowered, tears trickling down her face. "I know she's your sister, Shaun, but she acts like a crazy woman. She's going to get us both sent down."

Shaun slammed the suitcase lid shut and carried it to the bedroom door. "I won't hear another word against her," he said. "She'll act as go-between if you need to contact me, but be careful. If the cat ever comes out of the bag, we're all in the shit."

"Just how long do you think it's going to be before Bainbridge cottons on to her? He's not stupid."

"Neither is she," he said, making his way down the stairs. "If anyone asks, you don't know where I am, alright?"

"I won't be lying, will I? I don't know where you'll be."

"It's only 'til the Roberts lot get put down," Shaun said.

"What about Arron's funeral? You can't miss that."

"I have to," Shaun said, placing the suitcase in the car boot. "I'll be there in spirit."

He climbed into his Fiesta and turned on the engine. "Cheer up," he said as the car started to pull away. "It won't be for long." But Leanne couldn't hear him over the loud, rattling noise from the exhaust.

78

Freddie Roberts was in a wheelchair in Interview Room One. He looked tired and frail as he pulled a tartan rug up to his chest. Next to him was George Duvall, a senior partner in the firm Dodds, Duvall & Bright, a prestigious firm of solicitors from Newcastle.

“Before we begin, Mr Roberts,” Bainbridge said, “do you need the services of a doctor?”

Freddie shook his head. “Let’s get this farce over with. You’ve wasted enough of my time.”

“My client is not a well man,” Duvall said. “I fail to see why he has been dragged to the police station in his current state of health.”

“Mr Roberts is facing some extremely serious accusations,” Bainbridge replied.

“Even so, I...”

“Leave it, George,” Freddie said. “Let’s just get this over with.”

Bainbridge inhaled. “Very well, I will remind you that you are still under caution, Mr Roberts. For the purpose of the tape, the time is 9.30 a.m. and the interview is taking place in Interview Room One at Redcar Police Station. Those present are Mr Frederick Roberts, a person of interest, his solicitor, Mr George Duvall, Detective Constable Beaumont and Detective Chief Superintendent Bainbridge.”

Bainbridge opened a buff-coloured file which was on the desk and removed a sheet of paper, whilst Beaumont took out his notebook and pen.

"Let's start by going back to the day you were attacked at the racecourse," Bainbridge addressed Roberts. "Tell me exactly what happened."

"It's a matter of record that my client remembers nothing of that incident," Duvall answered.

"Is that still the case, Mr Roberts?"

"Like my brief said, what happened that day is a complete blank. All I remember is waking up in hospital with the mother of all headaches."

"Do you remember having your tote bag with you at the racecourse?"

"No, but I would have had it. I always did. I couldn't work without it."

"What were the contents of the bag?"

"It was the end of the working day. The usual takings from the Redcar races would be in the region of five to six thousand quid."

"I have been reliably informed it was nearer sixty thousand pounds. Why do you think that was?"

"DCS Bainbridge, do I have to remind you my client has no recollection of that day. Your insistence in questioning him on this is bordering on oppressive."

Bainbridge ignored the solicitor. "Tell me about the drugs found in your tote bag."

"What drugs? I don't know anything about any drugs."

"Your fingerprints were found all over the packaging. How do you explain that?"

"Where are these packages? Do you have them to present in evidence?" Duvall said.

"The packages were sabotaged," Bainbridge said, "by someone we believe to be a relative of your client."

"And who might that be?"

Bainbridge again ignored the solicitor and turned instead to face Roberts. "Tell me about your nephew, Paul Porter," he said.

"Paul's dead," Roberts said. "Him and Denise. Some sort of road accident up in Sunderland I believe."

"When was the last time you saw your nephew?"

Roberts shrugged. "I don't remember. My memory's not what it was since I got hit over the head with a hammer."

"I understand you gave Paul large sums of money. Can you tell me what these payments were for?"

"Who said I did? Can you prove that?"

"We have reason to believe that your nephew, PC Porter, was the person responsible for sabotaging the packaging which had been stored in our property store. Records show that immediately before this incident, a large sum of money had been paid into his bank account."

"I don't know anything about that. If he had a wad of cash, he could have got it from anywhere. You can't prove the ten thousand came from me."

"Oh, so you knew the amount?"

Roberts began wheezing and holding his chest. "I… I don't feel well," he said. "I'd like to rest now."

"We'll have a ten-minute break," Bainbridge said. "Do you require a doctor?"

"My client is clearly unwell," Duvall said. "I want this interview suspended indefinitely."

"Mr Roberts, do you want me to fetch a doctor?"

Roberts shook his head.

"I'll arrange for some tea," Bainbridge seethed, as he made to leave the room, followed by DC Beaumont.

"Get some tea sent in, will you?" Bainbridge asked. "I'm going to have a word with Sergeant Brown."

"Yes, sir," Beaumont replied, as he hurried away in the direction of the canteen.

79

Inspector Mason walked into reception at the same time as DCS Bainbridge.

"Ah, there you are, Jack. I was beginning to think you'd deserted us for the Durham police."

"I've just got back," Mason said. "I need to speak to you urgently, sir."

Bainbridge indicated for Mason to follow him into the sergeant's office. "What is it?"

"Terry Roberts has been spilling his guts out up in Durham. He's admitted getting a gun on the instruction of Freddie. He says Lee and Barry went after Paul and Denise." He handed Bainbridge a copy of Terry Roberts's statement. "It's all here, sir. Every last detail."

Bainbridge quickly perused the document. "This is good work, Mason. Very good work."

"Thank you, sir," Mason beamed with pride.

Bainbridge sighed. "I've got Freddie in custody at the moment. His lads are over at Middlesbrough waiting to be interrogated. I want you to get over there and start the interviews. I'll join you after I've finished with their old man."

"Don't you think we should bring Dyson into custody for his own protection?"

"Dyson's skipped Redcar early this morning. PC Jones was on surveillance and saw him place a suitcase in the car and head south. He's being followed down the motorway as we speak. It looks like he's heading for London."

"Christ! Things are moving fast," Mason gasped. "I'll get over to Middlesbrough and see what the Roberts brothers have got to say for themselves."

"See you this afternoon," Bainbridge said as Mason rushed out of the station, heading towards his car.

"Anything I can help you with, sir?" Sergeant Brown enquired, as Bainbridge plonked down on one of the two chairs in his office.

"Yes, sergeant. I'm expecting a package from Solomon Greaves Adoption Agency later this morning. I want you to sign for the package on my behalf."

Brown frowned. "Can I ask what it's about, sir?"

"I'm attempting to trace the whereabouts of a young woman whom I believe to be Shaun Dyson's sister. The Agency have been searching through their records in an attempt to find her."

"Of course, the kid he saved from the fire. I'd forgotten all about her," Brown said. "She must be in her twenties now."

"Twenty-three," Bainbridge said, "and possibly linked to the murders of Arthur Rhodes and Charlie Bull."

Sergeant Brown exhaled a soft whistle. "Bloody hell, I'll let you know as soon as it arrives."

"Thanks, Sergeant," Bainbridge said. "Make sure you keep it in your possession. Don't leave it lying on my desk."

"Very well, sir," the sergeant said.

"I'd better get back to Freddie Roberts and let him know his brother has well and truly dobbed him in it."

When Bainbridge and Beaumont returned to the interview room, Freddie had discarded the wheelchair and was sitting upright at the table next to George Duvall.

"Feeling better?" Bainbridge said as he took his seat and turned on the tape.

Roberts turned his head away and remained silent.

"Now, where were we?" Bainbridge said, looking at his notes. "Ah yes, you were going to tell me how your fingerprints were all over the packets of drugs we found inside your tote bag."

"Packets which you are unable to produce in evidence," countered Duvall, "and as my client has no recollection of that day, I suggest we move on."

"My colleagues have been interviewing your brother," Bainbridge said.

"Which brother? I have three."

"Your brother Terry," Bainbridge said. "It would be difficult to interview the other two as they're both dead."

Roberts huffed, but said nothing.

"We've also arrested Giles Nixon. You know Giles, don't you? He's the bloke who delivers the drugs around the north of England under the pretext of delivering Terry's dog supplies. Giles is singing like a bird."

"I don't know anything that Terry gets up to," he said.

"Oh, I think you do. In fact, I think you're involved right up to your neck."

"Prove it. You've got nothing."

Bainbridge held up Terry Roberts's statement. "Terry's not exactly the brains of the outfit, is he?" he said, glancing at the document. "I mean anyone stupid enough to catalogue every transaction is asking to be nicked."

"What do you mean? Catalogue every transaction?"

"Terry has been keeping a log of every delivery, didn't you know? Names, dates, quantities. It's all there, Freddie. And your name is right at the top of that list."

"You're lying. I don't believe you."

"Oh, it's true, and there's more. Much more. Terry told my colleagues you instructed him to get a gun."

Roberts inhaled deeply. "I don't know anything about a gun."

"We've located the gun and it's been confirmed that it is the same one used to shoot Paul and Denise Porter. Which one of your lads shot the Porters, Freddie? Do you know? They're both vicious little bastards, aren't they?"

Roberts gnashed his teeth. "You leave my lads alone, you bastard. They've done nothing, you hear. Nothing."

"They're being interviewed now," Bainbridge said. "We'll soon find out. Dealing in drugs is one thing, but killing a policeman, that's in a different league. It's a mandatory life sentence, did you know that? They'll never see daylight again."

Beads of sweat appeared on Robert's forehead. He wiped them away with the back of his hand.

"All right," he said, his voice trembling. "You win. It wasn't my lads who shot them, it was me. Now leave my lads alone."

"You couldn't shoot pool," Bainbridge scoffed. "You've barely left the house since your accident."

Roberts jumped to his feet and reaching over the desk, attempted to punch Bainbridge in the face. Bainbridge dodged to the side, grabbing Freddie's wrist.

"Sit down," he said. "You're in enough trouble without adding assaulting a police officer to the charge."

Breathless, Roberts sank back into his chair.

"I really must protest," Duvall said. "My client..."

"Shut up," Roberts said. "I've made my statement. I killed them."

"Tell me why?" Bainbridge said.

Roberts closed his eyes. His breathing became shallow. It was several minutes before he spoke. "Paul came to me about a year ago begging for a handout. He was in a terrible state. His wife squanders money like confetti. More was never enough."

"So, that's when you started demanding little favours from him?"

"Yeah. Nothing much at first, just the nod here and there. Then when the drugs ended up in the nick, I offered him ten thousand to destroy them. I gave him the acid solution and told him what to do."

"It must have been a shock when you realised, he was under suspicion."

"Like I said, the stupid bastard put the money I gave him straight into his bank to pay off a credit card debt Denise had run up. If he'd done what I told him and kept the money hidden, none of this would have happened."

"And once you knew he was under suspicion, you decided to get rid of him?"

"I'd no choice. The lad had no bottle. He would have led you straight to the family. I couldn't have that."

"But Paul was family too."

"He wasn't real family. He was related to that cow of a wife of mine. Besides he was a copper. You can never trust a copper. Everybody knows that."

Bainbridge turned to DC Beaumont. "Take Mr Roberts back to his cell," he said. "We'll resume this interview after I have spoken to his sons."

Roberts banged his fist on the table. "Leave my lads alone," he said. "I've told you it was me who killed Paul and Denise. It's nothing to do with them."

Bainbridge called into reception. Sergeant Brown was at the desk.

"Anything?" he said.

"No, sir," he said, "not yet."

"Very well, sergeant. I'm going over to Middlesbrough if anyone needs to contact me."

"Yes, sir," said the sergeant, "and good luck."

"Thanks," Bainbridge said as he hurried through the swing doors and out into the car park.

80

Jodie arrived at thirteen Walton Street, three o'clock that afternoon. She knocked briskly on the door and it was opened immediately by Leanne Dyson.

"Oh, it's you," Leanne said.

"I wanted to come round and pay my condolences," Jodie said. "I'm sorry I couldn't get to the funeral this morning, I had to work. Annika, one of the stylists has gone sick."

"Do you want to come in?"

"Thanks," Jodie said, as she followed Leanne into the lounge. "I can't stay long. I have to get back for a four o'clock appointment." She took off her coat and flung it on the back of a chair. "Maria sends her condolences. She'll get in touch in a day or two."

"This is my sister, Fi," Leanne said, indicating a fair-haired woman in her mid-thirties lounging on the couch holding a half-drunk bottle of Budweiser. "Fi, this is Jodie who I told you about. Her fella is a policeman."

"I just came to see how you were," Jodie said. "If there's anything I can do, Leanne. Anything at all."

"You can get your bloke and his mates to stop harassing our Shaun," Fi said. "The cops think he's responsible for everything that happens in Redcar. It's not fair." She lifted the bottle to her lips and drank the remaining liquid.

"Would you like a drink?" Leanne said, handing her a bottle of Budweiser. "I haven't got anything stronger I'm afraid."

"Thanks, this is fine," Jodie said, opening the bottle and putting it to her lips. "Where's Shaun? I thought he would be here with you."

"Our Shaun's gone," Fi said. "Somewhere the cops can't find him."

"Shut your gob, Fi," Leanne said. She turned to Jodie. "I don't know where Shaun is. He just wants to be by himself for a while. He's gutted about what happened to Arron. I don't think he'll ever get over it."

"I'm so sorry," Jodie soothed, gently patting Leanne's arm. "I meant what I said Leanne. If I can help you with anything."

"Thanks, but I have all the support I need with my family."

"Where is everybody? I thought they'd be here with you."

"They've gone to the pub for an hour. I've just about ran out of booze, but they'll be back soon."

"All right, love. If you're sure I can't do anything, I'd better get back." Jodie picked up her coat from the back of the chair. "Give me a call when you're up to it and I'll arrange for a night out. Me, you and Marie."

"Sounds good," Leanne said. "Book me in for my roots on Friday, will you?"

"Sure, I'll do them myself and there'll be no charge."

"Thanks," Leanne said. "I'll see you then."

Marie was waiting expectantly for Jodie when she returned. "How was she?" she asked. "Is Leanne all right?"

Jodie shrugged. "She says she's fine but… well I'm not sure. She didn't look at all well to me."

"What about Shaun? How is he coping?"

"Shaun wasn't there. Leanne said he's gone away for a few days. He's taken Arron's death hard."

The familiar 'buzz-buzz' sounded at the back of the salon.

"Oh, Mrs Java's perm is ready," Maria said. "I'd better get on."

"Have you heard any more from Annika?" Jodie asked. "What's supposed to be wrong with her?"

"She rang in yesterday to say she wasn't feeling well and needed a couple of days off. I've rang her a few times today, but got no reply."

"Maybe she's sleeping."

"Maybe she's skiving," said Marie. "I'm going over to her house tonight to see for myself."

81

Inspector Mason had just finished a 'no comment' interview with Lee Roberts, the youngest of the two brothers. Frustrated, he watched as Lee was led away back to his cell.

"Let's speak to Barry next," he said, addressing PC Jackson who had been present throughout the interview. "Maybe he'll be more forthcoming."

"Yes, sir," the constable said. "Barry said he doesn't want a solicitor either, like his brother."

"Perhaps he'll change his mind when we present him with the evidence."

Jackson left the room, returning a few minutes later with Barry Roberts.

"I remind you that you are still under caution," Mason warned as Barry threw himself onto the chair across from the metal table.

Roberts remained silent.

"It's not too late to request a solicitor," Mason advised.

"Why would I want a solicitor? I've done nothing wrong and you can't prove I have."

He folded his arms across his chest in a gesture of defiance. "Now ask your questions and stop wasting my time."

There was a sharp rap on the interview door and Bainbridge entered the room.

"For the benefit of the tape," Mason said, "DCS Bainbridge has now entered the room."

Bainbridge did not sit at the table, instead he chose to stand by the small, barred window. "So, you're Barry Roberts?" he said. "I was hoping you and I would meet."

Roberts raised an eyebrow. "Well, now you've met me. So what?"

"I've just left your father," Bainbridge said. "He's not looking at all well."

Roberts jumped to his feet. "You leave my dad alone! He's done nothing."

"Well, that's not strictly true, is it Barry? Now sit down and listen carefully to what I have to say." Barry returned to his chair and plonked down heavily. "That's better," Bainbridge said. "I've interviewed your father earlier today. He's made a statement admitting he killed Paul and Denise Porter."

"Bollocks. Dad did no such thing."

"Then if he didn't, who did? I don't think Freddie would take the blame for anyone else, do you?"

"Dad's not well. He doesn't know what he's saying."

"He seemed of perfectly sound mind to me. When I get back to Redcar, Freddie's going to be charged with Paul and Denise Porter's murder."

"You've no proof. Where's your proof?"

"Your Uncle Terry has provided us with all the proof we need. He's been singing like a bird. He's told us all about how Freddie instructed him to get a gun and..."

"You stupid bastard. Terry got the gun for me. It was me who shot Paul and his missus, not dad."

"Well, while you're in the mood for confessing, perhaps you can fill me in on who killed Benji Myers? Was that you?"

"No, it bloody wasn't. That was Shaun Dyson."

"How do you know it was Shaun?"

"I know because he told my dad. He also killed some old hag who had witnessed what had happened in Benji's shop."

"You heard him confess to that?"

"Yeah. Dad recorded him on his phone. Dyson was shit scared because he still hadn't found what he was looking for."

"And what exactly was he looking for?"

Barry shrugged, but remained silent.

"I take it what he was looking for was your dad's tote bag. The tote bag containing a large amount of heroin."

"Dyson stole it. He bashed Dad over the head and took it. Everybody knows that. Dad said he'd better return it or else there would be consequences."

"What sort of consequences?"

"What do you think?

"Barry, your whole family are in deep shit and the more obstructive you get, the harder it's going to be to get out of it. Do you understand? Now, be sensible. I need you to make a statement setting out exactly what happened going back to the day your dad was attacked. Do you think you can do that?"

Barry huffed. "Do I have a choice?"

"No, son, you don't" Bainbridge smiled. "Inspector Mason will take your statement."

82

It's all going wrong.

It's not supposed to be like this.

No-one's supposed to know about me. It's the fault of Bainbridge and that bitch Sophie. Especially Sophie.

If it wasn't for her, nobody would know anything about me.

I have to put this right. Teach her she can't interfere in people's lives without there being consequences.

And there will be consequences.

You can count on that.

83

Carrying a large bouquet of red and pink roses, Jack arrived home at seven o'clock that night. Annika was curled up on the couch watching television.

"Darling, I'm home," Jack said as he entered the lounge.

Annika got to her feet and rushed over to Jack, throwing her arms around his neck in an intimate embrace. "At last," she said. "I've missed you, darling."

"I've missed you too," Jack said, throwing the flowers onto an armchair as he embraced his wife. "Sorry it took a little longer than I thought it would, but we have the result we wanted."

"Oh?"

"Barry Roberts has admitted shooting Paul and Denise Porter and setting fire to their car."

"That's great news," Annika said.

"Ah, but that's not all. Freddie has implicated Shaun Dyson in the murder of Benji Myers and Sheila Thompson. The Met are about to pick him up."

"The Met?"

"Shaun's been followed to London. They should be making the arrest any time now."

Annika scowled. "Can you believe anything the Roberts family say? After all, they're all criminals."

"We've got the evidence," Jack said as he walked to the drinks cabinet. "Can I get you anything?"

Annika rushed over to her husband. "You sit down, Jack. I'll get the drinks," she said. "You must be exhausted. What'll it be?"

"Whisky," Jack said. "A large one."

It was seven-fifteen when the doorbell rang. Annika went through into the hall to open the door. She was surprised to see Maria on the doorstep.

"I've come to see how you are," Maria said. "I've been trying to get in touch with you all day. I was worried about you."

"I'm all right," Annika said. "It was just a nasty tummy bug. I should be fine tomorrow."

"That's good news. It's been manic in the salon." Maria moved forward in an attempt to get into the hall, but Annika barred her path. "Whilst I'm here, perhaps I could say hello to your husband? Jack, isn't it? I always like to meet my staff's other half."

"Jack's in the shower," she said. "Then he's having an early night. He's had a rough couple of days."

Maria looked disappointed as she moved back onto the step. "Never mind," she said, "I'm sure I'll meet him another time." She turned and began to walk down the drive to her car. "See you tomorrow," she called.

"Good night, Maria," Annika said as she firmly shut the door.

84

Climbing up the drain pipe and forcing the lock of the French doors to gain entry was easy.

The apartment was deserted. Empty clothes hangers were scattered on the bed.

So, the bitch has got away this time? Probably staying with her lover. He can't keep her safe though. Nobody can.

I can picture them now, huddled together over a glass of red wine, concocting ways to trap me.

How stupid people can be. They'll never catch me. I thought they'd have realised that by now.

No matter. There's work to be done here. A message to be left that even a criminal psychologist can understand.

85

Bainbridge was at Redcar police station at seven-thirty the following morning. Sergeant Brown was at the front desk.

"I take it our visitor has arrived safely?" asked Bainbridge.

"Yes sir. Dyson was delivered by the Met at four o'clock this morning."

"Has he requested a solicitor?"

"He rang Melvyn Kendall as soon as he got here," Brown said. "Kendall will be here at nine o'clock."

Bainbridge huffed as he made his way up the stairs to his office. "Get someone to bring me a cup of tea, will you sergeant?" he said, "and send Inspector Mason up to my office as soon as he arrives."

"Very good, sir."

It was eight-forty-five when Inspector Mason entered Bainbridge's office. He looked pale and slightly dishevelled.

"Good morning, sir," he said. "Sorry I'm late."

Bainbridge raised an eyebrow in annoyance. "I was hoping to discuss strategy before we interview Dyson," he said. "Kendall's already here."

Mason grabbed the back of the chair for support. "I'm sorry," he said, "I… I really don't feel well." He gasped and sank to his knees, clutching his chest. Bainbridge rushed towards him.

"What is it, Jack? What's wrong?"

Mason began panting. His body trembled violently as beads of sweat formed on his brow. "Doctor," he whispered. "I… I need a doctor."

An ambulance was called to take Mason to James Cooke Hospital. PC Walker got into the ambulance with him.

"Let me know the minute there's any news," Bainbridge ordered.

"Yes, sir!"

Bainbridge went into reception. Sergeant Brown was looking concerned.

"Is he going to be all right, sir?" he asked. "I thought the inspector was unwell when I saw the way he parked his car this morning." He nodded in the direction of the car park where Jack's Audi was parked at an obscure angle. "When he came into the station, he looked like he was in some kind of trance."

Bainbridge sighed. "Let's hope he's going to be all right," he said. "Where's Beaumont, by the way? I need him to assist me interviewing Dyson."

"I believe he's having breakfast in the canteen," the sergeant said, picking up the internal phone. "I'll tell him to come down to the interview room right away."

Dyson was sitting at the metal table when Bainbridge and Beaumont entered the room. Dyson looked exhausted with dark circles beneath his eyes. Sitting beside him was his solicitor, Melvyn Kendall.

The police officers took their seat at the table. Beaumont administered the caution and turning on the tape, introduced all those present.

"Before we begin," Kendall said, "my client wishes to make a statement."

"Oh?" Bainbridge said. "What is it your client wishes to say?"

"It was me," Dyson said. "I killed Benji Myers. I didn't mean to kill him. It was self-defence."

"You hit him over the head with what we think was a hammer," Bainbridge said. "That was no accident."

"It was Benji's hammer," Dyson said. "He kept it under the counter. He knew I would be coming looking for him so he kept it there for protection."

"I think you'd better start at the beginning, Shaun."

Dyson began to rock backwards and forwards in his chair. Slowly at first, then gradually faster. His breathing became erratic as tears began to roll down his cheeks.

"When I robbed Freddie Roberts, I hid his tote bag at the steelworks. I intended to go back when the heat had died down a bit and get the bag."

"But Benji got there first, eh?"

"Before I had the chance to retrieve it, I got nicked and sent down for assault. I told Leanne where the bag was hidden. She went to get it but the bag had gone."

"So, how did you know it was Benji and Arthur who had taken it?"

"Who else could it have been? The site was deserted, almost derelict. They were the only two still working there." He took out a handkerchief, wiped his eyes then blew his nose loudly. "Leanne went round to Benji's shop and told him she knew he had nicked the bag."

"What did Benji say to that?"

"He picked up the hammer and said if she wanted to keep her teeth she'd better get out of the shop and stay out."

"What about Arthur? Did she pay him a visit too?"

"Arthur said he knew nothing about it and shut the door in her face."

"So, when you got out of the nick, you decided to get the bag back, right?"

"Too bloody right I did. I went to Benji's off-licence. As soon as he saw me, he grabbed the hammer and came at me. Unfortunately for him, he tripped and fell down. I picked up the hammer and… well, you know the rest."

"So, he never said where the bag was?"

Dyson shook his head.

"Tell me about Sheila Thompson."

"That drunken waste of space? She was outside the shop and saw what I did through the window. She telephoned me later that night threatening to tell the police what she had seen unless I gave her fifty quid."

"So, what happened?"

"I told her to meet me at the boating lake near Majuba and I would give her the money."

"But you didn't give her the money, did you? You killed her instead."

"Sheila was a greedy cow. We'd agreed fifty quid, but after she heard Benji was dead, she demanded more. Much more."

"So, you lured her to the lake and killed her? I suppose that was an accident too?"

Shaun ran his tongue across his dry lips. "If the stupid bitch had kept to our agreement, none of this would have happened. It's her fault she's dead. Not mine."

Kendall placed his hand on Dyson's arm. "Careful, Shaun," he said. "You..."

Dyson pushed him away. "No, it's true. Sheila Thompson was a useless drunk. In time she would have bled me dry."

Bainbridge exhaled. "Tell me about Arthur Rhodes."

Dyson shrugged. "That was nothing to do with me. I have an alibi."

"So you do," Bainbridge said. "In that case, tell me about your sister."

Dyson's posture stiffened. "I don't know what you mean," he said. "What sister?"

"The one whose life you saved when you threw her from your bedroom window when your father had set fire to the house."

"She got adopted. I don't know where she is."

"Oh, I think you do, Shaun. I think she's the one who's been helping you."

"What do you mean, helping me? Nobody's been helping me."

Kendall banged his fist down on the table. "I really must protest," he said. "My client has answered your questions. He doesn't know the whereabouts of any sister."

"Did you find her or did she find you?" Bainbridge persisted. "If I were to make a guess, I would say it was her who made the initial contact. How did you feel, seeing her again after all these years?"

"That's enough," Kendall said. "This line of questioning is totally inappropriate."

"When did you realise that she was just as capable of murdering someone as you and your father had been? She did a proper job on Arthur Rhodes, didn't she? I bet that made you proud. And then poor Charlie Bull. Little sister protecting the family honour?"

Shaun leant back in his chair, putting his hands behind his head, a broad grin on his face. "She's got you lot chasing your own arse," he smirked. "You think what she did to Arthur and Charlie was gross? You haven't seen anything yet."

Kendall tutted. "Mr Dyson, I must advise you that..."

"Oh, shut the fuck up," Dyson gloated. "I'm enjoying myself watching these clowns running round in circles." He threw back his head and began to laugh. A loud, raucous laugh.

"What do you mean, we haven't seen anything yet? What is your sister planning next?"

"You'll see soon enough." He turned to Kendall. "I've finished here," he said. "I want to go back to my cell."

86

At seven o'clock that evening, Jack Mason was sitting up in a hospital bed eating steamed fish and vegetables. Annika was by his side.

"Have the doctors said what caused your seizure?" she said. "It wasn't a stroke, was it?"

"The doctor doesn't think it was anything like that. They've taken samples for toxicology. The results won't be back until sometime tomorrow."

"The doctor said you can come home tomorrow. A few days of bedrest and you'll be good as new."

"Sorry, love, but I won't have time for bedrest. When I get out of here, I'm going straight back to the office."

"Don't be ridiculous. You're not well. You need to get better before you think of going back to work."

Jack reached out and took Annika's hand in his. "Stop worrying, I'll be fine. It was probably something I had eaten which made me ill. Whatever it was, we'll know tomorrow."

"Let's hope so. Anyway, I must be going. I've..."

"Annika, there is something I wanted to ask you. Something you said about Arthur Rhodes."

"Oh, what was that? I don't even know the man."

"You commented on his eyes being gouged. Who told you about that? That information was supposed to have been kept under wraps."

"You did, darling. Don't you remember?"

Jack shook his head. "No, I'm sure I didn't. Bainbridge specifically asked that the details of Arthur's assault should not be disclosed."

"Well, if you didn't tell me, it must have been Jodie. She's always repeating what Wayne tells her about his work." Leaning over, she kissed Jack on the forehead. "I'll call for you tomorrow," she said. "Goodnight, darling."

87

It was eight o'clock that night when Sophie parked her car outside her apartment and removed the small suitcase from the boot. Staying at Andy's had been a knee-jerk reaction after the break-in, but it wasn't the solution, she knew that. She climbed the stairs to the first-floor and opened the door to her apartment.

Stepping inside, she gasped at the chaotic scene before her. "Oh, my god," she said. "This can't be happening." She quickly closed the door and rushed downstairs back to her car. She phoned Andy immediately.

"What is it, Sophie?" Andy said. "What's wrong?"

"My apartment, it's… it's been wrecked."

"Stay there, I'm on my way. Don't touch anything."

"I'm in my car," she said as tears began to trickle down her cheeks. "Andy, I'm scared. I'm being targeted by that mad bitch."

"Don't let's jump to conclusions just yet," Andy said. "Stay in your car and lock the doors. I'll be there soon. I'm bringing Cutts with me."

"Hurry," she said. "Please hurry."

After telephoning Leo Cutts, Andy rushed out of his office and through reception.

"Sir," Sergeant Brown said, "this came for you a few minutes ago. It's from Solomon Greaves."

"Hold on to it sergeant," he said striding towards the exit. "I have something urgent to take care of."

On sight of Andy's vehicle, Sophie got out of her car. She looked pale and frightened as she flung her arms around his neck.

"Thank god you're here," she said. "The mess is unbelievable in there."

Andy hugged her, then led her back to her vehicle. "You stay in your car and keep the door locked," he said. "Cutts should be here any minute."

Sophie handed Andy her keys. "It's her, isn't it?" she said. "She's coming after me next. I know she is."

"Sophie, I… oh, here's Cutts," Andy said. "I'm going up with him. You stay in the car; you'll be quite safe."

"Okay," Sophie said, climbing back into her vehicle and locking the doors behind her. "Be careful, Andy."

Clad in white forensic suits, Bainbridge and Leo Cutts entered the building.

"Wow, whoever did this has done a thorough job," Cutts said, gazing around the lounge. Furniture had been ripped open and overturned, ceramics and glass had been smashed and strewn over the carpet. Pictures had been ripped from the walls and green paint had been sprayed over everything. The kitchen and bedroom had received a similar fate.

Cutts made his way into the bathroom where the basin had been ripped from the wall and the shower screen smashed. "Ah," he said. "It looks like the intruder got cut during this mayhem. There are a few drops of blood on the floor." He indicated a small red stain on the tiled floor. "I should be able to get DNA from there."

"Quick as you can," Bainbridge said.

"Coming back here again, it's déjà vu, except this time they've left me a big fat clue," Cutts said, a broad grin on his face, as he opened his forensics case.

"I'm going down to speak with Sophie," Bainbridge said.

"That's fine, sir. The rest of my team should be arriving any time."

Bainbridge approached Sophie's vehicle and she wound down the window.

"Tell me the place is full of fingerprints," she said.

"Better than that," Andy said. "It looks like whoever was in your apartment has cut themselves. There are traces of blood on the bathroom floor. We should get their DNA soon."

"I hope you're right, Andy. I don't know how much more of this I can take."

"Go back to mine," Andy said. "I'll be there shortly. I have to collect something from the station first."

"All right," Sophie said, "but please don't be too long. I'm scared. I'm really scared."

88

Half-an-hour later, Andy was sitting next to Sophie in his lounge drinking red wine and reading the report from Solomon Greaves.

"It seems Shaun Dyson's baby sister, Joanne Connolly, was a troubled child," he said. "She caused mayhem in Dubai where she was accused of attempting to burn down the school."

"Ah, so that's why the Connolly's moved back to Europe?" Sophie said. "I did wonder."

"It seems her step-mother, Rosa, was Italian. When they left Dubai, they moved to Rome. They moved in with Rosa's sister. Unfortunately, it looks like Joanne's bad behaviour did not improve. In the end she was sent to a 'special school'."

"What sort of special school?"

"A type of institution they have in Italy for unruly kids. Short, sharp shock treatment, that sort of thing. We had something similar in the UK until a few years back when it was abandoned, more's the pity."

Sophie sighed, but said nothing.

"When Joanna was sixteen, she absconded. Nobody's seen or heard from her since."

"What about the adoptive parents? Are they still alive?"

"According to this, they both died when their car went over a cliff on the Amalfi coast road."

"Was the incident treated as suspicious?"

"There was nothing to indicate foul play, but there were a lot of questions unanswered."

"Such as?"

"Both victims were still in their nightwear for one thing, and nobody could explain what they were doing on that road in the middle of the night. The car they were in caught fire so there was no DNA to suggest a third party's involvement."

"Even so, it does look… it does look suspicious."

"I agree, but I don't think there's anything we can do about it now. Do you?"

"What I was wondering is how Joanne would know to come here to Redcar to be with her brother?"

"These days everything is recorded," Andy said. "I'm sure it wouldn't have been difficult for her to find out about her past, and the fact that she had a brother."

"A brother who saved her life," Sophie said. "That would create a special bond between them."

"A special but deadly bond. By the way, I didn't tell you Jack Mason was taken ill in the office today."

"Oh? What's the problem?"

"No idea. He came in looking like shit, then more or less collapsed. The medics don't think it was a heart attack but… they'll know more tomorrow when the get the test results. They're keeping him in overnight for observation."

"The workload you're under must be tremendous," Sophie said. "You've got confessions for two murders here in Redcar, then the shooting of PC and Mrs Porter in Sunderland. It's getting just like it did before, Andy."

"There are still two unsolved killings don't forget," Andy said. "Those of Arthur Rhodes and Charlie Bull. We know they couldn't have been committed by Dyson."

"Well, I'm sure you'll solve them," Sophie said, supressing a yawn. "I think I'll turn in. The sooner todays finished with the better."

Andy leant over and kissed her gently on her forehead. "You go up, love," he said. "I want to read through this report again. Make sure I haven't missed anything."

Sophie walked towards the hall. "Goodnight," she said. "My brave knight in shining armour."

Andy smiled. "Goodnight, Sophie," he said. "See you tomorrow."

89

It was nine o'clock the following morning when Jack Mason got to the station. He went straight up to DCS Bainbridge's office.

"Jack, good to see you up and about, but are you sure you should be working so soon?"

"I'm fine," Jack said. "Whatever it was I ate has passed through my system. I still feel a bit weak, but I'm ready to get back to work."

"That's good to hear," Bainbridge said. "Take a seat. I'll fill you in on developments."

Mason drew up a chair to the desk and sat down.

"It appears Dyson has had help from his sister. A woman known as Joanne Connolly."

"Do we know this for certain?"

"As certain as we can be. That smarmy little git, Dyson, as much as admitted it."

"And we've no idea who this woman is?"

Bainbridge shook his head. "We know she's a killer. A vicious killer. I believe she's responsible for wrecking Sophie's apartment the other night."

"Is Sophie all right?"

"Yes. She was staying at mine when the break-in happened, thank god."

"But why would she come after Sophie? It doesn't make sense."

"It does if she knew Sophie was helping me. In fact, it was Sophie who first came up with the possibility that Dyson's sister could be involved."

"But how would Joanne know that?"

"She wouldn't unless… unless someone told her."

"Surely you don't think she got information from someone involved in the investigation?"

"If you can think of any other way she could have found out, I'd be happy to hear it," Bainbridge said.

"I'm sorry, sir, but this doesn't make any sense to me. What do we know about this woman, Joanne Connolly?"

"We know that as a child she spent time in Dubai. We also know she was suspected of attempting to burn down her school."

"Anything else?"

"She moved with her adoptive parents to Rome, her mother was Italian. She spent time in some sort of institution for her untoward behaviour. When she was sixteen, she absconded and shortly afterwards, both her adoptive parents were killed in a car crash on the Amalfi coast road."

"You think the girl was responsible?"

Bainbridge shrugged, "Who knows? The car exploded on impact so there was no evidence to say exactly what happened, but it does look suspicious."

"Do we have any idea where this woman is? Any idea at all?"

"None. I don't think we will find her," he said. "We're going to have to wait until she finds us and hope we're ready for her."

90

After a brief appearance in Middlesbrough Court, Shaun was transferred to Durham Prison later that day to await his trial for murder. Leanne was released on bail, pending further enquiries. As she left the police station, a familiar figure was standing across the street. Leanne rushed over to join her.

"Are you alright?" Jodie asked. "I heard you and Shaun had been arrested."

"The bastards are charging him with murdering Benji. What am I going to do? They can't lock him up, not my Shaun."

"Come on, love. My car's parked down the alley. I'll drive you home."

"Home? It's not my home anymore, not without Shaun. It was bad enough losing Arron, but to lose Shaun too. I can't bear it."

Both women got into Jodie's car and she drove in the direction of Walton Street.

"What does your solicitor think? Can he get him off?"

"Kendall? He's bloody useless. Shaun got stitched up by that bastard, Freddie Roberts and his lads. They're getting done for murdering that copper and his missus up in Sunderland."

"Bloody hell," Jodie said. "It's getting like the wild west around here."

Leanne sniffed. "Can't you find out what's going on from that policeman you're shacked up with? He'll know what's happening."

"Me and Wayne are… well, I don't know what we are. Wayne hasn't been home for the last couple of nights and he won't take my calls."

"He's dumped you?"

Jodie shrugged. "It looks like it. He's been acting weird for days."

"You need to get him back, Jodie. Do what you have to but you have to get him back. He can be useful."

The car pulled up outside Leanne's house.

"Do you want to come in?" Leanne offered, getting out of the car.

"I can't, love. I have to get to work. My shift starts in half-an-hour."

Leanne shrugged. "Okay," she said. "Thanks for the lift and don't forget to make up with Wayne."

Jodie smiled weakly. "I'll try," she said. "I'll try."

91

Jack Mason was in his office when his mobile rang. It was the hospital.

"Sorry, I missed you this morning," Dr Simpson apologised. "I understand you discharged yourself early."

"That's right, doctor. I'm feeling absolutely fine this morning and I had to get back to work."

"I would have liked to have had a chat with you first," the doctor said. "Face to face as it were."

"You've found out what caused me to black out like that?"

"The test results have just come in. They're worrying, Mr Mason. Extremely worrying."

"Oh? I thought it was a dodgy prawn sandwich from the canteen."

"No, it was nothing like that."

"Then what?"

"Mr Mason, we have found traces of chloral hydrate."

"Chloral hydrate? I don't understand. That's a type of anaesthetic, isn't it?"

"Something like that," the doctor said. "What I do not understand is what it was doing in your system?"

"I've absolutely no idea," Jack said. "Are you absolutely sure? You can't be mistaken?"

"There's no mistake, I assure you," the doctor said. "There were also traces of alcohol. I presume this is how it was administered."

"That's nonsense," Jack said. "I only had one glass of whisky that night."

"Who gave you the whisky?"

"I poured it myself," Jack said. "I…"

The phone went silent.

"Mr Mason, are you still there?"

Jack raced through reception and out into the car park. Jumping into his Audi he headed towards the seafront. He pulled up a few minutes later outside Maria's Salon.

"Where's Annika?" he said to Maria, who was shampooing a client's hair.

Maria scowled. "Who are you?" she said, "and what do you want with my stylist?"

"I'm her husband," Jack said, looking around the salon. "Where is she?"

"Annika's still off sick," Maria said. "I thought you would have known that."

Jodie rushed over to Jack. "Is anything wrong, Jack? "I'm Jodie, Wayne's girlfriend."

"I need to find my wife," he said. "It's urgent."

"Isn't she at home?"

"I've tried ringing, but there's no reply," he said. "I have to find her."

"Well, you can see she's not here," Maria said. "She hasn't been in most of the week."

Jack gave one last look around the salon, then strode to the door. Jodie followed.

"Are you alright?" she said. "You look awful."

Jack ignored her as, making his way to his Audi, he drove off in the direction of home.

***

The house was deserted. Jack rushed upstairs to the bedroom. He could see at once that Annikas clothes were missing from the wardrobes and drawers. Propped up on the dressing table was a white envelope with the word 'Jack' scrawled across it. Jack ripped it open and took out the one sheet of paper which it contained. He perched on the edge of the bed and began to read.

'Darling Jack, my sweet. naïve, unsuspecting Jack. I'm sure you would have worked it out for yourself eventually that it is me you've been looking for all this time. I'm the one who killed Arthur Rhodes and Charlie Bull.

I'm sorry I had to drug you the evening I went to see Arthur, but you would have asked too many questions about where I was going. The stubborn old bastard wouldn't say where the drugs were hidden. I gave him every opportunity. But then he turned. He went for me. He tried to kill me with his stick. I was only defending myself.

I hope you can understand that, my love. It was him or me. But let's go back to the beginning. To the day I discovered I had a big brother. A brother who had saved my life at the risk of his own. When I found out about Shaun, I had to meet him, to get to know him. I wrote to him in prison a few times, but that wasn't enough for me. I had to meet him. To be close to him. That's why I persuaded you to come to Redcar.

When Shaun was released, I met up with him every week. It was our little secret. When his son was killed by Charlie Bull, Shaun was devastated. It was left to me to get revenge. I'm sorry I had to drug you again, Jack. I meant you no harm, but I had no choice.

The compulsion to kill the bastard who had caused harm to Shaun was too great. I hope you can understand that. I should tell you I have taken all the money from our bank account. I hope you'll forgive me. I will send you the money back sometime in the future, believe me. I'm a lot of things, Jack, but I'm not a thief.

I'm sorry to have to be leaving in a way. We have a comfortable life here, but my brother has to come first. You need to set him free. I'm begging you to persuade Bainbridge to set him free. We'll leave and you'll never see either of us again. I give you my word on that. Goodbye my love. I'll probably never see you again but remember,

I do love you in my own way. Love Annika."

Breathing erratically, Jack made his way downstairs and plonked into an armchair, his head lowered, resting in his hands. He sat motionless for several minutes, beads of sweat running slowly down his face. He felt numb. He could hear his heart thumping in his chest. Slowly he got to his feet and meandered across the room towards the front door. He turned, looked around the hall and then opened the front door, locking it behind him.

92

Bainbridge was on the telephone when Inspector Mason arrived at his office.

"That's great news," he said. "Great news."

He put the phone down and turned to Mason. "That was Leo Cutts," he said. "The DNA in blood we found in Sophie's bathroom has definite similarities to Dyson. We can safely assume that it was Joanne Connolly who trashed Sophie's apartment."

Mason, looking pale and tense, remained silent.

"Are you all right, Jack? You still look a bit peaky to me."

"Sir, I… I have something to tell you. Something that is so horrible I can't believe it myself."

Bainbridge leant forward, steepling his fingers. "What is it, Jack?"

"It's Annika," Mason said. "I… I think she's Dyson's sister."

"Annika? That's ridiculous. She's… well, she's your wife for goodness sake. Surely, you'd know if you were living with a creature like Joanne Connolly?"

Jack began to slowly rock backwards and forwards on the chair, biting into his bottom lip.

"What makes you suspect Annika is involved?"

"I know she was the one who sedated me the night Sophie's flat was trashed," he said. "The doctor rang me this morning. He said my system showed traces of chloral hydrate."

"And you're sure it was your wife who administered the drug?"

"It couldn't have been anyone else. According to the doctor, the drug was mixed with alcohol. Annika poured me a whisky that night." He removed the envelope containing Annika's letter from his pocket. "Then there's this," he said, handing it to Bainbridge. "It's all in there."

Frowning, Bainbridge read the letter. "Where is she now, do you know?"

Jack shook his head. "I've no idea. I've been to the salon, but she's been off sick for a few days. I've checked the house, but she's gone. She's taken all her clothes and emptied the bank account."

"We'll have to get a sample of her DNA," Bainbridge said.

"I've already done that," Jack said. Opening his briefcase, he handed Bainbridge a hairbrush. "This is Annika's. I'm sure Cutts can get her DNA from that."

Bainbridge took the hairbrush and put it into an evidence bag he had in his desk drawer.

"There's something else," Jack said. "Something I should have picked up on much earlier."

"Oh? What's that?"

"Yesterday, Annika was talking about the attack on Arthur Rhodes. She mentioned that both his eyes had been gouged."

"How would she know that? You sure you hadn't mentioned the injuries to her?"

"I'm positive I didn't. I still have nightmares about the poor man's injuries. There was no way I would discuss his injuries with my wife. Besides, you gave firm instructions the extent of his injuries were to remain confidential."

Bainbridge leant back in his chair and inhaled deeply. "Jack, I'm sorry, but I'm going to have to take you off the case. You can't possibly stay involved with this enquiry."

"I understand," Mason said. "I will offer my resignation with immediate effect."

"There's no need for that," Bainbridge said, "not yet. What we have to do is figure out what her next move will be. Do you have any ideas?"

"None," Jack said. "Until I heard about the chloral hydrate, I never suspected a thing."

"Tell me what you know about Annika's background."

"I don't know much," Jack said, "in fact it's surprising how little I do know about her. Annika told me her adoptive parents were dead and she had no siblings. She didn't like to talk about her past really."

"So, you took everything at face value?"

"I know this looks bad, but I had no reason to doubt what she told me. Annika's a beautiful young woman. I fell in love with her, we got married two months after we met."

"Tell me again why you came from Leeds to Redcar? Was it your idea or hers?"

Jack was hesitant for a moment. "I suppose it was hers," he said at last. "Annika said she had always wanted to live by the sea and when she saw, on Force Orders, that there was a vacancy for an inspector in Redcar, she insisted I apply."

"Were you in favour of the move?"

Jack shrugged. "I'd no preference," he said. "I enjoyed the hustle and bustle of the city, but Annika convinced me that the Redcar posting was a good career move."

"Did Annika have any friends in Redcar? Anyone she saw on a regular basis."

Jack pouted in concentration, "Not really," he said. "There were her colleagues in the salon of course, but apart from them… Oh wait, there was the weekly Book Club. She enjoyed going there."

"Book Club? Where was that held?"

"The Galleon," Jack said. "Eight o'clock every Monday."

Bainbridge exhaled. "Well, it might interest you to know that every Monday at The Galleon, they hold an 'open mic' session. There's no way you could hold a book club there at the same time."

"I… I don't understand," Jack said. "Annika went without fail every Monday night."

"I'm sure she went somewhere," Bainbridge said, "but I can assure you it was not a book club at The Galleon."

93

Sophie Barrett arrived at The Parkside Bar & Grill at exactly twelve-fifteen. As she entered the dining room, Annika was already seated at a table by the window.

"Hi, Annika," she said. "It was a nice surprise, your invite for lunch today."

"I wanted to meet you again," she said. "The last meeting was a bit rushed really, wasn't it? We didn't really have the chance for a proper chat."

"I suppose not," Sophie said, "but we all have busy lives. We don't always have time for the things we would like to do."

The waiter came to the table.

"I'll have the salmon," Annika said. "What about you, Sophie?"

"Salmon sounds good," Sophie agreed.

"I've already ordered a bottle of Shiraz," Annika said as she began to pour out two glasses.

Sophie raised her hand in protest. "I'm working this afternoon," she said. "I really shouldn't be drinking red wine."

"Oh rubbish. A small glass won't hurt you," Annika said, handing Sophie a glass. "Cheers." Sophie took a sip of the wine.

"Annika, is there something in particular you want to discuss with me?" Sophie said as she sipped her wine. "Is there anything bothering you?"

"What makes you ask that?"

"You seem a little… a little tense, as if you have something on your mind."

"Nonsense. I just thought maybe we got off on the wrong foot at our last meeting, that's all."

"In what way?"

Annika shrugged. "I don't know, just a feeling, I guess. How's things going with you and Andy?"

"We're fine," Sophie said, taking another sip of her wine. "Why do you ask?"

"I got the impression he's very fond of you."

"I'm fond of him," she said.

"I was thinking maybe… Sophie are you alright?"

She rushed to Sophie's side and grabbed her arm "You look terrible," she said. "Let's go outside and get some air."

Sophie's head lolled to one side as she allowed herself to be steered out of the restaurant by Annika.

"My car's just over there," Annika said as they made their way across the street to her Fiesta. "Get in, Sophie and I'll take you to the hospital."

94

It was three-thirty in the afternoon. Bainbridge was busy in his office when his mobile rang.

"Bainbridge!" he answered distractedly, one eye on the report in front of him.

"I'm sorry to bother you, Mr Bainbridge," said the caller. "My name's Veronica Harper, I'm a colleague of Sophie Barrett."

Bainbridge put down the document, giving his full attention to the caller. "What's happened? Is Sophie all right?"

"I'm not sure," Veronica said. "She hasn't returned from lunch. She's missed two appointments this afternoon. It's just not like her. I'm worried."

"I presume you've tried her phone?"

"Yes of course, but it's been switched off."

"Did Sophie say where she was going for lunch?"

"Her secretary said she received a phone call this morning from some woman inviting her to lunch at The Parkside. I've tried telephoning them, but got no reply. I think they close in the afternoon."

Bainbridge strode to the door. "Ring me straight away if she contacts you," he said, as he raced down the stairs, two at a time.

It took nearly five minutes of constant banging on the door of The Parkside before someone made an appearance.

"We're closed," the man said. "We open again at six."

Bainbridge took out his warrant card and held it to the glass door. The man opened the door immediately.

"What is it?" he said. "What's happened.?"

"Two women had lunch here today just after twelve," Bainbridge said. "Do you remember them?"

The man shrugged. "It's been a busy day. There've been lots of women in here."

"The older of the two women had auburn hair. The younger one was blonde."

"Oh yes, I remember them. They ordered salmon but before it could be served, the older lady took a turn. To be honest, she looked terrible. Her friend helped her to her car and said she was taking her to the hospital."

"What time did they leave, can you remember?"

"Just before twelve-thirty," the man said.

Bainbridge turned and rushed from the restaurant. He headed straight to Walton Street. He hammered on the door of number thirteen. He could hear bolts being drawn back before the door was finally open. Leanne glared at her visitor.

"What the fuck do you want?" she said.

Bainbridge roughly pushed her into the house, closing the door behind him.

"Where is she?" he demanded.

"Where's who?"

He brought back his right hand and slapped her across the face. “Don’t fuck with me, you scummy bitch,” he shouted. “Where’s Joanne?”

Leanne winced in pain as she tried to free herself from Bainbridge’s tight grip. “Get off me,” she yelled. “Get out of my house.”

Bainbridge put his hand around her throat and shook her violently. “Where is she? I won’t ask you again.”

Leanne tried to scream, but Bainbridge put his hand over her mouth, pressing hard. She struggled to free herself from his grasp, but ended up on her knees with Bainbridge’s large, strong hand around her throat.

She tried to speak. “I… I don’t know,” she managed to say. Bainbridge brought his other hand crashing down once more across her face.

“Yes, you do know,” he snarled. “Where is she?”

Tears rolled down Leanne’s face. “You bastard. You’ll pay for this,” she sobbed.

“Probably, but not before you tell me where she is.”

He brought his fist back as if to strike her once more.

“All right,” she begged. “Please stop. I’ll tell you.”

Bainbridge roughly dragged her to her feet. “Well? Where is she?”

Leanne plonked down on the couch, rubbing at her swollen cheek. “She had you fooled, didn’t she?” she leered. “Right under your bloody noses and you didn’t have a clue.”

“If anything happens to Sophie…”

"She's mad, you know, quite mad. She can turn on a sixpence can Joanne, or Annika as she prefers to be called. If she wants Sophie dead then believe me, she's dead."

"Why has she abducted her? What does she want?"

"You'd better ask her that. She'll be up at the steel plant. I don't know where exactly. It's where she would meet up with Shaun every week."

"And you never went to these rendezvous?"

Leanne shook her head. "I was never invited," she said. "Shaun was obsessed with her. There was no room for me when they got together."

Bainbridge took out his mobile phone and brought up the image of Annika. "Is this her?" he said. "Is this Joanne Connolly?"

Leanne looked at the image. "Yes, that's Joanne," she said. "She has a look of Shaun around the eyes, don't you think?"

Bainbridge raced to the door. "You stay here and keep your mouth shut," he said. "You'd better hope nothing has happened to Sophie."

Bainbridge was halfway to the derelict steel plant when his mobile rang. It was Annika.

"You're wasting your time going to the plant," she said. "We're not there. Leanne lied."

"What the hell are you playing at, Annika? Is Sophie there? Is she all right? Can I speak to her?"

"Sophie's not dead, if that's what you're worried about. Not yet anyway."

"What is it you want?"

"You know what I want. I want you to free my brother."

"I can't do that. You know I can't."

"If you want to see your criminal psychologist friend again, that's exactly what you will do."

"You don't understand. You can't just take someone out of jail like that and set them free. There are rules."

"You're a clever man, DCS Bainbridge. Everybody says so. I'm sure you'll think of something."

"Let me speak to Sophie," Andy said. "I want proof of life."

"Andy," Sophie said softly. "Andy, I'm all right. Please, do what she wants. I'm begging you. I..."

"There, you've had your proof of life. Now, I suggest you get the wheels in motion to get my brother out of jail by eight o'clock tonight. Otherwise, I'm going to have great pleasure in carving up your friend here."

"Where do you want the exchange to take place?"

"I'll ring you."

Before Andy could respond, the line went dead.

His mood, like the clouds above, darkened

95

I suppose you're thinking I'm some kind of Monster?

The truth is, you're probably right.

I'm not a good person. I never was. From my first attempt at arson back in Dubai, I've always had this irrepressible urge to destroy, to kill.

All the money spent on doctors and psychiatrists by the Connolly's – what a waste!

Didn't they realise I was bad… damaged, that I bore the Dyson DNA?

I think it was the day I found the file in the psychiatrist's office that tipped me over the edge.

No kid wants to read about how their father killed their mother and almost killed me and Shaun. My big brother saved me. He's my hero.

There's nothing I won't do to keep him safe. If that means killing Sophie Barrett, well, so be it.

96

"Come on, Jack, think. Where can Annika be holding Sophie?" Both men were in Bainbridge's office.

Jack exhaled, shaking his head. "I've no idea," he said. "I'm beginning to think I don't know my wife at all. I never did."

"What about friends? Surely there must be someone who she would confide in?"

"She wasn't the type to make friends easily. She preferred to keep her own council."

"I'm clutching at straws here, Jack. I have every copper out there looking for your wife's car. She seems to have disappeared off the face of the earth."

"What about the phone? Can't you trace that?"

"She rang me on a pay-as-you-go," Bainbridge said. "She probably has half-a-dozen SIMs. Annika has planned this carefully. Probably since we first picked up Shaun Dyson."

Bainbridge's internal phone gave out its sharp, piercing ring. "Bainbridge," he said.

"Sir, it's Sergeant Brown. I've just had a call from Jacob Foster. He says a woman, wielding a knife, stole his boat down at South Gare."

"Is he at The Gare now?"

"Yes, sir. I was about to send a squad car."

"Don't bother. Inspector Mason and I will attend."

He turned to Mason. "Hurry up," he said. "It looks like we're going sailing."

Both officers raced from the office and were soon driving in the direction of South Gare.

The thunderstorm, which was forecast for later that day, suddenly appeared. Lightening illuminated the grey sky and thunder roared menacingly overhead. The rain began to fall, lightly at first, then turned to a torrent.

To the right of The Gare were a collection of green wooden huts which were used by the local fishermen. A tall, athletic man with long dark hair tied back in a ponytail, was standing on the track alongside the huts. He was frantically waving his arms. Next to him was an older man.

Bainbridge pulled up alongside, and quickly got out of the vehicle.

"I'm DCS Bainbridge," he said, flashing his warrant card. "This is Inspector Mason."

"I don't care who the fuck you are," the younger man said. "Some mad bitch threatened to knife me and my dad if I didn't give her the keys to my boat."

"And you are?"

"Jacob Foster," he said, "and this is my dad, Marcus."

The older man waved an acknowledgement.

"Tell me exactly what happened," Bainbridge said.

Jacob huffed his exasperation. "I came over to The Gare for dad to fix my boat. The engine keeps cutting out."

"I'm an engineer," Marcus said. "I'm always fixing people's boats."

"When dad went into his hut to get some tools, this woman was hiding inside."

"She gave me a fright, I can tell you," Marcus said. "She was brandishing a knife and another woman, a bit older than her, was huddled on the floor. I thought she was dead at first."

"What did the woman say?"

"She demanded the keys for the boat. I said I didn't have the keys. My son had them. The 'Happy Wanderer' was his boat after all."

"She was holding a knife to dad's throat and told me to hand over the keys."

"What did you do?"

"What could I do. I gave her the keys. Then she told us to help the other woman onto the boat."

"What shape was the other woman in?"

Jacob shrugged. "She was alive," he said. "It looked to me like she was drugged. I can't be doing with druggies."

"So, you got both women onto the boat? Then what?"

"She turned on the engine and off she went."

"Did you see in which direction she went?" Bainbridge said.

"That way," Foster said, pointing to the left. "She'll be heading towards Hartlepool."

Marcus grinned. "She won't get that far," he said. "There isn't a full tank of fuel for one thing, and the engine needs urgent attention. I wager she's just around the headland."

"So, why don't get your police motor launch out there?" Foster said. "That cow is dangerous."

Bainbridge took out two photographs from his pocket. "Are these the women?" he said.

"Yes, that's her," he said, pointing to the image of Annika. "That's the bitch with the knife."

"What about the second photograph? Is this the older woman you mentioned?"

Foster squinted at Sophie's image for a few seconds. "I think so. What do you think, dad?" he said, handing the photograph to Marcus.

"Yes, that's her," Marcus said. "No doubt about it. That's the woman who was half-conscious that we put into the boat."

Foster took out an envelope from his pocket. "The mad bitch told me to give this to the police when they arrived," he said, handing it to Bainbridge.

Bainbridge tore open the envelope. Inside was a note.

"Bring my brother to The Gare tonight. I'll exchange Shaun for Sophie. Any tricks and as God is my witness, I'll carve her up into so many pieces. Bring Shaun over to me in the Coastguard's boat."

97

Mason's phone rang. "Sir," he said, handing the phone to Bainbridge, "it's the Coastguard."

Bainbridge briefed the Coastguard on what was happening. "I want you to keep 'The Happy Wanderer' under observation," he said, "but don't intervene." He handed the phone back to Mason, then walked back towards his car. "I need to make a couple of calls," he said.

It was eight o'clock when the small, black van pulled up on The Gare. One of the two prison guards jumped out of the van and rushed towards Bainbridge.

"He's here," he said, handing Bainbridge his clipboard. "If you could sign, sir?"

Bainbridge scribbled his signature on the form which released the prisoner, Shaun Dyson, into his custody.

"This weather looks like it's in for the night," the officer said, pulling up his collar for protection from the rain that was lashing down.

"Have you brought the item I asked you?"

"Yes, sir," he said, handing Bainbridge a carrier bag. "It's in here."

"Good man," he said. "You'd better bring Dyson out then."

The officer returned to his vehicle and opened the rear door.

"Out you get," he said, leaning in and grabbing Dyson's right arm.

Clad in a bright-orange waterproof cagoule, Shaun Dyson jumped out of the van onto the rough ground. On sight of Bainbridge, a broad smile spread across his face.

"Detective Chief Superintendent Bainbridge," he said, "fancy seeing you here."

"Shaun, why don't you tell Annika to stop this madness. It's not too late and..."

Dyson gave a raucous laugh. "She had you fooled, didn't she?" he said. "She had you all fooled." He turned to Mason. "Especially you. She played you like a fiddle. Call yourself a policeman? You couldn't see what was going on right under your nose."

Mason lunged forward, punching Dyson below the right eye. "You evil bastard," he growled.

"Enough!" Bainbridge commanded. "That's enough, Jack. The important thing right now is to get Sophie back safely."

"You'd better not forget that," Dyson sneered. "If you try anything, Annika will kill her, you know that?"

The Coastguard vessel had been moored close by and Bainbridge, Mason and Dyson strode towards it. When all three men were aboard, the boat roared into life and headed to the headland where 'The Happy Wanderer' was anchored.

***

Sophie was slouched on the makeshift couch inside the small cabin of the fishing boat. Her hands were bound with cord and a cotton scarf was wrapped tightly across her mouth. Annika was pacing nervously around the cabin.

"It won't be long now," she said. "Bainbridge is bringing Shaun so we can do a swap."

Sophie wriggled wildly on the couch making inaudible noises.

"Oh, you have something to say, Sophie?" Annika belittled her as she leant over and pulled down the gag. "And what might that be?"

"Annika, this is madness. Please, let me help you. I want to help you."

Annika gave out a shrill cry. "You think I'm mad? A crazy woman? Let me tell you, I've never been saner." She took out a bottle of beer from the small fridge and throwing back her head, began to drink its contents.

"What are your plans when this is over?" Sophie asked. "You know the police will find you."

"The police? For fuck's sake, I've been married to a policeman for two years. He's supposed to be extra clever yet he didn't have a clue who I was. I could wrap him around my little finger."

"Jack's a good man. He loves you. Of course he would never suspect his wife of..."

"Of what? Of murdering two old men?" She put the bottle to her lips and drank more beer. "They weren't my first kill, you know. My so-called parents were the first."

"I thought they died in a car accident."

"I drugged them and got them into the car, then I drove them along the Amalfi coast road. Have you been there? The views are wonderful."

"So, you deliberately caused the car to go over the cliff?"

"Of course I did. It was easy. I was only about three miles from a village so I didn't have too far to walk. I got out of the car and then just a little push and… It was like bonfire night watching them burn."

"But why did you kill them?"

"Because they lied to me. They told me my family, my real family, were all dead, and all the time I had a big brother. A brave, wonderful brother who saved my life when I was a baby."

"How did you find out?"

Annika gave a shrill laugh. "I found out when Dr Phillip Osmond, to whom my parents paid dearly to psychoanalyse me, was stupid enough to leave his office door unlocked one night. I found my file and discovered I had a brother. Ten minutes research online and I knew the whole story."

"I take it Shaun was the reason you came to Redcar?"

"What other reason? Like I said, I can wrap Jack around my little finger. It was me who persuaded him to go for the post of inspector in Redcar when the vacancy occurred."

"How did you manage to meet up with Shaun?"

"Oh, that was easy. I pretended I was going to a book club every Monday. Instead, I would go to the abandoned steelworks and meet my brother. We just talked and talked. It was wonderful."

"So, the great plan now is for you and Shaun to go on the run? What about his wife? Doesn't Leanne have any part in your plans?"

"Leanne doesn't understand Shaun like I do," she said. "Nobody does."

"But you can't seriously think..."

Suddenly Annika sprang forward and pulled the scarf once more around Sophie's mouth. "Shut up," she said, "you're boring me." She looked through the grimy porthole. "They'll be here soon. Not long now."

Annika was standing on the bow as the Coastguard vessel approached alongside the fishing boat. The orange garbed hostage jumped up and down, waving his arms with excitement.

"Well done, Sis," he said above the sound of the howling wind. "You're a bloody genius."

Bainbridge moved forward, holding his prisoner tightly by his arm. "I've kept my part of the bargain," he said, "now you keep yours. Where's Sophie?"

"Give me your keys," Annika said.

Bainbridge took the keys from the ignition and threw them into the fishing boat.

Annika picked them up and dropped them into the sea before going down into the cabin. "Get up. It's time to go," she said, roughly grabbing Sophie's arm.

Sophie struggled to her feet and was half dragged up on deck by Annika.

"Are you all right, Sophie?" Bainbridge said.

"I… I think so," Sophie said, the howling wind biting into her face.

The orange-clad figure moved towards the edge of the Coastguard vessel and jumped down into the fishing boat as Bainbridge reached over and pulled Sophie safely aboard.

Annika turned on the engine of the boat. "Come on, Shaun," she said. "Let's get out of here fast. We'll be out of the country by this time tomorrow."

"No, Annika, I don't think so," said a familiar voice.

Annika spun to see Jack pulling back the orange hood on his cagoule. "You… you bastard," she shrieked, racing forward and thumping his chest with her fists. "Where's Shaun? What have you done with him?"

"Shaun's back there with the Coastguard," Jack said, "in fact if you look back, you'll see them approaching. They do have more than one set of keys."

Annika grabbed Jack's arm. "Darling, you've got to protect me. You will protect me, won't you, Jack? I'm your wife, remember. You can't let them lock me up again. I…"

Jack turned off the boat's engine as the Coastguard vessel pulled alongside. Bainbridge jumped onboard. "Are you all right, Jack?" he said.

"Yes, sir. I was just about to caution the prisoner."

"Leave that to me," Bainbridge said. "You take this boat back to The Gare and I'll take Annika back with the Coastguard." He turned to Annika. "Come on," he said. "Time to go. You can say goodbye to your brother on the way."

98

Four weeks later, Bainbridge was in his office sitting across from Jack Mason.

"Are you sure it's what you want to do?" he said. "You're entitled to compassionate leave, Jack if you want to think things through."

"No, sir. My mind's made up. I've decided the academic life is what I really want."

"I suppose teaching law at Oxford's not a bad gig," Bainbridge conceded. "When do you start?"

"In two weeks. I'm having some of the furniture taken down tomorrow. I've been given a nice flat on campus but it's too small to take everything."

"Well, I wish you well," Bainbridge said. "It's been a privilege working with you these last few months, Jack."

"Thank you, sir. I appreciate you saying that."

"Have you been to see Annika since they moved her to Broadmoor?"

"I tried. Twice in fact, but she refuses to see me. I've written letters, but they've been returned unopened."

"Give it time. She might come round."

Jack sighed and slowly shook his head. "I can't believe I didn't realise I was living with such a… a monster, because that's what she is."

"She's sick. She has the same sickness as her brother and father. The girl can't help herself. It's in her DNA."

"I still have flashbacks seeing Arthur Rhodes's body for the first time. The frenzied attack upon him will stay with me forever."

"Charlie Bull was much the same. It shows what anger must be inside her head, boiling away until one day, boom. It explodes."

"How's Sophie doing? No ill effects after her ordeal?"

"She seems fine. She's in Corfu at the moment. She wants me to join her for a couple of weeks."

"You should. It will do you good."

"Perhaps," Bainbridge mused, "but… well, when I was down at South Gare, it brought it all back."

"You mean what happened to Inspector Cooper?"

Bainbridge nodded. "I thought I'd got over her, that she was out of my system and I could move on, but…"

"Sophie's a lovely person," Jack said. "You look good together."

Bainbridge raised an eyebrow. "We'll see," he said.

Jack got to his feet. "Well, sir, it's time I was going." He leant over the desk and shook Bainbridge by the hand.

"Goodbye, Jack and good luck."

"Goodbye, sir."

99

"Are you sure?" Wayne Beaumont said. "Are you absolutely sure?"

"Of course I'm sure," Jodie said, wrapping her arms around Wayne's neck. "We're going to have a baby."

"Oh my god. I… I'm going to be a father," Wayne said, plummeting heavily into his armchair. "I can't believe it. Me, a dad."

"It'll mean me giving up work," she said. "Can we manage on one wage?"

Wayne's grin widened. "Of course we can," he said. "I've got transferred into CID permanently now, so that's a bit more money, and I'm going to take the sergeant's advice."

"What advice?"

"Study," Beaumont said. "I'm going to study to get more promotions. I'll be a superintendent before you know it."

"That's great news," Jodie said.

"That's not all." Wayne put his hand into his jacket pocket and removed a small box. He walked towards Jodie, then got down on one knee, taking out a solitaire diamond ring from the box. "Darling," he said. "I love you. Will you do me the honour of becoming my wife?"

100

Well, now you know the full story.

Do you still think I'm mad? Truthfully, wouldn't you have done the same to protect your own flesh and blood?

My poor brother's been locked away for life. It's so unfair. I hear Leanne doesn't visit him in prison any more, in fact she's got herself a new bloke. Shaun will kill her when he gets out. If he doesn't, maybe I will.

Jack keeps writing. The stupid fool. Doesn't he realise he was merely a means to an end? I don't think I'll ever see him again.

As for Bainbridge. How I hate that man for what he did. When I get out of this dreadful place I'm going to tear him limb from limb. I'll gouge out his eyes. Cut off his tongue. I'll…

But no, I must stay calm. If I get into one of my rages they'll stick me with one of those damned needles again and I won't be able to think straight for days. And I have to think straight. Keep my mind clear to plan, to plot.

Enjoy yourself whilst you can, Bainbridge.

I will be back!

About the Author

Eva Carmichael followed her dream to live by the sea when, along with her husband and miniature schnauzer, she moved to Redcar in 2016.

Eva comes from a legal background, working first as a shorthand typist for the West Yorkshire police and then as a Special Constable. More recently, Eva worked as a legal PA in Leeds.

Although she has always enjoyed writing fiction, it wasn't until she came to live in Redcar that Eva took her writing seriously. She became a member of the U3A in Saltburn and joined the novel writing group in Guisborough, where she was encouraged to pursue her dream of writing a book.

Eva's first novel, "Bad blood Rising" was published towards the end of 2019, followed by her other novels. Her current book "Frenzy" is set in her idyllic hometown where the peace has been shattered by several brutal murders.

EVA CARMICHAEL'S BOOKS

BAD BLOOD RISING

A NORTHERN CITY… MONEY… GIRS… CRIME… MURDER… AND BAD MEN. AN EXCITING ROMP THROUGH THE CRIMINAL UNDERWORLD…

When a young prostitute is murdered by her pimp, Karl Maddox, he thinks the terrible secret she had threatened to expose is buried with her.

But when the murdered prostitute's daughter arrives in Leeds eighteen years later, she is seeking answers.

Slowly but surely, Karl's life as the wealthy, powerful kingpin of his clubland empire begins to unravel as loyalty is replaced by treachery, and friendship is replaced by hatred.

Is Karl about to find out that no secret can remain buried forever?

……

MORE BAD BLOOD

MORE MURDER… MORE GIRLS… MORE BAD MEN

A thrilling gritty novel which delves into the seedy underbelly of the sex trade in the North of England.

Karl Maddox is content with his lot as kingpin of the sex industry. His beautiful, estranged wife is now back in his life, along with his son and daughter. However, when one of his escorts dies after stealing a briefcase from a client, Karl finds himself caught up in the sinister and dangerous world of sex trafficking.

When danger knocks directly on his door, Karl needs every ounce of his ingenuity to keep those close to him safe. However, the real danger is much closer than he realises. A danger which threatens everything he holds dear.

……

LET THERE BE BLOOD

BETRAYAL… VIOLENCE… BAD MEN

Filled with drama, violence and betrayal, life has never given Karl Maddox an easy ride, but with several attempts made on his life, things move to a new and frightening level.

The pressure builds when Karl learns an investigation is being undertaken into events in his past – events he thought had been buried forever.

With his back to the wall, Karl is at his most dangerous as he begins to retaliate in the only way he knows how.

……

A TWISTED MIND

When a young girl goes missing from a crowded each, Detective Inspector Andy Bainbridge of Cleveland Police, is put in charge of the case. Despite endless enquiries, no trace of the child is found, and it is assumed she has been swept out to sea.

Sixteen years later, when a number of young women go missing from the same resort, Bainbridge is horrified to realise that their disappearance, and that of the young girl years earlier, are connected.

Bainbridge comes up against the worst type of evil – the pure evil of a twisted mind.

……

Printed in Great Britain
by Amazon

30258798R00196